WITH A MINOR IN MURDER

What Reviewers Say
About Karis Walsh's Work

Sit. Stay. Love.

"I definitely enjoyed this sweet, funny romance. ...Loved that the couple were upfront in their communication and expectations! With all of that out of the way, I could enjoy their relationship and love the doggies."—*C-Spot Reviews*

"All the characters are well developed, even the minor ones. There is a lot of snarky and sarcastic dialog (always hooks me immediately!) and just enough drama to keep things interesting. It's an engaging love story between two women who truly complement each other. ...I'm going to pile up on the couch in a warm robe, thick socks, and a cup of hot chocolate and read it again this winter."—*Bookish Sort*

"This book is just a delightful little feel-good summer read."—*Istoria Lit*

Love on Lavender Lane

"The writing was engaging and I enjoyed the slow burn attraction between the two leads."—Melina Bickard, Librarian, Waterloo Library (UK)

"One thing I love about Karis Walsh's novels is the way the setting is as important an aspect of the story as the characters."—*The Good, the Bad and the Unread*

Seascape

"When I think of Karis Walsh novels, the two aspects that distinguish them from those of many authors are the interactions of the characters with their environment, both the scenery and the plants and animals that live in it. This book has all of that in abundance…"—*The Good, the Bad and the Unread*

Set the Stage

"Settings are an artwork for [Karis Walsh] as she creates these places that feel so real and vivid you wish you could hop in a car or plane to go walk where her characters are to experience what they get to on the pages of her book. …Her character work is as good as the places she's created so they feel like realistic people making the whole picture enjoyable."—*Artistic Bent*

"…a fun romance. It made me want to go to this festival, which I'd never had any interest in before. *Set the Stage* is worth a read for fans of romance or theater."—*The Lesbrary*

You Make Me Tremble

"Another quality read from Karis Walsh. She is definitely a go-to for a heartwarming read."—*Romantic Reader Blog*

Amounting to Nothing

"Karis Walsh is known for quality books. Her characters are likable and well developed, her stories have interesting/realistic dialogue. She is one of my go-to authors for an easy, enjoyable read."
—*Romantic Reader Blog*

Tales From the Sea Glass Inn

"Karis Walsh has an appealing and easy writing style that always makes her stories a pleasant read and a keen eye for human frailties that captures the interest. Here she pulls out the quirks of each woman and shows us who they are and what they struggle with in swift brush strokes."—*Lesbian Reading Room*

Love on Tap

"*Love on Tap* by Karis Walsh is a contemporary romance between an archaeologist and an artisanal brewer. That might sound like an odd match, but thanks to the author's deft hand, it works very well and makes for a satisfying read."—*Lesbian Review*

"I liked this book, I really did. There was something about it that pulled me in and held my attention. Karis Walsh is an expert in creating interesting characters that often have to face some type of adversity. I love that she gives them strength to persevere in spite of this."—*Romantic Reader Blog*

Sweet Hearts: Romantic Novellas

"*Sweet Hearts: Romantic Novellas* is just what it says it is: SWEET. Insert "awe" here, and feel free to really draw it out like us Southerners do, AAAWWWWEEE. This is a quick read, distinctively broken up into three well written, compelling novellas. All three authors are quite frankly amazing writers, and it shows time and time again in the works that they produce."—*Romantic Reader Blog*

Risk Factor—*Novella in* Sweet Hearts

"Another satisfying and exciting short novel. This one was set in an unusual setting, and covered an emotive and at times emotional subject. The characters although strong were very different women, and both had individual weaknesses. The author used these differences to create an interesting and touching story line."
—*Inked Rainbow Reads*

Mounting Evidence

"[A] well paced and thrilling mystery revolving around two enigmatic women."—*Rainbow Book Reviews*

"...great characters and development, a wonderful story line, lots of suspense and mystery and a truly sweet romance."—*Prism Book Alliance*

Mounting Danger

"Karis Walsh easily masters the most difficult pitfall of a traditional romance. Karis' love for horses and for the Pacific Northwest is palpable throughout and adds a wonderful flavor to the story: The beauty of the oceanside at Tacoma, the smell of horses, the dogs, the excitement of Polo, the horses themselves (I am secretly in love with Bandit), the sounds of the forest. A most enjoyable read for cold winter days and nights."—*Curve*

Blindsided

"Their slow-burn romance is a nuanced exploration of trust, desire, and negotiating boundaries, without a hint of schmaltz or pity. The sex scenes are sizzling hot, but it's the slow burn that really allows Walsh to shine. …The deft dialogue and well-written characters make this a winner."—*Publishers Weekly*

"Karis Walsh always comes up with charming Traditional Romances with interesting characters who have slightly unusual quirks."—*Curve*

Wingspan

"As with all Karis Walsh's wonderful books the characters are the story. Multifaceted, layered and beautifully drawn, Ken and Bailey hold our attention from the start. Their clashes, their attraction and the personal and shared development are what draw us in and hold us. The surrounding scenery, the wild rugged landscape and the birds at the center of the story are exquisitely drawn."—*Lesbian Reading Room*

The Sea Glass Inn

"Karis Walsh's third book, excellently written and paced as always, takes us on a gentle but determined journey through two women's awakening. …Loved it, another great read that will stay on my re-visit shelf."—*Lesbian Reading Room*

Worth the Risk

"The setting of this novel is exquisite, based on Karis Walsh's own background in horsemanship and knowledge of showjumping. It provides a wonderful plot to the story, a great backdrop to the characters and an interesting insight for those of us who don't know that world. …Another great book by Karis Walsh. Well written, well paced, amusing and warming. Definitely a hit for me."—*Lesbian Reading Room*

Improvisation

"Walsh tells this story in achingly beautiful words, phrases and paragraphs, building a tension that is bittersweet. As the two main characters sway through life to the music of their souls, the reader may think she hears the strains of Tina's violin. As the two women interact, there is always an undercurrent of sensuality buzzing around the edges of the pages, even while they exchange sometimes snappy, sometimes comic dialogue. *Improvisation* is a true romantic tale, Walsh's fourth book, and she's evolving into a master romantic storyteller."—*Lambda Literary*

Harmony

"This was Karis Walsh's first novel and what a great addition to the LesFic fold. It is very well written and flows effortlessly as it weaves together the story of Brooke and Andi's worlds and their intriguing journey together. Ms Walsh has given space to more than just the heroines and we come to know the quartet and their partners, all of whom are likeable and interesting."—*Lesbian Reading Room*

Visit us at www.boldstrokesbooks.com

By the Author

Harmony

Worth the Risk

Sea Glass Inn

Improvisation

Wingspan

Blindsided

Love on Tap

Tales from Sea Glass Inn

You Make Me Tremble

Set the Stage

Seascape

Love on Lavender Lane

Sit. Stay. Love

Liberty Bay

With a Minor in Murder

Mounted Police Romantic Intrigues:

Mounting Danger

Mounting Evidence

Amounting to Nothing

WITH A MINOR IN MURDER

by

Karis Walsh

2022

ISBN 13: 978-1-63679-186-9

THIS TRADE PAPERBACK ORIGINAL IS PUBLISHED BY
BOLD STROKES BOOKS, INC.
P.O. BOX 249
VALLEY FALLS, NY 12185

FIRST EDITION: MAY 2022

CREDITS
EDITOR: RUTH STERNGLANTZ
PRODUCTION DESIGN: SUSAN RAMUNDO
COVER DESIGN BY TAMMY SEIDICK

Chapter One

Clare Sawyer hurried up the hill toward the University of Washington's Campus Police Headquarters, her reluctance to arrive late beating out her desire to show up looking relatively fresh and unsweaty. She had spent the past weeks leading up to her first day on the job worrying about making a good first impression, hoping to prove she was able to quickly adapt to her new work environment and the routines in place at this new department. Even through all her fretful moments when she imagined herself making mistakes or standing out in a bad way, she hadn't spared a single stressful thought on the possibility of arriving late. She had naturally assumed that she would be on time. She was *always* on time.

She tried to ignore the worry and regret that had been gaining momentum since the day she had quit her old job. Maybe she was late because subconsciously—and increasingly, uncomfortably *consciously*—she didn't want to be here. She had marched out of her former department with confidence, sure she was heading on a path toward the moral high ground, and her steps had been gradually faltering every day since. Now, she was about to face her first day of actual duty on campus, and she felt as if she had somehow landed herself in a pit of doubt rather than on the lofty hill she had been aiming for. She increased her pace, outwardly defying her bleak thoughts. She had to make this work, had no choice but to make this work.

She plucked at the front of her black uniform, trying to get a little cooling airflow on her overheated skin. September seemed determined to continue the summer's trend of bright sun and high temperatures, reluctant to yield to the more expected rainy Northwest autumn. Not the ideal weather conditions for a near-sprint along the steeply sloping sidewalks that made up the University District. Her black wool uniform and heavy-soled black boots weren't helping, either.

Clare veered to the right, opting to cut across the southwest edge of campus because it offered more shade and gave her a chance to avoid waiting for lights at crosswalks. On her constantly updating hierarchy of potential disasters on her first day, being caught jaywalking by her new colleagues ranked higher than bursting into the morning meeting after it had already started. Arriving sweaty and out of breath was moving farther down the list, toward the rank of inevitable disasters on her first day.

Clare ran her hand through her short hair as she walked quickly along the meandering path, her eyes focused on the pavement in front of her and determinedly away from the beautiful trees and austere buildings surrounding her. She had escaped from college with her degree nearly fifteen years ago, and her mind had happily and with much relief shed the need to follow an academic calendar—or, in fact, to care about anything even remotely academic. Her interviews and early training sessions had taken place at odd hours and on weekends over the summer, and she hadn't had any trouble finding places to park in the lots near the police station. She berated herself for not anticipating how much different it would be on a September morning, at the beginning of the fall quarter. She had circled through several lots and garages before finding a spot near Portage Bay, on the outskirts of the U District. She should have realized she'd be competing for parking real estate with thousands of students and staff, not to mention all the people who worked at the local shops and restaurants catering to the university crowd. She'd have to adjust to this new world, since she had to treat this move from her former city police job as a long-term one. She had come here for the career opportunities that were missing from her old department, so she had to do her best to find them. She couldn't go back, and she was getting too far into her life as a police officer to develop a habit of flitting from job to job. She had wiped out a worldful of viable options with one decision, and she no longer had the luxury of exploring options. She had one career route ahead of her now, and she sure as hell was going to make the best of it, regrets be damned.

Of course, she had to actually get to the station before she could embark on her meteoric rise through the ranks. She gave a brief laugh—which sounded more like a gasp for air than she liked—at the way her carefully scripted career plans had been boiled down to the essential first step of merely getting to the damned department building.

"Officer? Officer! Excuse me, Officer."

Clare's eyes flickered shut in annoyance for a brief moment before she assumed what she hoped was a pleasant, professional expression and turned around to see a man jogging toward her and waving, his face red from exertion as if he had been following her for a while. She estimated his age in his midseventies, and he was wearing a brown tweed jacket and gray pants—two neutral items of clothing that somehow managed to clash rather horribly. If he wasn't a professor, she'd eat her duty belt.

"Can I help you?" she asked politely, even though she realized she had limited ways to be of assistance. She still had more training sessions to complete, and today she was meant to shadow another officer on her first day on campus in uniform. The chasm between her present position as a not-yet-fully-qualified rookie and her past as an experienced Seattle police officer and detective suddenly loomed in front of her. She was fairly sure she could direct him to the police station—at least she hoped so, since she was currently aiming for it—but she was sanctioned to do little else.

He came to a stop in front of her and rested his hands on his knees, pausing to catch his breath. "It's too damned hot out here."

"I'm afraid weather is out of my jurisdiction," Clare said. "Above my pay grade. I'd be happy to call the paramedics for you, though, if you need them."

The man stood up and put his hands on his hips. "You're a cheeky one," he said, but he looked like he was trying not to smile. "I'm perfectly fine, just not used to chasing down speeding police officers in the heat. Now, come with me. A burglar broke into my office and stole some of my books."

He turned and walked away, obviously expecting her to follow, but Clare didn't budge. "Sir, wait," she called, fishing her phone out of her pocket and opening a note-taking app. He came back, all traces of his smile gone. She tried to come up with a reason why she couldn't help him right away that didn't include the phrases *I'm new here* and *I don't think I'm allowed to solve crimes on my own yet*. "I really want to help, but I'm not…I don't have the correct paperwork with me for filing a police report. If you'll tell me what building and office you're in, I'll come back and…I mean, I'll get someone to come to the scene right away."

He frowned. "Who needs paperwork? I just need you to come help me find my books."

Clare bit her lip, torn between her professional instinct to solve problems for other people and her very personal need to get to the station for her first morning meeting. She hadn't been this lost while in uniform since her rookie year on the Seattle force, and she hated the feeling. She looked over the shoulder of the increasingly impatient civilian in front of her and saw two campus police officers walking toward her. She felt as relieved to see them as if she had backup coming while on a dangerous call.

"How are you today, Professor Arnault? Not another robbery, I hope?" One of the cops, a woman with short black hair, ignored Clare completely and spoke to the professor, leading him a few yards away. Leaving her partner to deal with Clare, apparently. Judging by his expression, he felt he had gotten the worse end of the deal.

"You're the new lateral, right?" he asked. "From Seattle PD?"

He managed to make the question sound as flattering as if he had asked if she had just crawled out of the nearby dumpster. She wondered if his opinion of laterals was the common one in this department. She'd find out eventually, if she ever made it to her first meeting. For now, she would ignore the slight and take his query at face value. "Yes. I'm Clare."

"Derek. And that's Cappy," he said, nodding toward his partner, who was laughing at something the professor had said.

"Was there really a burglary?"

"He's a professor emeritus," Derek said, not answering her question. "That means he's retired, but he's still involved with his department. He teaches a class on Chaucer every fall."

Clare fought the reflexive urge to go on the defensive and tell him to stop being condescending because *of course* she knew what a professor emeritus was. She doubted the retort would change his opinion of her, and besides, she really hadn't known what it was. She had never cared to learn more than the basics of university hierarchies. There were students, there were teachers, there were grades. Beyond that, she hadn't cared.

"He teaches Chaucer? His books must be hot sellers on the black market, so no wonder they were stolen."

Derek frowned at her. "He sometimes misplaces things, and we help him look for them. We're a community here, unlike big city departments. We know our people and take care of them."

There was some truth to what he was saying—although Clare had gotten to know some of the people in her sectors, she certainly wasn't on a first-name basis with the entire population of Seattle. Still, the implication of his words was unfair since she had always done her best to treat each person she met with compassion and fairness, even if she only was in contact with them once. She was well-practiced at only revealing what she wanted others to see, though. She hid her annoyance at his insinuations—and her growing panic that she might always be considered an outsider in this department—behind a composed mask and lied with a smile.

"I'm looking forward to getting to know this community, too, and to being a part of it. Right now, though, I need to get to the day shift meeting, so I'll leave Professor Arnault in your capable hands."

She turned and started on her path again. "You're going to be late. It's almost shift change," Derek called after her.

She wanted to flip him off but settled instead for less-satisfying sarcasm. "Thank you, that's useful information," she said, giving him a tight smile over her shoulder as she walked away.

She tried to muster the same sense of haste she had felt before, but the realization that she had made a huge mistake coming here was slowing her down like weights in her boots. If Derek's attitude was indicative of the rest of the department, she was going to have more to worry about than merely impressing her bosses and earning promotions. She was also going to have to earn the respect of the other officers, and the prospect of that was looking bleak. At least the other officer, Cappy, hadn't said anything negative to her. Of course, Cappy had completely ignored her, but maybe Clare could pretend that she had done so in a friendly way.

Yes, she had made a *huge* mistake.

Clare finally jogged down a set of stairs leading from the campus pathway to Fifteenth Avenue and hurried across the road toward the campus police station. The building itself was a physical representation of her new life. It was similar in appearance to the Seattle Police headquarters—fairly nondescript and modern, blending in with the stores and businesses surrounding it, not standing apart from the community it served. But as a miniaturized version of the SPD, it looked more like a precinct substation than the main station. Clare had already been given a tour of the various satellite offices spread throughout the university grounds, and she had compared them—in her mind, of course, and never out loud—to the size of SPD's storage closets.

She wasn't trying to be critical of her new department with her focus on the size differences between the two. The campus police structures were neat and well-appointed, perfectly suited to the community's needs. And the reputation of the officers inside those buildings, as well as the work they did on campus, was undeniably impressive. But the department was—also undeniably—smaller than Seattle's. She had come here because she wanted less prejudice and more fairness in opportunities. But what good was a department with no glass ceiling when there simply weren't a lot of floors available above it?

Still, she had no choice but to push through the wide glass door and enter the blissfully cool foyer. Her sigh of relief turned into a quiet groan when she saw her new sergeant standing by the public reception desk with her arms crossed over her chest.

"Sawyer. Come with me." Sergeant Adriana Kent turned with parade crispness and headed down the hall.

Clare trotted after her, waving toward the meeting room door as they passed it. "Aren't I supposed to be—"

"Barging in halfway through the meeting? No. That would be disruptive. You're supposed to be coming with me."

Delightful. Clare waited until they were inside Kent's miniscule, tidy office before launching into her apology for being late.

"I'm sorry I'm late, Sergeant Kent. It won't happen again, and I—"

"Oh, sit *down*, Sawyer. This isn't a formal disciplinary hearing. Landry called and told me you were held up by Professor Arnault."

Clare had unconsciously snapped into her stiff posture, standing at attention with her hands clasped behind her back, and now she tried to ease gracefully into the chair across from her sergeant. Her surprise at Derek's kindness made her feel awkward as she balanced on the edge of the seat. She was under no illusion that he had called Kent because he liked her as a person or colleague, but he had probably done so because it was the right thing to do. It was what she would have done for another officer, but she hadn't expected the same treatment. He had seemed genuinely irritated by her presence and possibly biased against laterals, but he was a decent guy. Not ideal, but Clare could work with that.

"And it most likely will happen again," Sergeant Kent said, leaning back in her chair and looking far more at ease than Clare felt. "You won't be an anonymous officer here. You'll become familiar to a lot of people, and they'll be more inclined to talk to you than the average Seattle citizen would be. They'll ask for directions, they'll question you about campus policies, and they'll ask you to escort them across campus at night. And sometimes, if they're lonely because their wife of over fifty years recently passed away, or if they are getting older and changing from absentminded professor to just plain forgetful, they might ask you to help them search their office for glasses or papers or something else they claim was stolen. And you will smile and do your best to help them because we take care of our people. All of them. Just call in and let someone know if you're going to be delayed."

Clare nodded her acceptance. She wouldn't have followed this career path if she didn't like helping people, and she had always done her best to pay attention to the needs of those she met when she was working in the city, but she could tell that Taking Care of Our People was a mission here in a different way than it had been in her old department. These people practically chanted it like a mantra. Clare wasn't about to complain about the campus police's priority, though. It was why she had quit and come here, because she had heard that the truth of those words didn't just apply to the citizens the department served, but to the members of its own force.

As if sensing the route her thoughts had taken, Kent leaned forward in her chair, resting her elbows on a desk that was bare of everything except a single overflowing in-box tray and a handmade-looking mug full of pens. "I know why you're here," she said. "You're not the first lateral to come here searching for a place where qualities like race, gender, or sexual orientation won't be seen as barriers to promotion. Unfortunately, sometimes laterals truly aren't capable of becoming leaders and weren't being promoted in their former departments because of the way they did their job, not who they were as people."

Clare swallowed, desperately trying to do so subtly and not as an audible gulp. Kent knew her background, knew what accommodations she had requested for her qualifying exams. And now she was going to tell Clare that she was one of those sad laterals who had come here searching for opportunities that would never be within her grasp. That her decision was even more misguided than she had realized.

"Calm down, Sawyer," Sergeant Kent said, continuing with her disturbing ability to read Clare's emotions. "I believe you have the potential to do well here. But right now, it's nothing more than potential, and if this department and its community don't prove to be a good fit for you, then you won't go far, no matter how many theoretical opportunities are available. And if I find out you're half-assing this job?" Kent continued, her voice somehow getting more powerful as it got quieter. "You've put yourself out on a limb, leaving Seattle to come here, and I won't hesitate to chop that limb off if I don't believe you're doing your best to be an asset to this department."

She opened a drawer and took out a small box, handing it to Clare. "Here's your new work cell. It has recording and note-taking apps loaded, but feel free to add whatever you need to it. Now get out of here and find Dayton," Kent said as she straightened in her seat, her voice now back in a normal and relatively friendly register. She pulled a few papers out of her in-box and somehow managed, even with a nearly empty desk, to look far too busy to be bothered with Clare anymore. "You'll be shadowing him today."

Clare mumbled a thank-you and good-bye, neither of which seemed to have been heard, and stepped out of the office, sagging against the wall with a mixture of relief and dread. The sergeant had managed to terrify her and give her hope at the same time, and she wasn't sure how to process their short conversation. She pushed off the wall and set off toward the meeting room, hearing the louder conversations and sounds of chairs scraping that signaled the end of preparation and the beginning of the shift. She'd mull over Kent's words and their meaning later. Right now, she had to find Officer Dayton and start taking care of the people in this community, who now seemed to hold her future in their hands.

CHAPTER TWO

L ibby Hart chose an off-white poplin shirt and a pair of brown wool trousers with a faint cream-colored plaid pattern and hung them on her closet door. She glanced out her window at the sun filtering through the pointed leaves of a large horse chestnut tree and added a dark brown blazer to her outfit. It had been unusually warm for September, but the afternoon might bring unexpected clouds and rain, and she didn't want to be caught on campus without an extra layer.

She got dressed and ran a brush through her shoulder-length hair while she mentally reviewed the two classes she would be teaching today—Gender and Architecture, a seminar that she was excited to offer this year, and Women in Rome, an entry-level course that would include both Classics majors and a variety of other students who had chosen it as an elective. The second class might be less stimulating, without the same opportunities for in-depth discussions as the first, with its smaller size and more advanced participants, but she loved teaching the more basic classes because of the interdisciplinary nature of the students. Some needed the class for their major, while the rest came from all sorts of other departments just because they were interested in the topic. Conversations in those classes were unpredictable and wide-ranging, and she often felt as if she was learning along with her students instead of merely teaching them what she already knew.

She went into her second bedroom, which had no space for a bed since floor-to-ceiling bookshelves lined each wall, and retrieved her satchel from where it was hanging off the pointed ear of a stone gargoyle. She had packed it the night before with the books and supplies she would need for the day, but she spent an extra ten minutes digging through a pile of old journals, searching for an article she had just remembered about the patriarchal symbolism of architectural details on the Roman Colosseum. The article would be useful in today's classes, especially as an interesting tie-in for the few students who were in both.

Libby left her apartment and started her leisurely three-block commute to school. She didn't have to rush, despite her last-minute quest for the vaguely remembered article. She had found herself tracking down suddenly remembered books and journals often enough that she padded her morning schedule with enough time to plow through her library and still make it to class on time. She hated rushing through her walk, especially on beautiful fall mornings. Even though she technically lived off campus, her neighborhood was full of Greek and special-interest housing for students. The tree-shaded sidewalks blended seamlessly with those on the university grounds, and from her doorstep to her classroom, she was surrounded by people of all ages wearing U-Dub's purple and gold colors. She'd still be living in a dorm room if they'd let her, but her apartment was the best substitution that she was able to get. Dorm rooms were small and easily manageable, and they were usually mere steps away from cafeterias. Putting a plate of food on a tray and walking it over to a table was the closest Libby wanted to get to cooking.

Luckily, she could still take advantage of campus meal plans, even as a professor. Her route to Gould Hall took her conveniently past Odegaard Undergraduate Library, with its ground-floor café. As long as she averted her eyes as she walked toward the building and ignored its bland red-brick, boxy exterior, it was a great place to grab a quick breakfast. Brutalist style architecture was not to her taste, and she preferred the sweeping design elements of Suzzallo, the collegiate Gothic graduate library. But Suzzallo didn't have as many food options.

Libby got in line at the café behind a campus police officer. Someone new, she decided, since she wouldn't have forgotten seeing her before. She had short hair the color of fall leaves caught between gold and red, and a uniform that fit extremely well. Very pretty, Libby thought vaguely, her mind mostly on breakfast and her upcoming classes. The officer ordered and moved aside, leaving Libby to return her thoughts to breakfast and her upcoming classes.

"An Earl Grey tea and lemon bar, please," she ordered as she stepped forward, resisting the urge to turn and stare at the officer who was now next to her, waiting for her coffee. Libby didn't recognize the young woman at the register either, which was to be expected this early in the school year when new faces were everywhere.

"I'm sorry, but I just sold the last of the lemon bars. Can I get you something else?"

"You're sold out?" Libby repeated, cringing as her voice sounded louder than she had intended. She turned to face the officer, who was in the process of taking a big bite out of what should have been Libby's lemon bar. Libby decided that the woman looked even better from the front, with her captivating combination of wide green eyes and red-gold hair, full lips, and a uniform that must have been specially tailored to fit her curves so snugly. Well, both sides of her offered much to admire, but her beauty didn't excuse pastry thievery.

The officer swallowed her bite and grinned at Libby. "Sorry about that. I didn't know it was already spoken for. I'd give it back to you, but I've sworn to protect and serve the people on this campus, and I don't think that giving you a germy, half-eaten pastry would be in compliance with that moral code."

Libby raised her eyebrows. Banter, really? When the fate of her breakfast was at stake? She gave the officer what she hoped was an unruffled smile. "It's okay."

The officer leaned closer to her and said in a low voice, "It doesn't look okay. That's the second time you've glanced at my gun, so I should warn you that you wouldn't be able to get it out of the holster without knowing how."

Good to know, Libby thought, filing away the information so she'd remember to research it later. Not because she'd ever seriously try to steal an officer's gun, but because she liked to learn new things. "What makes you think it was your gun I was looking at?" she asked, matching the officer's quiet tone.

She was rewarded with a burst of musical laughter, which dissipated the last of her lingering irritation.

"Really, it's not a big deal. I'll just order something else," she said with a smile, raising her voice to a normal level. She peered in the pastry case and frowned in annoyance—not at the café for being out of her usual Monday breakfast or even the officer, but at herself for feeling indecisive about what to choose as a replacement. She had two doctorates. Surely she could handle this pastry dilemma with some degree of grace. "I suppose I'll have a chocolate croissant, I guess? But not with Earl Grey, so maybe English Breakfast instead?"

Well, maybe not grace, but at least she had picked something. The woman serving her was just putting the croissant into a paper bag when another walked behind the counter. She had worked here last year, as well, and Libby remembered her from one of her classes.

"Here's your coffee, Officer," she said, handing a large to-go cup to Libby's new nemesis.

The officer thanked her and flashed another of her brilliant smiles at Libby. "Sorry, again," she said.

"No problem," Libby answered with an innocent grin. "I hope you enjoy your breakfast and that it doesn't cause any severe intestinal distress."

The officer laughed again before walking away. Libby had to make an effort to drag her attention back to the counter.

"Good morning, Professor Hart," the young woman continued before turning to her coworker. "I put the last lemon bar aside for her—it's over there by the espresso machine. Professor Hart always has a lemon bar on Monday mornings."

Libby wanted to protest that she wasn't as predictable as that, and that she hadn't been shamefully upset about the lack of lemon bars, but she was glad to have her usual breakfast restored and decided not to press the point. Besides, she was too busy trying to remember her savior's name to speak. An art history major. Her final paper had been on architectural details in Edward Hopper's paintings—nothing too brilliant, but an interesting paper...

"Thank you, Cassie," she said, relieved when the name popped into her mind. She stuffed several bills into the tip jar next to the register and smiled at both of them. "See you tomorrow."

Tomorrow. Tuesdays in the autumn meant a piece of pumpkin bread and a soy latte. Yikes—maybe she did have a problem. She took a bite of her tangy pastry and brushed powdered sugar off her lips. Oh well, if being predictable meant that people kindly reserved her usual order behind the counter, then why change? Maybe she should post her weekly menu at the police department to ward off any future altercations, although she might be willing to forgo an occasional usual breakfast if it meant she could talk to that beautiful officer again. She tried to pretend that her charitable attitude was a sign of her emotional maturity and not a direct result of getting what she wanted.

She arrived at the crosswalk at Fifteenth Avenue and realized she had caught up to the lemon bar thief. She tried to blend in with the crowd when the officer glanced over her shoulder and caught Libby staring—unfortunately at a place much lower than the back of her head—but there were too few people to provide much cover. She came back to Libby's side.

"Do I need to bring you in to the station on suspicion of stalking?"

"You wish," Libby said with a haughty flip of her hair, before she grinned. "I was just admiring the view on my way to work. I teach over there." She gestured at Gould Hall, across from the police station. It was one of the two buildings housing UW's School of Architecture. All glass and concrete and straight lines. She grimaced with disappointment at its lack of imagination and turned back to the officer who was visually much more appealing. She was trying to think of something else to say to prolong their conversation, but the walk light came on, and they followed the rest of the pedestrians across the street. She might have been imagining it, but she thought the officer's sigh matched her own.

"Well, good-bye."

"Bye," Libby said with a wave before she turned and crossed the side street toward her building.

By the time Libby's second class ended, she felt exhausted. Mondays and Wednesdays were her lightest days of the week, with only the two classes to teach, but the early days of the quarter were always tiring for her. Every batch of students was unique, with different names, goals, and communication styles, and she struggled to learn them in the first few weeks. Although each course would basically follow the syllabus she had created—with scheduled readings, assignments, and exams—she left room in them to be able to adapt to the students themselves. She spent the first weeks of the quarter with part of her attention focused on teaching and the rest on observing the class as they learned and determining how to best adjust to them. Once she had a month or so with a class, she settled into the flow of teaching more easily.

She stuffed a notepad and folder full of handouts into her satchel and slung it over her shoulder. She had held office hours between classes today—with the usual start-of-term nervous students asking questions about quizzes, grading, and the particulars of assignments—so now she was free to go. She headed straight to Denny Hall, walking around the building to enter through the front doors instead of taking the shorter route through one of the side entrances which had boring concrete stairwells. She preferred climbing the wide staircase, flanked by cylindrical towers, that led to the main doors. The revivalist building's arched windows and spires soothed her after the starkness of Gould and the modernist fiasco that was Padelford Hall, where her Women in Rome class was held.

Libby scanned the facade of the building, with its beautiful blend of curves and points, and felt the tension of the day drain from her, before she climbed the stairs and entered through the somewhat incongruous light wood door. The inside of Denny had been thoroughly renovated into near-sterility before she had come to the university, but she was less concerned about interiors—preferring them to be functional and clean—than exteriors, where she appreciated anything *but* those qualities.

She went to the second floor, where her friend Tig's office was. The wood of the door was barely visible under a chaotic collage of photos from trips to Greece, poetry fragments by Sappho scribed in Tig's elegant handwriting, and a flyer advertising the opportunity to spend the summer rowing around the Aegean Sea in a replica of a trireme. The last one sounded quite awful to Libby, and she tapped on the partially open door and walked into the office, ready to ask Tig about it.

She came to a halt just inside the doorway, her questions fading from her mind when she saw that Tig wasn't alone. Ariella was sitting in one of the chairs across from her, and Jasmine was perched on the edge of Tig's desk. They were Libby's three closest friends, and they were often together at restaurants or in one of their homes, but she couldn't recall ever having their entire group crammed into the same office. The surprise of seeing them all at once wouldn't have been as jarring, except that they were looking at her with expressions that somehow made her feel like a prey animal that had stumbled into a predator's den.

"Hello," she said, her voice rising enough to make the greeting sound like a question.

Ariella gave her a little wave in return, but Jazz pointed at the empty chair. "Shut the door and sit down, Libby."

Something about Jazz's voice always made Libby mentally add the phrase *or else* to whatever she had said. Jasmine was the director of Suzzallo Library, and she seemed to live her life as if it was her personal mission to completely remove the stereotype of librarians as meek little old ladies from the American psyche.

Libby shut the door and sat down.

"You three are giving me the creeps," she said. She set her bag on the floor at her feet and crossed her legs. "What's going on?"

"We just wanted to talk to you," Ariella said, patting her on the arm in a way that was unusual rather than comforting.

Libby looked at the three of them in turn, confused. "So, you all came here? Why not corner me in my own office?"

"Because we knew you'd be here, but we weren't sure what your offices hours were." Tig shrugged. "You always visit me on Monday afternoons."

"Except for the quarter when she had a late afternoon class on Mondays," Ariella added. "Then she switched me to Mondays and saw you on Thursdays instead."

"And I'm Fridays because that's when she comes to the library to check out books for the weekend."

Libby was definitely *not* going to bring up the morning's story of her near-assault on a police officer because of a Monday lemon bar. "So I have a few routines I follow. Would you rather I came to see you on random days?"

"They're ruts, not routines, Libby dear," Jazz said. "And we expect you to break out of them."

"Not *expect*, Jazz. We would like to *encourage* her to change them," Ariella said in a whisper loud enough for Libby to hear. Because she was sitting Right. Next. To. Her. Libby crossed her arms, too, turning herself into a defensive pretzel. The movement called her attention to the sleeve of her blouse. Her *Monday* blouse, she realized uncomfortably.

"Is this some sort of intervention just because I visit you on certain days? We have predictable class schedules, so—"

"You're getting too hung up on that part of it," Jazz said. "We're worried about you because you rarely leave campus. You need to find some new hobbies. Make some new friends."

"I leave campus every day when I go home. Plus, I go downtown all the time." *All the time* was a slight exaggeration, but not much. She'd taken the bus to Pike Place Market just a week or so ago. Or was it a month?

"You live five minutes away," Tig said dismissively. "And you spend most of your time when you're in the city wandering around and staring at buildings. That's hardly a change of pace from what you do on campus."

"I'm an architectural historian. Staring at buildings is what I do for a living. I'm not going to move to the other side of Seattle just for a change in scenery." She glared at each of her friends in turn, but they didn't seem intimidated by her. "Although the suggestion that I find three new friends is starting to look better by the minute."

"We don't mean for you to replace us," Jazz said, gently kicking the leg of Libby's chair. "Just to maybe add some new people to your world. People who are different."

Perhaps a beautiful woman in uniform? Libby pushed that thought as far out of her mind as she could get it, not because she wouldn't be interested in pursuing the idea, but because the memory of her morning interaction only seemed to serve as proof of what her friends were saying. She had been standing close to an attractive stranger, actually having a conversation with her, but too much of her attention had been focused on the potential break in her routine rather than on any romantic possibilities that the chance meeting might have provided. Still, her friends didn't need to know how uncomfortably close to the mark they were. Libby stuck to her defensive position with determination.

"But you're all very different, and the four of us wouldn't be friends if I hadn't brought us together." Libby loved her small group, even if they were being annoying and intrusive at the present moment.

Tig snorted, adding weight to the annoying side of the scales. "Your three best friends are all lesbian Humanities professors. Fine, two professors and one librarian, so stop hissing at me, Jazz. My point still stands that we're not exactly a microcosm of the diverse American population."

Libby shook her head, still unconvinced. "I'm happy. Why should I change?"

Ariella rested her hand on Libby's forearm. "Are you really? You seem content, but you don't seem truly happy to us."

The warmth and concern in her friend's voice broke through some of Libby's stubborn resistance to their suggestions. If she was being honest with herself, she hadn't been feeling particularly joyous lately. She loved her work and her friends, but at the end of the day, when she was in her apartment reading with only a stone gargoyle and a cat for company, she felt something was missing from her life. Maybe this talk—invasive as it was—would spur her on to find that spark of passion again. In a safe way, though. Not in a way that involved chasing down an officer.

"Maybe you're right," she admitted reluctantly. "I wouldn't mind adding something new to my life. I've always wanted to learn Russian, so maybe I could audit a class. Or get a book and teach myself. Or sign up for Duolingo."

"No," all three of them chorused, making Libby startle.

"Nothing academic," Jazz added. "If you really want to take a class, you could go off campus and learn how to do something like bread baking or cooking."

"Not bread," Tig said. "She'll just use that as an excuse to stay home in the evening." She switched to a falsetto and said, "My bread is rising. I'll have to stay in my apartment and read for the next five hours."

"I really don't think I sound so shrill," Libby protested, trying not to laugh at Tig's exaggerated impression of her. It didn't help that she had been thinking almost those exact words when Jazz had made her suggestion. "And I don't wave my hands like that when I talk."

"You do when you're talking about buildings," Jazz said, pushing herself off the desk. "So it's settled, then? You'll find something interesting to do, or else we'll find something for you. And trust me, if you heard some of the suggestions these two were dreaming up before you got here, you'd be quick about signing yourself up for hot yoga or bonsai pruning or whatever. Otherwise you'll find yourself engaged in some embarrassing activity that involves other singles who are looking for love. Now, let's go get dinner because I'm starving. You usually have falafel from that little restaurant on the Ave. on Mondays, don't you?"

Libby sighed. Had she accidentally emailed everyone her weekly itinerary? They seemed far more aware of her routines—or ruts, as they so impolitely called them—than she herself had been. At least they weren't forcing her to start by switching her normal dinner routine, because now that Jazz had mentioned falafel, she was having a serious craving for some. She got up, and they headed toward University Way, thankfully talking about subjects other than her life. She wasn't going to admit it to them, but she felt a little electric ping inside, a flicker of interest in the idea of pushing her boundaries and trying something new. Besides, Jazz had moved from veiled threats to outright pronouncements of the *or else* consequences. Trouble was, unless it involved books or taking academic courses or staring at buildings, she had no idea what interested her, or what hobby could possibly make her evenings a little less lonely. Libby had better find her own activity, though, before she was forced into an evening of speed dating or an awkward Lonely Hearts Birdwatching Club outing.

CHAPTER THREE

Clare only had to drive around the block three times before she found a great spot on a nearby side street. Her Hyundai might be old and ugly, but it was a dream to parallel park, practically scooting itself sideways into impossibly tiny gaps between other cars. And its garish lime-green paint made it easy to spot in any sea of more tastefully colored vehicles. She had chosen it because of its low price, and the fact that it had turned out to be a perfect city car was a bonus. She manually locked the door—the key remote had stopped working years ago, despite battery changes and repeated smacks against the dashboard—and gave the hood a pat before walking around the corner to the restaurant.

Lassi, one of the city's trendiest new dining locations, was distinctive even on this eclectic and bright street, its windows glittering with lights and gilded statues. The warm smell of spices wafted around the doorway, changing to an aromatic punch in the face when she stepped inside. Clare knew her friends hadn't chosen this meeting spot in the Fremont neighborhood in north Seattle because they wanted her to have an easy drive from her Greenwood apartment. They had picked it because it was far from the casual pubs where they used to hang out when she was still with Seattle PD. They might run into a stray cop from their precinct here, but it would likely be someone on a date or dining with the family. Not a crowd of officers getting together for a drink after their shift ended. She wasn't sure if they were trying to protect her from her own feelings of regret and no longer belonging, or if they suspected that some of her old coworkers wouldn't be shy about commenting on her defection from the force.

Either way, their choice of venue and obvious attempt to protect her had made her feel a little sad, but one whiff of the place and sadness shifted toward gratitude. And hunger.

She made her way through the crowded lobby to the restaurant's bar. She paused under the arched entrance and scanned the room, as much looking for her friends as noticing and marking the positions of the other people in the room. It was a habit she had picked up soon after joining the force, and she knew it would always be part of her.

Erin noticed her first, and then Zeke. They both smiled at her, and she felt the impact of their expressions in her gut, as if she had forgotten what it was like to have anyone be glad to see her when she walked into a room. Three weeks with the campus police had been harder on her than she had realized. Everyone in the department was polite to her, answering her questions and offering to help with paperwork or with finding her way around campus, but *polite* could sometimes be miles away from *friendly*. She blinked a few times— ready to blame the oily scent of chiles in the air for any tears that might show in her eyes—and made her way to the small booth in the back of the room where her friends were sitting.

They hugged, then spent several minutes getting settled and making the expected comments about how wonderful the place smelled, and what amazing reviews they had read about it.

"How's your dad?" Clare asked Erin once they had given their orders to a waiter. Clare had glanced over the menu, but the lighting was too dim to read easily, so she had ordered her favorite, saag paneer, having already checked the restaurant's online menu to make sure they served it.

"Still tired after chemo, but the treatments are finished. His doctors are hopeful." She fidgeted with her napkin even as she relayed the hopeful news, a small physical sign of how stressful the year had been for her family. "He wanted me to thank you for the Seahawks jersey. He said it was a much better present than all those damned flowers other people sent."

"Hey!" Zeke said.

Erin mouthed *oops* at Clare before patting Zeke on the shoulder. "He didn't mean your gift, of course. Besides, you gave him a plant, not flowers. He loves that plant. Carries it everywhere he goes." She laughed when Zeke gave her a skeptical look. "Okay, he doesn't. But seriously, my mom loves it and keeps it on the dining room table. This has been tougher on her than anyone, I think, and she said that having so many growing things around the house makes her feel better."

Their conversation moved to Zeke's daughter, who was excited to be in first grade and obsessed with the idea of getting a puppy, then on to Clare's car and whether they should have a tow truck on speed dial in case it didn't start when it was time to go home. Clare found the familiar topics and playful teasing comforting. She had avoided getting together with her friends since she had left the department, rationalizing her self-imposed isolation with a variety of excuses. She had worried that seeing them might make her transition harder to bear, and then once the sense of regret had settled inside her belly, she had convinced herself that she'd feel awkward and sad around them. Only minutes into their conversation, she knew she had been wrong to keep her distance. She had been needing this. Their talk flowed naturally, and they paused only while their drinks were delivered. Two beers and one masala chai.

"I'm on call tonight," Clare said, answering an unspoken question and picking up her cup, taking a sip of the warm, milky tea with its strong accents of cardamom and star anise. She had kept her status as detective when she switched jobs, but on the small campus force, she would be spending much of her time as a regular patrol officer and stepping into the detective role on an as-needed basis. According to Kent, she was permanently on call until told otherwise. Clare had thought her sergeant was joking when she said that, but she wasn't entirely sure, so she was sticking to nonalcoholic drinks when off-duty until she was certain. Sergeant Kent wasn't an easy woman to figure out.

Zeke and Erin shared a look, confirming Clare's suspicion that they had been avoiding the subject of police work until she brought it up. "So, you're happy there?" Erin asked.

She was somewhere between happy and sinking in a pit of despair and regret. She moved along the scale, depending on the day. "I'm fine. It's fine," she said. "The people are nice, but I miss you two."

"We miss you, too," Erin said. "Now, without using the word *fine*, tell us how it's really going."

Clare began with the story of her first day, emphasizing the ridiculousness of her mad dash to the police headquarters and making her conversation with the professor sound sillier than it had been by focusing on her feeling of being a rookie again. Her friends laughed with her, but she could tell they recognized the less positive emotions lurking beneath the surface of her tale. She added the lemon bar story because it was the only one she had that was completely fun, untainted by her current work stresses. Zeke and Erin laughed again, as she had expected, but they exchanged a look with each other that she couldn't quite read.

"What?" she asked.

Erin shrugged with a grin. "Nothing. She just sounds pretty."

Clare had been careful not to mention any physical description of the woman, sticking to the humorous aspects of their interaction. She didn't want her attraction to leak into her story, and she definitely wasn't going to share how often she had scanned the crowded paths when she was at work, hoping for another glimpse of the stranger. She had spotted her from a distance several times, but unfortunately, her days had been too busy to allow her to linger and make contact, as she was either being rushed from one area of campus to another or was locked away in one of the department's small offices doing online training.

"I don't think I described her appearance at all."

"You didn't have to," Zeke said. He rubbed the bridge of his nose. "You had one of your special Clare smiles when you talked about her. Your nose crinkles when you like someone."

"We haven't seen one of those smiles for a long time," Erin added. "So maybe it's not all bad there?"

One brief and unrepeated meeting wasn't enough to heal Clare's broken career. "Sorry, Erin, but since those first days, *fine* is the best way to describe what it's been like. Everyone has been helpful, and no one has been overtly rude or shunned me." She shrugged, twisting her cup and sloshing a little liquid into the saucer. "They're cautious and somewhat cool toward me, but I'm new, and they don't know me yet. It's nothing unexpected, and probably a better reception than I'd get as a newcomer at a lot of other departments. I'll eventually be treated as less of an outsider as I earn their trust. Even if I never feel like a true part of the team, I'll be okay." She paused, caught by her own words and suddenly aware that she had been resigning herself to never truly fitting in at work. She had her old friends, and being liked by her coworkers wasn't her priority. Her career plans meant she needed to be respected, but not necessarily loved. She'd be fine if they never became more than acquaintances. Better than fine. Super. Fantastic.

"Still, it's a small force with a lot of good people on it," she continued, getting to what she was sure was the heart of her problem. "Promotions are going to be hard to come by, even if I don't have to worry about some of the barriers I'd face in a more old-school situation."

To their credit, her friends just commiserated silently with her and didn't offer any unrealistic solutions to her problem. What could they suggest, anyway? That she quit and return to her old job? Impossible. That she quit and find a job somewhere else? Not impossible, but damaging to her career. She would either look flighty to prospective employers, or they would suspect that she had left quickly because she had personality issues and didn't fit in well with others. She propped her elbows on the table and rested her forehead in her hands. "I made a mistake," she said softly, unsure whether they would even hear her muffled voice.

"Well, yeah," Erin agreed with her.

"You did," Zeke said at the same time.

"Thanks a lot," Clare said, lifting her head. She had to laugh, though. After so many days living with a shield of politeness between her and the other campus officers, her friends' brutal honesty was welcome. They would call her on her mistakes but would support her through each and every one, without a doubt. Clare appreciated that level of trust, but still, *ouch.* "Couldn't you even pretend to disagree with me?"

"Oh, sure, I can do that," Erin said. "I think you made a great decision." She cleared her throat and assumed a falsely cheery tone of voice, continuing, "It sounds like a wonderful place, and I wish I worked there, too."

"Then apply, and I'll write you a letter of recommendation," Clare said, matching Erin's fake enthusiasm. "I'm sure my opinion will carry a lot of weight with the hiring committee."

"I'll do that. And I'm sure Zeke will pretend to apply, too. Right?" She poked him in the ribs. He smiled at the joke but shook his head.

"I won't pretend, but I'll add a disclaimer to my agreement about this being a mistake," Zeke said, pausing while their dinner plates were set in front of them. Clare, sensing she was going to need fortification before she heard his speech, speared a chunk of paneer and chewed it slowly, savoring the heat of chiles and strong spices that had been infused in the soft cheese.

"All three of us understand what it's like to be a member of an underrepresented community in a career that has a tradition of embracing stereotypes," Zeke continued. "We've all experienced subtle and overt discrimination, and the way I see it, there are two options for handling it. The first is to accept it for what it is—not to condone or ignore it, but to persevere, and to take responsibility for speaking against it whenever possible and to use our power to change the status quo when we rise in the ranks. The second is to do your research and find another position that matches your career goals, where the system for determining advancement will be more supportive and unbiased."

"Which is what I did," Clare said.

"No. You angry-quit. UW's department has a reputation of being less discriminatory than most others—we've all heard that. But did you really research the opportunities available, or find out what promotions would actually mean in terms of job duties and transferability to other forces? Do you know what percentage of officers rise above the rank of sergeant or lieutenant, or how many positions open on average in a year?"

Clare toyed with the bright green sauce on her plate. She didn't answer because she didn't have to—both Zeke and Erin had been there the day she had decided to resign. Yes, she had been angry at the time. And no, she hadn't done any more research than looking online for open positions with the campus police since she had heard positive things about them.

"Are you getting to the disclaimer anytime soon?" Erin asked. "Because you just seem to be making things worse."

"Here goes," Zeke said, resting his hand over Clare's and meeting her eyes with his kind brown ones. "I agree that it was a mistake to quit in anger without researching your options. But you don't know yet whether it's a mistake to be there or not. Even though you weren't careful about making the choice, it still has the potential to be the best one you could have made. Only time will tell." He shrugged one shoulder and turned his attention to his plate of tandoori chicken.

Erin, looking unsure if Zeke had made the situation better or not, watched Clare while she considered his words. Clare wasn't good at waiting, and she had nearly handed in her resignation more times than she could count in just a few weeks on campus. Zeke's words didn't so much give her hope as they gave her a dose of realism, and she decided that was exactly what she had needed.

"I suppose regret-quitting would be even worse than angry-quitting."

"Career suicide," he said with a nod of affirmation.

Clare scooped up another piece of paneer. "I guess I'll just have to be patient, then, and see how it goes."

"You? Be patient?" Erin laughed. "We'll have to meet weekly for dinner, so you can let us know how *that* goes."

Clare laughed along with her friends, and then changed the subject and asked about some of the other cops from her old precinct. She wanted to reassure them that they could talk about Seattle PD and not tiptoe around the topic when they were around her. She also wanted to set aside her worries about her new job, at least for the rest of the evening. Somehow, here with her friends, it seemed easier to put her anxious thoughts out of her mind than it had been lately.

Several hours and numerous mugs of chai later, Clare made her way back home, feeling more settled than she had for weeks. It wasn't until she was in her bed and sound asleep in the early hours of morning that she got the text from the campus police station. Apparently she really had been on call that evening.

❖

She parked on a side street two blocks from the edge of campus, careful to pick a spot without a parking meter since her days of having a take-home patrol car were over. University Avenue was dark and silent for the most part—only the occasional all-night eatery or theater casting a dim light onto the sidewalk. If she didn't mind getting to work four hours early every day, she'd never have to worry about finding a place to park again.

She jogged across the street and up a short staircase, slowing to a walk as she was enveloped by the shadows of the large oaks on the university side of the road. After spending plenty of hours memorizing maps and walking around campus, she easily found her way to Red Square, the red-brick plaza surrounded by several buildings, including Suzzallo Library, her destination.

The university was well-lit at night for the safety of its students and staff, and bright spotlights now illuminated the area in front of the library. Clare paused on the edge of the false daylight where the police had cordoned off Suzzallo's entranceway and took in the sight in front of her. She had worked every shift so far, in a standard rotation intended to familiarize her with the job as a whole, but the majority of her time on night shifts had been spent near the dormitories and campus-owned housing. Those had been fairly active at all hours, and she had felt more like a nanny than a cop as they escorted students around, warned fraternities and sororities to turn down their music, and hauled drunk kids to the campus infirmary. The only thing that had set the university setting apart from a standard city one was the ridiculous proportion of young people who seemed far too enthusiastic about being on their own and unsupervised.

Standing here in the middle of the night, though, gave her an unanticipated shift in perspective. The library, with its regimented rows of ornately decorated, arched windows, seemed suddenly massive and ancient. The spotlights only made the shadowed areas seem darker and more mysterious than they were with the regular campus lighting. There was an otherworldly feel to the place, as if she had somehow stumbled on a University with a capital *U* instead of the collection of buildings that made up this particular campus, and the rest of Seattle—really only steps away—might have been in a completely other country. She wasn't quite sure why the square she had walked through hundreds of times by now seemed different tonight, but it did. Maybe it was in contrast to the rest of her evening, spent in a city that birthed trendy new places nearly every day, but she had crossed a barrier when she stepped over the boundary from the U District and onto the campus proper. This place was somehow out of step with real life in a way she hadn't recognized before.

What was she doing here? Now more than ever, she felt as if she didn't belong. In her sleep-deprived and anxious state, she had the weird sense that the buildings themselves felt it, too.

She shook off her unexpected reaction to the sight of the library and hurried toward the crime scene. If she didn't arrive promptly enough, Sergeant Kent's anger would no doubt send her reeling out of her imagination and back into the real world.

CHAPTER FOUR

Clare ducked under the crime scene tape and walked around one of the two campus police vehicles parked at angles in front of the building, blocking the crime scene from the view of anyone passing by. She heard Sergeant Kent and Cappy talking before she saw them, and the anger in their voices naturally made her hesitate before stepping into their line of sight.

Why her? Were the first words Clare could distinguish clearly. If Cappy had said them with anguish in her voice, Clare would have assumed they were meant for the murder victim, whoever it was. Instead, her obvious irritation made Clare's stomach tighten with the certainty that she was the *her* in this situation.

"Because she has experience as a homicide detective," Sergeant Kent snapped back, proving her right.

"But she doesn't have experience here. With us. She doesn't deserve to work on this case."

Clare hadn't personally spoken to Cappy since the day they had first…well, since her first day on the job, when they hadn't spoken a word to each other. Cappy had always managed to look busy with something else or to suddenly need to sit on the other side of the room when she saw Clare. Clare had wondered if it was personal or just a coincidence, but now, listening to her angry tone, Clare no longer had any question.

"Listen, Flannery. This murder happened on my campus, and my team will be the one to solve it. If we don't seem qualified enough, the chief will pull us and call in Seattle PD, and it's bad enough having their forensics people swarming over our turf. I'm letting you take point, but she's on the case. If you push me to choose between you, she's in and you're out. Got it?"

Cappy's silence seemed to indicate her acceptance of Kent's threat. Clare rubbed her eyes wearily. She had been thrilled to get this call, to have a chance to prove herself so soon after starting with the department. Now she had to face a partner who hated her and a sergeant who expected her to have more expertise than her short time in homicide had actually given her. Solving the murder would hopefully be the easiest part of this assignment. Still, she couldn't hide behind the police car for much longer.

She walked into the circle of brightness cast by the nearest spotlight, and both Cappy and Kent snapped their heads around to look at her.

Kent frowned at her, and Clare steeled herself for a tirade about eavesdropping, but it didn't come. "It's probably for the best that you heard that, Sawyer," she said instead. "You know Cappy doesn't want to work with you—"

"I don't," Cappy said with a shrug.

Kent sighed and continued. "And I'm sure you'd rather be the lead in this case and not answering to her."

"I would," Clare said, mimicking Cappy's dismissive shrug. She actually wouldn't, but she wasn't about to admit it to these two. Under normal circumstances, she might have felt more hurt and confused by Cappy's negative opinion of her, but her sense of overwhelm because of Kent's expectations overrode any personal considerations. She had spent the bulk of her time as a detective working in Seattle's criminal department, mainly with vandalism and theft, and had been temporarily promoted to homicide when an unexpected retirement had opened up a slot. After only two months, a detective with less experience had replaced her as a permanent member of homicide, and she had been bumped back to her old job. Hence the angry quitting. Those two months' worth of experience seemed woefully inadequate right now.

"Good," Kent said. "Now we all know how the two of you feel, and you know that I don't care. You're going to put aside whatever personal issues you have and get the job done. Now, let's get to work."

Clare wanted to protest that she didn't really have any issues with Cappy—she didn't even know the woman—but she recognized an invitation to shut the hell up when she heard one. She kept her silence as they approached the library entrance, getting her first glimpse of the crime scene.

Three large archways were perfectly centered in the front of the building, leading to the main entry doors, and the body was lying under the center one. She felt a sudden and unexpected twist in her gut when she saw the body from a distance, her mind conjuring up a disturbing image of the lovely lemon bar fanatic lying dead before her, and she had to fight to keep from audibly sighing in relief when she saw that the victim was male. She didn't even know that woman, so what difference did it make to Clare if the body was hers? Well, it definitely *did* make a difference, but Clare wasn't going to examine that fact right now. She was going to do her job.

She stepped closer and observed the man. His ankles were crossed, and his arms were resting at his sides. He looked to be in his early forties and was neatly dressed—aside from the blood drenching his neck and chest. His throat had been slit—*hacked*, Clare amended as she took in the details of the scene. It didn't look like a quick, professional murder, but a messy and laborious one. The man's serene pose struck her as odd given his gruesome wounds. No, not odd, she thought. Significant? Possibly.

Clare squeezed her eyes shut and took a deep breath before opening them again. She needed to slow down and be more careful with her observations. Her tendency to jump to quick conclusions wouldn't benefit her here. She took a physical step back and scanned the scene, trying to see it as a whole before she focused on the details.

"James Turnbow," Kent said, reading from a small notebook. "Recently granted tenure, promoted to associate professor in the Department of Architecture. Lives on Mercer Island with his wife and two teenaged sons."

Clare turned on the recording app on her phone and quietly gave herself a reminder to learn more about the tenure process. She knew it meant the ultimate in job security, and television shows and movies sometimes portrayed it as a position worth killing for, but she wasn't sure how much of an exaggeration that was. The mention of his department triggered something in her mind, probably because she had been thinking of this building as some sort of symbol when she had first arrived on the scene. She looked away from the body and let the columns on either side of the victim lead her gaze upward.

"Oh wow," she said, not realizing she had spoken out loud until Cappy and Sergeant Kent spun in her direction. She pointed at the statue above the archway. "He's posed like her."

The sculpture was a woman, ankles crossed and arms at her side like the corpse. Clare briefly admired the way her robes seemed to flow around her, even though they were carved from stone. Her face was turned toward the heavens with a peaceful expression. She had what looked like a stylized sunburst behind her.

Cappy glanced at Clare, her face unreadable, before pulling out a notebook identical to Sergeant Kent's and writing quickly. Kent called the crime scene photographer over and pointed out the sculpture. They moved aside so he could take pictures, and one of the forensics team followed them. Clare had seen her before, at crime scenes in Seattle, but Clare was relieved that she didn't know the officer by name. She'd rather just be an anonymous campus officer right now, and not have even more attention called to her in-between status.

"Preliminary report," the forensics officer said briskly. "Likely cause of death is loss of blood from the lacerations on the victim's neck. Blood spatter suggests he was killed here, but he was probably dragged to this spot, possibly on some sort of tarp. Stay right behind me."

She turned and walked away, continually pointing at the ground beside her as she went. Clare and the others followed in single file, careful not to disturb the path she was indicating. The evidence that the body had been dragged was slight, but once she was paying close attention, Clare could see signs of disturbance along the path between a low, decorative stone wall and the building. Smudged footprints, compressed dirt, crushed leaves. As they got closer to the corner of the building—where daily foot traffic was lighter and there was more plant matter and debris on the pathway—the signs became clearer. They were lucky the weather had been so dry lately, Clare decided. Even a light rain would have hidden the clues.

A ramp with a green-painted metal railing provided access to the walkway and entrance, otherwise only accessible by the stone steps leading up to the body. The ramp was partially obscured by shrubs and the low-hanging branches of an evergreen tree, probably meant to minimize the sight of such a modern and utilitarian feature. Clare didn't know much about buildings, but even she was able to see how jarring the green metal was when juxtaposed with the elegant stained-glass windows and old-fashioned look of the rest of the library. Unfortunately, the attempt to hide the ramp made its base a perfect location for a crime.

Clare edged forward, avoiding the drag marks as they became more pronounced. The forensics expert stopped where the ramp met a paved sidewalk. At the base of the tree next to it, the dirt and layers of fir needles were clearly flattened.

"The victim has multiple contusions at the base of his skull, seemingly indicative of blunt force trauma with upward strikes, possibly delivered by someone shorter than him. Those might have occurred here, before the unconscious victim was moved."

"So someone whacked him on the head, dragged him up the ramp, posed him like the statue, and then chopped at his throat until he died, with what seemed to be a dull butter knife," Cappy said. Clare had to cover her mouth to keep from laughing, even though the situation was about as far from funny as one could get. Her exhausted mind just appreciated the way Cappy cut to the chase, especially after listening to all the forensic disclaimers. She had been telling herself to remain open to possibilities and not jump to conclusions too quickly—apparently her partner had similar tendencies.

"Maybe. Maybe not. I'm forensics. I give you details about the clues, but you detectives piece them together into a narrative. Now, I need to get back to the body."

"And I need to get back to HQ," said Kent, after the other woman left them. "You two play nice."

Once they were alone, Cappy crossed her arms over her chest. "All right, you're the big-city expert. You start."

Clare resisted the urge to roll her eyes and instead focused on the ground at the bottom of the ramp. Cappy was being defensive, but she was also giving Clare the chance to form and voice her opinions first. Clare had to prove herself with this case—she couldn't let herself get sidetracked by anything or anyone.

"There aren't any signs of a scuffle in the dirt, so a struggle either took place on the pavement, or he was struck from behind and didn't see it coming. The drag marks start way over here"—she pointed at a spot about three feet from the cement—"so the second scenario seems more likely. What was he doing out here in the middle of the night?"

"Sex, obviously," Cappy said. "Show me any shadowy spot on campus, and I can probably give you at least three examples of people I've found there having sex."

Ugh. Clare hadn't faced that particular type of incident yet while on duty. Yet another delight to look forward to while she did her time in this department. She forced her attention back to the crime scene. "And whoever killed him had a weapon to knock him out, a tarp or blanket, and a knife. Not the usual school supplies you find in a college backpack."

Cappy nodded, finishing Clare's thought. "Premeditated. Most likely the person he was here to meet."

"Or the one he *wasn't* here to meet. Wife? Ex-lover?"

They took the long way when they returned to the front of the building, climbing the steps instead of using the ramp again and risking disturbing the evidence. Clare looked up at the statue again before walking closer to the victim. She crouched beside the professor's body, carefully avoiding the forensics markers that outlined the spray of blood. She took out her flashlight and shone it on the neck wounds.

"I think the knife was sharp," she said. Cappy knelt on the other side and looked where Clare illuminated the slash marks. "But the cuts are tentative. See how some of these are shallow? If you've only seen a throat slit on television, you wouldn't realize how much force it would take to break through skin and muscles."

"Not an experienced killer, then," Cappy agreed. "A crime of passion that turned out to be more difficult than imagined."

"Hopefully, hiding the evidence will also prove to be a challenge, and they'll make mistakes that will lead us right to them."

Cappy shook her head this time, resting back on her heels and surveying the ground around them. "Inexperienced, but careful. There aren't any bloody footprints leading away. They probably changed clothes here and hauled everything away wrapped in the tarp."

"That's a lot of evidence to hide."

"There's a lot of water around here," Cappy said with a shrug. "We're surrounded by dozens of lakes and inlets where a bundle of weapons and clothes could be sunk, and then they'd be near impossible to find."

Clare stood up. "Someone always messes up, somehow. There's no such thing as a perfect crime."

"Does that make you a pessimist or an optimist?" Cappy asked, standing up as well, and jotting some more details in her notebook.

Clare smiled somewhat grimly as they walked down the steps and returned to the police vehicles, where she rested her hip against the car. She had to believe they would find the killer. If she botched this, her reputation with her sergeant and the department might be permanently set in stone before she had even had a chance to make a start here. "I'm optimistic about our chances of solving this. Besides, even if it was the perfect crime—which it's not—there are too many people on this campus for this to have happened entirely without witnesses. Once the news spreads, we'll have people jamming the phone lines at the department. Surely one of them saw a person hauling a bloodstained tarp toward Lake Washington."

"Well, until your eyewitness calls and gives us a name, and until we get the ME's full report, we should make a list of possible suspects and start interviewing them. Mrs. Turnbow seems to be a good place to start."

Clare appreciated the way they were bouncing ideas off one another while looking over the crime scene, but she couldn't shake the memory of Cappy telling Kent that Clare didn't belong on this case. Would Cappy try to undermine her every step of the way? Would she pretend to be amiable but go behind Clare's back and make her look bad? She would trust Cappy with her life if need be— the same as she would with anyone on the force with her—but she wasn't ready to trust Cappy with her career. Clare needed to keep control over her own performance while investigating this murder, and that meant working alone as much as possible.

"A list of suspects is a great idea. We'll probably end up with quite a lot of names, so it'll be quicker to divide them up and do the initial interviews separately instead of both of us talking to each one. Then we can compare notes. And we'll be able to talk to twice as many people as we would if we interviewed them together."

She recognized that she was rambling and forced herself to stop. It didn't help that Cappy was observing her with a closed expression, as if she had shut off the animation that she had been showing earlier, whether in anger over her forced partnership with Clare or her curiosity as they discussed the scene.

Cappy remained silent for a few long moments, and then she flipped her notebook to a clean page. "Okay, we'll split the work. I'll interview the wife as soon as Kent lets me. I'd also like to talk to admin and see if there have been any harassment or misconduct insinuations about him. If he was here for an inappropriate tryst, it likely wasn't his first. What about you? What's your grand plan?"

Clare tried to ignore Cappy's sarcastic tone, but now she needed to come up with a line of investigation, and quickly. She had made a fuss about wanting to work alone, and she couldn't admit that she wasn't sure where to begin. She latched on to the initial thought she had when she heard the victim's credentials. She still wasn't sure how the tenure process worked, but she understood careers just fine. If someone was promoted, there was likely someone else who wasn't. Jealousy was a powerful emotion—this wouldn't be the first murder with envy at its core. "I'll start with the other professors in his department, especially the ones who might have been passed over when he was advanced."

Why had she picked professors—the very demographic most likely to make her uncomfortable and unsure of herself—as her initial interview subjects? She had backed herself into a corner with her play to work alone.

Cappy finished writing and tucked her notepad back in her pocket. "We'll give this a try for now," she said. "You do your thing, I'll do mine. But we talk every day, and we don't hide information from each other."

Clare agreed to Cappy's terms. If she had been assigned to work with anyone from her old department, even someone she didn't like, she wouldn't have insisted on going separate ways. This lone wolf act wasn't like her, but panic about her future and regrets about her past were clouding her mind.

"All right, then. There's enough daylight now to examine the scene more closely. Do you care if we do this part together, or would you rather we staggered our start times?"

"Let's just get this done," Clare said, getting out her phone again for recording her observations. She pushed aside her irritation as they got back to work. Yes, Cappy had started this by fighting against Clare's assignment to the case, but Clare had only herself to blame for making the situation worse.

CHAPTER FIVE

L ibby shifted her bag from her left side to her right as she hurried toward Odegaard Library for breakfast. This morning's last-minute additions to her teaching supplies had been three hardcover books with illustrations of Antoni Gaudí's neo-Gothic buildings. She could have stopped by Suzzallo to make copies of similar photos—thus lightening the laden satchel that was currently digging into her shoulder—but she had wanted to avoid running into Jazz. Two weeks after her friends' intervention, and she still hadn't come up with a plan for expanding her horizons or building character or whatever they thought she'd gain from adding a new hobby to her already busy life. She was afraid their patience might be wearing thin, and she expected to be unwillingly signed up for some ridiculous activity soon. For the moment, she was relying on avoidance, but she doubted it would work much longer.

Damn, she thought, spotting the very librarian she had been hoping to dodge. Jazz was standing by the bike racks in front of Odegaard, her arms crossed tightly over her chest, and glaring across Red Square toward her library. Libby frantically scrambled to come up with a pretend plan that would buy her some more time, but then she realized that Jazz didn't seem to be waiting for her at all. In fact, she didn't notice Libby's arrival even when she got within a yard of her. She considered sneaking past Jazz while her attention was focused elsewhere, ducking inside Odegaard to eat her morning lemon bar in peace, but her friend was obviously distressed. Well, *pissed off* might be a more accurate phrase, but the two emotions often went hand-in-hand with Jazz.

"Jazz? Are you okay?" Libby asked, resting her hand on Jazz's tense arm.

"Of course I'm not okay. They closed my library." Jazz didn't shift her focus off Suzzallo. "God knows what sort of mess they're making on my landing."

Libby looked away from her friend and toward the building, inhaling with a small gasp when she saw the bright yellow crime scene tape cordoning off the front of Suzzallo, from side ramp to far corner. Two police vehicles were parked like dark and silent sentinels, hiding the steps leading to the entryway from view. Several officers were stationed at intervals, their backs to the library. The tape and guards seemed invasive, somehow, as if they were scabs covering some unseen wound on the beautiful old building.

"What happened?"

"Jimmy Turnbow was murdered. *On my steps.*"

"Oh, that's…" Libby paused, searching for the right word. Awful. Horrible. What a tragedy. Those were the types of things convention dictated she say. The word she really felt was *wrong*. Not something that happened here, in the safe confines of her university. It wasn't true, of course—she knew the world of academia certainly wasn't immune from crime, everything from murder to petty theft.

She let her sentence remain unfinished. Jazz wasn't really listening, anyway. Libby knew Turnbow—had known him—but they had never moved beyond a lukewarm acquaintance. They were different types of academics, and she had sensed his disapproval of her less conventional, more multidisciplinary approach to learning. He wasn't someone she would mourn in more than a universal, alas-for-humanity kind of way.

"Did the police catch who did it?" she asked, watching as one of the police officers spoke into the walkie-talkie mic clipped to the shoulder of his uniform.

Jazz shrugged. "I don't know. They just released his name a few minutes ago, and I haven't heard anything else."

Libby snuck a peek at her watch. She didn't mean to be callous, but she really needed to get going if she was going to be on time for her class. She wasn't sure if she was supposed to stand vigil out here for a certain amount of time, or if normal life could resume. "I should probably get going..."

Jazz waved vaguely in her direction. "Yeah, you need to get to class. I'm going to go ask that officer when I can get in my building. He told me to stop asking him every five minutes, and it's been at least ten."

"Well, if he arrests you on the charge of annoying an officer, let me know. I'll come bail you out."

Libby had only taken a few steps toward Odegaard when her cell rang. She had to set her bag on the ground and tug the phone out from under the heavy books she had thrown on top of it right before she left her apartment. She didn't recognize the number on the screen. Probably a scam, but she figured she might as well answer it since she had gone through the effort of digging it out.

"Hello?"

"Professor Hart?"

"Yes." Scammers usually didn't address her as *professor*. The voice sounded too mature and confident to be one of her students, and she had a nagging feeling she had heard it before. Low but not soft, and carefully modulated. An alto, if she was singing.

"This is Detective Clare Sawyer. I need you to come to the Campus Police Headquarters and answer some questions."

"Now? I have class in..." Libby checked her watch again. Darn it—no time for even a cup of coffee, let alone breakfast. "Eight minutes. I'll be right across the street in Gould Hall. Can I come after, about eleven?"

There was a pause, and Libby cringed. She hadn't been asked to tea, but to an interrogation. This was the first phone call she had ever received from the police. Was it okay to set her own timetable?

"Yes, that's fine."

The call ended abruptly, and Libby felt a twinge of relief. She probably wasn't under arrest, then, since the cops were unlikely to allow her to saunter in at her earliest convenience if they were going to throw her in jail. Not that she had done anything illegal, but still...A summons from the police tended to invite a person to scour her conscience for forgotten past misdeeds. She halted midstep, suddenly realizing where she had heard that voice. At the pastry counter in Odegaard. *Clare Sawyer* went from being just a name to a fully fleshed-out vision in Libby's mind. Her breath quickened at the memory, and she replayed their conversation in her mind, sure she hadn't made any overt threats that would get her arrested. Besides, the incident had taken place weeks ago.

Two encounters with police in one morning was too much to be coincidence, though, so the call was likely connected to Professor Turnbow's murder rather than anything pastry-related. Not that Libby could help with the case. The only thing she had witnessed was a potential harassment claim when she had watched Jazz march over to the police officer, demanding to be allowed into her library. And Libby definitely wasn't going to rat on her friend.

Libby hoisted her bag onto her shoulder again and hurried toward her class, bypassing Odegaard's cafeteria. She'd find out what the police wanted soon enough. Right now, she had a class to teach.

❖

Walking through the door of the police station felt like going through a portal to a different world—one of glass and steel, metal detectors and scanners. She was told to leave her satchel in a locker, and then was escorted into a small room with only a metal table and chairs in it. She perched on the edge of the cold, hard seat and looked around. Very nice decor, if one was going for the Early Aluminum Foil design style. From her vast experience with police interrogations—from TV shows and movies—she had expected to see a two-way glass masquerading as a mirror, but the walls were bare and beige. A camera was perched in one corner of the ceiling, with its lens pointing at her and an illuminated red light, making the statement that they weren't even bothering to pretend not to be watching her. Whoever *they* were.

She wasn't kept waiting long before an officer entered the room. Libby recognized her immediately, of course, even though they had only met the one time, and she saw the moment when she was recognized in turn.

"Oh, it's you." The officer raised her eyebrows slightly, but otherwise didn't show any expression on her face.

"Yes, we met on the first day of class. You weren't in class, of course, but you were at the café, stealing my lemon bar, and then I followed you here. Well, I didn't actually follow you, I was just behind you." Oh my God, what was wrong with her? Libby had to laugh at herself—she was apparently more disconcerted by the unusual circumstance of being questioned by the police than she had thought. "You probably haven't noticed me lately, because I've been staying behind pillars, with binoculars."

"You've been...what?" Clare's professional mask hadn't slipped entirely, but her raised eyebrows were now drawn together in an expression of confusion. Libby couldn't really blame her.

"That was a joke. Remember, you asked if I was stalking you when we were waiting at the crosswalk? Well, I really wasn't. I was going into Gould to teach, not following you, but I added the part about the binoculars to be funny, because then it—"

The officer held up her hand. Once Libby stopped talking, she gestured with the phone she had in her other hand. "Okay, I get the joke. Would this be a good time to tell you that everything you say is being recorded?"

"Thirty seconds ago would have been better," Libby said, irrationally proud of herself when the officer's lips quirked in a brief smile.

"Let's start over. I'm Detective Clare Sawyer." She sat across from Libby and set her phone and a yellow legal pad on the table. "Please state your name."

"Libby Hart." Wait, legal name? Nicknames didn't seem suited to police interrogations. "Olivia Hart. Olivia Jane Hart. But you can call me Libby."

Detective Sawyer exhaled audibly. She didn't reciprocate and tell Libby to call her Clare, but Libby was going to anyway—in her mind, at least. Thinking of her as Detective Sawyer was making her nervous and overly chatty.

"I don't know if you've heard, but one of your colleagues, Professor James Turnbow, died last night. This is a homicide investigation, and I would like to ask you some questions that might provide insight into the case. Did you know the deceased?"

"Yes." Libby said, relieved when she managed to stop after the simple affirmative instead of launching into a detailed account of their acquaintance. Her self-control had come a little late—she would have preferred for it to have kicked in before she told Clare she had been watching her from behind—but better late than never. She doubted it would last long, but she could hope.

Clare watched her in silence for a moment, as if she, too, expected Libby to say more than one word. "You are also an assistant professor in the Architecture department?"

"Yes. Sort of. I mean, yes, I am, but I also teach for several other departments. I have doctorates in Architecture and Art History, but my research incorporates Classics and Gender Studies. I'm an architectural historian, but classes related to my specialty are offered through all four departments." She recognized the look on Clare's face—she had seen it plenty of times, when she first told people about her academic credentials. *You've studied what?* Followed often by *Why?* "I like school," she added.

"Apparently." Clare paused and wrote some notes on the legal pad. Libby watched, more interested in Clare's slow and measured handwriting and less in trying to decipher the actual words on the paper. "Professor Turnbow was recently granted tenure and promoted to associate professor. You interviewed for that tenure-track position, but he was chosen over you. Correct?"

Libby frowned. Why were so many of these questions about her? She had expected to be asked about Jimmy, not herself. Questions such as *Was he such a boring teacher that one of his students might have killed him just to avoid hearing another of his lectures*? Yes, it was possible. Why would the police care about her repeated failures whenever tenure-track lines opened? "Well, yes, but...hey, wait a minute. Do you think I killed him because he got promoted over me? I doubt that adding murder to my CV would improve my chances on the academic job market." She laughed, imagining telling Tig, Jazz, and Ariella about this interview. "Although my friends have been telling me to find a new hobby. I don't think they had homicide in mind, but they weren't really specific."

Clare picked up her phone and wiggled it back and forth before returning it to the table. "Recording. Remember?"

Libby leaned forward and enunciated clearly. "I did not kill James Turnbow." She sat back again. "Is that better? Besides, like I said, I teach in four departments. If I killed someone every time they got tenure and I didn't, this campus would be piled with dead bodies. Plus, these positions are open to everyone, so I'd have to take out the competition from other universities. I'd have to go on some sort of interstate killing spree, and who has time for that?"

Clare tapped her phone's screen, turning off the recording, and rested her forearms on the table. "Unless you're seriously trying to confess something here, how about you stop using phrases like *piles of dead bodies* and *interstate killing sprees*?"

She looked as if she was wavering somewhere between being frustrated as hell and trying not to laugh. Libby found Clare's expression endearing. Okay, she found it sexy—just like the rest of her—but that didn't seem like an appropriate response in this situation. Not to say she wasn't enjoying the response, but she probably shouldn't dwell on it too much at the moment.

She gestured toward the phone. "You can turn it back on," she whispered. Clare hesitated, then started recording again. Libby cleared her throat and launched into an explanation of her professional life at the university. An explanation that hopefully wouldn't include any mention of dead bodies, but she wasn't about to make any promises to herself that she might not be able to keep. "My position at the university is unusual because of the multidisciplinary nature of my research and the departments I teach in. I'm not the only person in this situation, of course, but we're far outnumbered by the professors who are more focused on a single subject, and often on a very specific subcategory within that subject." Libby stretched her hands apart, up and down, and then side to side. "They go deep, but I go wide. Anyway, that often means that I don't really seem to belong anywhere. If a tenure-track position opens up in the Art History department, I'll often hear that I'm really more of an Architecture scholar, and vice versa. Even though I've published just as much if not more than others who are being considered, the articles I've written that don't directly apply to the subject in question are discounted or given less weight, making it seem as if I'm not as well-credentialed as those who stick to their disciplines."

Libby shrugged, trying to slough off the hurt and frustration she usually kept hidden. Even with her eclectic training, she could have chosen to concentrate on a single subject area for a while, giving herself a better chance at tenure within a specific department. She hadn't been willing to sacrifice her Renaissance approach to learning and teaching, even though the bias against her wide-ranging approach sometimes bothered her. "My point is, I've accepted this as the way universities work. And I've made the choice to continue working the way I do in spite of it, knowing I'll likely spend the rest of my career as a contract appointment. So while Turnbow got a job I might have liked, I certainly wasn't anywhere near next in line."

Clare silently made some more brief notes on her pad before speaking again, changing the topic slightly. Libby wasn't sure if it was because her explanation had been sufficient, or if Clare was trying to keep her from perjuring herself. "Do you know anyone who would have benefitted from his death? Anyone with a grudge against him?"

Libby shook her head. Both Avery and Johnson had been more likely to be serious professional competition for Turnbow, but neither struck her as the type to kick him in the shins, let alone murder him, to increase their chances, so she wasn't going to give their names to the police. Besides, if Clare knew this much about her, she had probably already called them for interviews.

Clare kept her eyes on her paper. "What did you think of him on a personal level? Did he have any relationships that might not have been…appropriate for a married man?"

Libby flinched. She hoped Clare hadn't noticed, even though she had looked away from her notepad and directly at Libby as she finished her last question. "No," Libby said. "I knew he had a wife, but I never heard of him having an affair or anything. He seemed nice enough, but I didn't socialize with him, so I didn't really know him well."

Clare narrowed her eyes. "You made a face when I asked that question. What did that mean?"

"I didn't make a face." At least, she had tried not to.

Clare jabbed her pen toward the camera. "Do you want me to play back the recording and show you?"

"I really don't have anything specific to say on the subject, and it seems wrong to speak ill of the dead." It was a trite and common phrase, and one Libby was certain she had never said out loud before. Still, she felt it would be cruel to criticize someone who was unable to defend himself.

Clare didn't seem to agree. "I'm investigating his murder, not composing his eulogy. If you have something to say about him, then you need to tell me."

Libby sighed. "It's nothing. When I first started teaching here, he got in an empty elevator with me in the library. I made an excuse and got off again and took the stairs instead."

"You don't believe it was nothing. You got off the elevator."

Libby half shrugged, half nodded. "Gut feeling. I listen carefully to them. I've never heard of him acting inappropriately with students or anyone else, and he never did anything to me beyond making me uncomfortable. If he had, then I would have done more than just walk off the elevator." Libby paused and replayed her last sentence in her mind. She leaned toward Clare's phone again. "I meant that I would have reported him or kneed him in the groin or something. I didn't mean I would have killed him."

Clare groaned and rested her head on her crossed arms for a moment. When she raised her head, she picked up her phone. "This concludes our interview. If we have any more questions, we'll contact you." She stopped the recording again and shook her head in Libby's direction. "You probably shouldn't leave the country."

CHAPTER SIX

Clare tucked her phone back in her pocket, relieved that she was no longer recording their conversation, but strangely reluctant to say good-bye. Her interview with Libby—with Professor Hart—hadn't gone the way she had expected. She had a feeling nothing about Professor Hart would be as expected. Clare had interviewed two other professors before her, while waiting for Libby's schedule to open up enough to accommodate her summons to the police station, and both of them had seemed to think she might be the guilty party. Neither had come out and voiced their suspicions, but they had managed to give Clare the impression that Libby was a conniving recluse who would do anything to get ahead in her career. After meeting the real person, the vivacious and quick-witted woman who was seated across from her, Clare was no longer inclined to believe anything they had said. She figured most of their misdirection was caused by the shock of having a colleague murdered and fear that if they didn't throw someone else under the bus, they might be considered suspects. After hearing about Libby's experiences with departmental politics, she decided some of the reason she had been used as a scapegoat was because they thought of her as an outsider in their department.

Clare understood all too well how Libby must feel in her peripheral position at work.

"That was fun," Libby said brightly, resting her elbows on the table and propping her chin in her hands. "It's interesting to think of reasons why I might decide to murder someone."

Jeez, the woman was going to talk herself into a jail cell if she wasn't careful. "This isn't an academic exercise. It's a homicide investigation."

It didn't help matters that Clare had to struggle not to laugh at Libby's comments. She had a guileless sense of humor that made Clare wish they were anywhere but a police interview room, talking about anything but a murdered man. Her wish for them to be elsewhere was deepened by Libby's long, sexy legs and a soft mouth that settled naturally into a smile. Clare's habit of mentally describing people she met, as if she was preparing to put their vitals on a police report, had kicked in the second they had met at the café. Brown hair, just brushing her shoulders and shimmering like polished mahogany in the harsh light of the room. Classic trousers and shirt with just enough wear and off-trend style to seem truly vintage and not vintage-inspired. And intense, just-after-dusk blue eyes that were startling, given the rest of her understated, earth-toned look.

Yeah, Clare was going to need to edit her description before she actually filled in the police report for today's interview.

"Same thing, really," Libby countered, seemingly unaware of Clare's assessment of her. "Logic and imagination intersect. It's stimulating."

Clare at least agreed that Libby herself was stimulating, which was why Clare wasn't following a sensible course of action and hustling her out of the station before she started raving about piles of dead bodies in front of other officers. Instead, she was *lingering*. Allowing their conversation to continue even though the interview was supposed to be finished. Was she merely desperate for human company after feeling so out of place at this department for the past weeks? No. She hadn't stayed in the room for a friendly post-interrogation chat session with either of her other interviewees. She had been self-conscious during those interviews, just as she had expected she would be, and had been hyperaware of everything she did or said that would prove how far from an academic she was. Libby had managed to make her relax and not worry about what judgments were being made about her.

"It's work," Clare said, capping her pen and sticking it in her breast pocket. "Speaking of which, I should get back to the investigation. Thank you, again, for coming in today."

She stood up, but Libby didn't. She crossed her legs, stretching the subtle plaid fabric across her thigh. "Remember how I said my friends want me to find a new hobby?"

"Oh, please don't say murder. Or private investigation. It's really not as glamorous as it looks on TV."

"Neither of those. I want you to be my hobby."

Okay. Clare's shameless body was ready to jump at the chance to be Libby's hobby. Better yet, her full-time job. "Me?" she asked weakly. She used to believe she was skilled at conducting interviews, but this one had somehow gotten away from her.

Libby waved her hand vaguely. "Not you, specifically," She paused and grinned at Clare, her mouth curving in an all-too-inviting way. "Well, I'm not opposed to the idea, but it's not what I meant."

Why had Clare stupidly insisted on her and Cappy doing these interviews separately? She desperately needed some backup in here.

Libby laughed. "Don't worry. What I meant was that I can help you with this case. I'll be your assistant. No, maybe a junior detective? Ooh, freelance expert. That's what I'll be."

"What's your area of expertise? Self-incrimination?"

"Very amusing, but no. I'm an expert in university life. I can show you where Jimmy Turnbow ate lunch every day. I can introduce you to his friends and point out his enemies. I can take you inside his life in a way only another faculty member could do. Think of me as a tour guide of sorts. You might know the buildings and streets on campus, but I'm more familiar with what's going on inside."

Clare paused, intrigued in spite of herself. "I thought you said you barely knew him."

"We weren't friends, but I saw him around campus enough to learn some of his habits. And if I don't know something, then I'll know the right people to ask and find out."

It wasn't conventional, but neither was Libby. Neither was Clare. And Libby was correct that the campus police were on the edge of the university. Clare could find her way around campus fairly easily now, and she was becoming familiar with more and more people in the community, but she and the other officers didn't belong to the school the same way someone like Libby did.

"I'll have to think about it," Clare said. "And it wouldn't be more than familiarizing me with his habits and schedule. I'm not going to jeopardize your safety."

"That's great." Libby smiled and slid the legal pad across the table. She flipped to a blank page and started scribbling. "I never really expected you to even consider it, but I figured it was worth a shot since we'll be doing each other a favor. I'll give you knowledge, and you'll save me from being signed up by my friends for a singles bowling league or something equally awful."

Clare tried to concentrate on her curiosity about these strange but caring-sounding friends of Libby's, but her brain seemed unable to think anything besides *Hey! She's single!*

Libby stood and handed Clare the legal pad, with its top page now covered with her weekly schedule written in surprisingly legible printing. "I've been told I'm unbearably predictable, so this will let you find me on campus any day of the week."

They shook hands, lingering a few seconds longer than a normal handshake.

"It was nice seeing you from the front again," Libby said. "Although I have to admit, I'm rather partial to the other view."

Clare shook her head, laughing at Libby's playful reference to her stalker joke. "Careful. Flattery won't keep you from being arrested."

She walked out to the foyer with Libby and retrieved her bag for her. Clare watched her walk away from the station—two could play at that game—and then headed back to the interview room. Along the way, she tried to compose herself, returning her expression to the careful, neutral mask she wore while on duty. She sat in the chair Libby had just vacated, the metal still warm to the touch, and Cappy joined her after a few minutes' wait.

"How'd it go?" Cappy asked without preamble, tossing her notebook onto the table and dropping into the empty chair.

Clare sighed. She really didn't want to spend time chitchatting with Cappy about the weather, but she wished some of her interactions with her new coworkers could feel less clinical and cold. Her interview with Libby had felt friendlier than anything she had experienced since coming to the university. She started to smile, remembering one of Libby's answers to her questions, and bit her lip to try to hide it.

"I talked to the three faculty members whom Turnbow beat out to get his job. A few years later, he's got tenure and a promotion, and they're still contract workers. Trouble is, the process is more complex than I realized. There wasn't a clear-cut second choice back then, and now there's no guarantee Turnbow's vacated position will be filled anytime soon."

"So if one of them had killed Turnbow, they'd need to be prepared to possibly take out the other two as well."

"Yes, along with who knows how many candidates from outside U-Dub." Clare tried to clean up Libby's description of the interstate killing spree that would be required to clear out the competition. "Even without considering the tenure track as motive, they aren't likely suspects. Professor Avery is over six feet tall and volunteers as an assistant coach with the rowing team. He wouldn't have needed multiple blows to knock out Turnbow."

The man had been huge. He had also practically jumped under the table when someone outside the room had accidentally banged an equipment cart against the door and had spent most of the interview fretting about getting home to his dog that was about to have puppies. He hadn't struck her as a cold-blooded killer.

"Professors Johnson and Hart fit the physical profile more than Avery. Johnson just had a knee replacement in July, and he's still using a cane, so I doubt he would have been able to haul Turnbow up that ramp."

"And Professor Hart is far too gorgeous to have killed anyone," Cappy said.

"She's…wait, what?"

Cappy made a derisive sound. "Please. I saw you walking her out after your interview. It was like watching the end of a date. A really awkward date. I was worried you might try for a bumbling good-night kiss, but luckily you showed some self-control."

"I would never—"

"I'm teasing, Sawyer," Cappy interrupted with a frown. "Didn't people tease each other in Seattle PD?

"Well, yes, my..." Clare hesitated, about to say *my friends did*, but that seemed to imply *and you're not a friend so you're not allowed to tease*, which seemed rude. And also untrue, when Clare thought back to her days on the force. Everyone had been fair game for pranks and playful banter, no matter how close they were personally. Clare didn't think she had ever walked into the station at the start of her shift without hearing someone loudly—and with more hysteria than the tired joke warranted—complain about her car, as in *that lime-green monstrosity someone just dumped on police property*. She had been missing the feelings of camaraderie that she was accustomed to from Seattle PD, attributing the lack of it to her position as a lateral and rookie with this department—but her instinctive, defensive response to Cappy's comment made her wonder if she was partly to blame for the distant way the other officers on campus communicated with her.

She crossed her arms and leaned back in her chair, assuming the most prudish sounding voice she could manage. "Call me old-fashioned, but I don't believe in kissing after a first interview. I usually wait until the second or third."

Cappy laughed, and Clare realized with some shock that it was the first time anyone here had done so while carrying on a conversation with her. Just how prickly had she been?

"Good one," Cappy said. "So, I suppose they all said they were asleep between two and four in the morning? Can anyone corroborate?"

"A wife, a pregnant dog, and no one. Still, I'm not seeing professional envy as a viable motive," Clare said, returning to the investigation. Moments of connection were fine, but she had to keep her focus where it mattered most—on solving this case and proving herself on the job, not on becoming best friends with her coworkers. She could try to lighten up with them, but her goals weren't about to change.

"The payoff just doesn't seem sure enough to make it worth committing a murder for the sake of their careers," she continued. "I'm sure jealousy and pettiness are common, but I get the sense that any sabotage these three planned would be more along the lines of taking the last doughnut in the staff room. Plus, to hear Hart tell it, she's sort of an outsider in the department and doesn't see herself as a contender for serious advancement."

Given time, she was sure Libby could come up with several compelling reasons why she might have wanted to murder Turnbow. She probably would enjoy the challenge of raising herself higher on the list of suspects. Clare decided not to mention any of that, and instead told Cappy about Libby's reaction to Turnbow on the elevator. Omitting the kneeing him in the groin threat, of course.

Cappy nodded thoughtfully when Clare finished. "She's got good instincts, in my opinion. I felt the same way about him just from talking to his wife. Apparently he was on campus last night because he had to stay late and grade some papers. Who grades papers at three a.m., especially this early in the quarter? She kept saying how busy he was lately, with so many classes to teach and meetings to attend, as if she was trying to convince herself that he was legitimately working. When I asked if she thought he was having an affair, she broke down crying. She didn't say he was, but she also didn't deny it. She said she was home and in bed when it happened, but her sons weren't there. They had spent the night with a school friend after a party."

Clare was starting to regret her rash plan to have them work separately on the case, since Cappy had spoken to what sounded like their most likely suspect. The jealous wife, pushed to the limit by one too many late-night trysts. The dream of revenge that turned panicky and messy when faced with the reality of bone and blood and muscle. If Mrs. Turnbow did turn out to be the killer, then Cappy would be the one who got the credit for uncovering her motives.

Would Clare switch places with Cappy if she could go back in time? Would she have chosen to go see the widow and to leave Libby and Cappy together in this interview room? Clare wanted to think she would have taken the path leading toward the more advantageous professional move, or the one that had her interviewing civilians instead of intimidating academics, but truthfully, she would have picked Libby all over again. Cappy probably would have arrested Libby. Or asked her on a date. Clare wasn't sure which was the most upsetting to her, but neither should matter as much as her own career.

"Mrs. Turnbow stands to gain the most financially by his death," Cappy said. "An amazing house, not to mention his life insurance and pension."

"Hmm," Clare mumbled softly, something in her mind snagging on Cappy's introduction of monetary gain to the equation.

Cappy remained silent, thankfully letting her collect her thoughts, while Clare reviewed her mental pictures of the scene, the body, and now the fancy Mercer Island house.

"Why pose the body, then? Why risk moving it out of the shadows instead of finishing the job where he had fallen unconscious? Think about it. Pretend you're Alicia Turnbow." Clare shook her head slightly, trying to get Libby off her mind. This was exactly the kind of mental exercise Libby would have thought was a superfun game.

"You're tired of your husband's affairs, and you've decided to kill him. Get the money, the house, the sympathy for being the grieving widow. You gather the weapons, then either lure him to a secluded place or follow him when he's meeting someone else. Then you hit him in the head."

"You're right," Cappy said, continuing with Clare's logic. "Why drag him into the light, where she has a good chance of being seen? She has the home, her kids are there. She had everything to gain by killing him, and nothing to gain by posing him and making some sort of symbolic point."

"It still might be her," Clare said. "Maybe she wanted to humiliate him, or make a spectacle of him. Kill him in a public place, but close enough to his hidden spot to bring his affairs to light. If he was really having an affair."

"We need to find out. Was he meeting someone last night? Who was it? Did they kill him, or did they witness a murder and are afraid to come forward and admit why they were there? Unfortunately, he didn't write *Meeting with Ms. X in the bushes by the library at three a.m.* on his calendar."

Clare hesitated. This was the best opportunity she was going to get to bring up Libby's offer, but she didn't know Cappy well enough to guess how she would respond.

"I might have a way to find out more about his personal life— where he taught, the people he spent time with. Professor Hart offered to be sort of a tour guide to his life on campus."

"I'll bet she did."

Clare rolled her eyes at Cappy's suggestive tone but otherwise let the comment go. Personal growth.

"I might have a better chance of learning about him from his students and colleagues if she's introducing me, and she'll have a better idea of his daily life than we could piece together through interviews and guesswork."

Cappy was quiet, one side of her mouth pulled down in a thoughtful frown. "Actually, it's a good idea," she said after a few moments. "Give it a try. Just remember, she's not a cop, and she's not your partner on this case. No pillow talk about our lines of investigation or sharing details of the case that aren't public knowledge."

"I would never…" Clare managed to stop her indignant reply when she saw Cappy smile and shake her head. So much for personal growth.

"Don't worry, Sawyer. I know you're the perfect professional."

Was that the impression she was putting forward in this place? Inside, she was desperate to prove herself, and maybe outwardly she was coming across as overly formal and stiff. "I'm not perfect," Clare said. She reached over and patted Cappy condescendingly on the arm. "I probably just seem that way from your perspective."

Cappy's burst of laughter warmed Clare. The thought of spending more time with Libby brought a completely different kind of heat. The prospect of having new friends—and the barely acknowledged hope of something more with Libby—made her road more pleasant but didn't change her end goal. She would need to be careful when around Libby, not letting her personal insecurities get in the way of her investigation. They might enjoy a few moments of laughter together, and Clare might already be looking forward to the prospect of spending time with her outside of the police station, but she couldn't imagine someone like Libby, with her numerous degrees, being friends, or more, with someone like her.

CHAPTER SEVEN

L ibby sat on the floor of her office, surrounded by piles of old academic journals. She had come up with the grand idea of doing some decluttering during her office hours, so she'd pulled every issue off her bookshelves, where some had been stacked two or three volumes deep on the shelf. Her goal had been to only return to the bookshelf the issues with articles that were relevant and timely, and to repurpose the rest. She had been sitting here reading through each table of contents and imagining classroom scenarios in which she would need one of the articles to prove some fascinating point or to inspire her students to broaden their approach to the subject at hand. She had one slim journal in the giveaway stack, and that was only because she had a duplicate copy to keep.

She was aware that she was trying to distract herself from the memory of her interview with Clare, which only made her more annoyed because she hadn't been able to move Clare far from her thoughts during this project, and now she had a huge mess to clean as well.

Her time at the police station had felt so far from her usual routine, and she had gotten carried away with the freedom of feeling as if she was someone else, doing things that Libby Hart never did. The Libby at the police station was a potential suspect, someone enough unlike her true self to be a criminal. Someone dashing and dangerous. Under the influence of her alternate self, she had found herself flirting with Clare and even offering to help with the investigation. She had mentioned Clare's backside more than once, for God's sake. Alternate Libby had gone rogue.

Libby sighed and returned the duplicate copy of the journal to her keep pile. What if one of her students decided to do a dissertation on the architecture of twelfth century Cistercian abbeys? They would definitely need one of the articles from this issue, and if she had two copies available, she could give this one away instead of lending it.

If Libby was honest with herself—which she was trying not to be at the moment, hoping Kondo-ing her office would keep her mind too occupied for self-analysis—she would admit that Clare had changed her mindset more than the change in venue had. There had been something so poised and controlled about her, and Libby found herself wanting to know more about the woman beneath the uniform and job. She and Clare had seemed to be such different people, and probably it was just the novelty that attracted her to Clare.

No. Libby had been intrigued by more than that. Clare had been smart and confident. Obviously very good at her job, since it wasn't as if murders occurred at the university every day. The campus police weren't going to put their least competent officer on the case. She surely would be able to solve the crime without needing Libby to show her around, although she had been tactful enough to say she would consider the offer instead of laughing in Libby's face.

Libby's friends were right about it being stimulating to expand her horizons, but they hadn't warned her about it being dangerous because she might lose her inhibitions. She was better off sticking with the comfort of her routine, with its predictable pastries and outfits.

A tap on the door dragged Libby's attention back to the present. She looked up to find one of her students, Angela Whitney, hesitating in the doorway, as if unwilling to disturb her if she was busy.

"Come in, Angela," she said, sliding a pile of journals to one side. The tall stack toppled into the next one, creating a small avalanche. "Just step over all this and have a seat." Libby got to her feet and stumbled over the books, landing heavily in her chair and trying to appear as if she had meant to fling herself forward that way. "How can I help you?"

Angela held her phone up so the screen faced Libby. "I've been working on topic ideas for my final paper," she said in her soft-spoken way. Libby had to lean forward and concentrate on her to catch every word. "I thought maybe you could look at them for me and give me some advice about which would be best?"

"Of course," Libby said, "email the notes to me right now, and we'll go over them together." She wasn't surprised that Angela was already working on a paper that wasn't due for weeks—it was the same thing Libby would have done when she was a student. She had been shy and lonely, engaging only with her teachers and with books, until she got to college. Then she had suddenly been surrounded by interesting and intelligent people her own age, and her newfound ability—and desire—to make friends had been a revelation.

Since becoming a professor, she tried to notice the students who seemed like her younger self, the ones who were interested in their classes but lacked the social skills and confidence to fully take part and connect with their classmates. Ariella called them her special cases. She held informal office hours on the steps of Denny Hall once a week, which ended up being wild and free-ranging discussions, since so many of her students—and ones she hadn't yet had in a class—came to them. She made sure to invite those special cases of hers, and they usually slowly became part of the group, making friends who shared common interests and gaining more confidence. They often started to speak up in class as they became more familiar with her and the other students. Angela had attended every week since spring quarter. She still hadn't broken out of her shell and rarely spoke in class even though she was very bright, and Libby expected she would have a lot to contribute. Libby was hopeful that she would eventually begin to develop friendships with the other students, although for now she still only talked with any sort of animation when she was one-on-one with Libby.

She helped Angela combine two of her ideas, then narrow the focus until she had a strong thesis that seemed to excite her for her paper. Libby remembered seeing a useful article for her in one of her journals. She didn't mention it yet, though, since her relatively neat stacks were now a shambles, and she was going to have to dig for the one she wanted. She'd rather not have a witness to her chaotic searching techniques, so she'd bring it to class for her later.

Angela was just getting ready to leave when Libby heard another knock on her door. She looked up and saw Clare pop her head around the partially open door. "Oh, sorry," she said. "I don't mean to interrupt. I can come back later."

"No, now is fine," Libby said, amazed that her voice sounded normal when her heartbeat was anything but. She felt flushed with the surprise of Clare's unexpected appearance—partly because she was a little embarrassed about how she had acted in their previous encounters, but mostly because she was just happy to see her. She wasn't sure why. She didn't know Clare except for that brief time at the police station and the café, but somehow her arrival managed to make Libby feel settled and excited at the same time. She smiled at Angela, not wanting her to feel like she was being shunted out of the room, although Libby irrationally wanted to push her out the door and drag Clare inside. "We were just finishing up here. Angela, once you've had a chance to start your research for the paper, let me know if you need help fine-tuning your thesis."

"I will, thank you, Professor Hart," she said. Clare gave her a friendly smile and said hello as they passed in the doorway, and Angela mumbled a greeting in return and ducked out of the office.

"She's kind of shy," Libby said after Clare had shut the door.

"I was, too, when I first started college," Clare said, maneuvering her way across the room. "I didn't really make any close friends until my third year. By the way, I love what you've done with the flooring in here. Most people would go for throw rugs or carpets. Books are an unconventional choice."

"Very funny," Libby said, relaxing back in her chair as Clare sat in the seat Angela had just vacated. "I was organizing the journals and just haven't put them back yet."

She gestured at the empty shelves, and Clare looked at them skeptically. Libby couldn't blame her—the journals seemed to have multiplied since she had taken them out, and she had no idea how she was going to cram them back into what now looked like inadequate shelf space. "They fit just fine," she said, not sure which of them she was most trying to convince.

"Did they?" Clare asked. She shrugged and crossed her legs. "Anyway, I'm not here to critique your office decor. I wanted to take you up on your offer to show me around and give me a sense of Professor Turnbow's habits and surroundings."

"Really?" Libby hadn't expected to ever see Clare again, except for the occasional glimpse of her around campus, and she could hear the note of pleasure in her disbelieving question.

"Yes, really. If you're still up for it, of course."

"Absolutely." Libby paused, trying to remember the promises she had made to Clare about her ability to shed light on Turnbow's activities, and hoping she hadn't exaggerated too much. She cringed inwardly, willing to bet she had, given how little she had interacted with the man. If all else failed, she might have to make something up. *Yes, Jimmy ate a meatball sandwich every Friday at lunch.* Still, she had her own skills to contribute to their collaboration, and what she lacked in actual knowledge she could make up for with logic.

"I've never tried to solve a murder before, except those dinner theater ones. I've always been the first to discover who the killer is, though, so I don't see how it will be much different in real life." Usually because she treated the games like a class assignment that it was imperative for her to pass, while everyone else seemed focused on having fun and drinking. She didn't mention that part to Clare.

"You are not trying to solve anything," Clare said, leaning forward and glaring at her. Libby didn't feel very intimidated since she could only think about how adorable Clare was when she tried to look so stern and police-like. "If I find out that you're playing investigator when I'm not around, or if you start rounding up suspects, or if you do anything beyond showing me where his office and classrooms were, then I'll have you thrown into a holding cell until this case is closed."

"Can you really do that?" Libby asked, quite certain the answer was no, especially when Clare remained silent. "Yeah, I didn't think so. Don't worry, I'll behave. Well, for the most part."

Alternate Libby seemed to be making a reappearance. Libby felt her cheeks flush with heat at the comment she hadn't meant to make, but she didn't worry too much about it since Clare went a little pink, too.

"So, where do we start?" she asked, excited to begin and anxious to get them out of the office that suddenly seemed very small and intimate. "My office hours are over, so I'm free for the afternoon."

Clare stood up. "Let's start with the crime scene." She held up a hand. "Not to look for clues, so you can leave the fingerprint kit and magnifying glass from your junior detective set here. I'd just like to get your perspective on a few details about the location."

"I can do that," Libby said, picking up her bag and following Clare across the room. She shut the door behind them, gratefully locking away the mess of journals. She'd deal with them tomorrow. "Suzzallo is one of my favorite buildings on campus. Well, one of my favorites, period. I've given entire two-hour lectures on it."

Clare muttered something that sounded suspiciously like *Oh, goody*.

"Hey," Libby said. "My students love my lectures."

"I'm sure they do. I'll bet they spend the entire class period with their eyes closed, so they can better absorb your words of wisdom." Libby playfully punched her in the arm, and Clare laughed. "You just assaulted an officer in uniform. *Now* I can put you in a holding cell if I need to."

Libby's office was at the end of a quiet wing of Architecture Hall, but once they reached the central open-plan area of the building, they were surrounded by students and professors who were making their way to and from classes. Clare's teasing demeanor changed completely, and Libby covertly glanced at her now and then as they walked the short distance to Suzzallo. At first, she attributed Clare's stiffness to her being a cop in the midst of crowds of people— she probably always felt on guard and watchful around so many strangers. Eventually, however, Libby decided it was something more. Clare seemed more tense than alert to her, and Libby wasn't sure why. She didn't know her well enough yet to ask, or even to be sure that her impressions were correct. She was curious enough to want to find out.

Clare had warned her not to investigate the murder. There was nothing stopping Libby from investigating Clare.

❖

Libby stopped when Clare did, at the foot of the steps leading to Suzzallo's entrance. Jazz had told her where the body had been found. She had fumed for over half an hour about the bloodstains on the stone pathway, and the struggle it had been for the campus maintenance workers to scrub them clean. She said there was still a hint of darkness near the central column that might always be part of the building. Libby hadn't gone there to check for herself.

She was tempted to launch into The History of Suzzallo, but instead she asked Clare. "What do you want to know about the building? General style, building materials, history?"

"The statues," Clare said, gesturing toward the three arched entrances to the library. Each was perfectly bisected by a column with a human figure at the top. "Can you tell me about them?"

"Sure," said Libby, wondering how they could possibly be connected to the murder. "They're terra cotta, sculpted by a local artist named Allan Clark in 1924. He made all eighteen of them."

"Eighteen?" Clare looked at her with a quizzical expression. "Where are the others?"

"Look up." Libby pointed at the upper stories of the building. In between the tall neo-Gothic arched windows were niches, each with a carved figure in it.

"Oh. I had only noticed the three on this lower level."

"The ones up there are famous people. Darwin, Dante, Shakespeare. These three in the entry arches are abstract concepts. Thought, Inspiration, and Mastery. Inspiration, in the center, is the only woman out of all eighteen."

Clare pulled out her phone, swiped at it for a moment, and then handed it to Libby without comment. She gasped in surprise at the unexpected sight of Turnbow's body lying on the steps. Right in front of where she was standing now. His death had seemed as abstract as the figures above her until now, but being confronted by his corpse—even a digital version—made it seem suddenly real and far too close.

She frowned and looked at Inspiration, and then back at the photo. "Is he a sacrifice to her?" she asked, handing the phone back to Clare.

"A sacrifice? I thought he was meant to *be* her. Or to somehow be connected to her, since he's in the same position."

Libby stared at the entryway, unable to shake the image of Turnbow, which had somehow become superimposed over the bare stone walkway in front of her. "He's on the ground, at her feet, in an abased version of her pose. If he was meant to be an inspiration, or to be elevated somehow by this kind of positioning, he'd need to be upright."

Clare watched her for a moment, as if trying to figure out how delicate she needed to be. "Dead bodies aren't easy to move, especially if you're in a hurry because someone might walk by at any moment and see you."

"Yes, but couldn't you sort of...prop him up? Right there, against the column. If we're talking about this positioning as a symbolic act, then he'd only need to be a little bit upright to make the point. Flat on one's back sends an entirely different message."

Clare nodded thoughtfully as she put her phone away. She rested her hand on Libby's arm. "I'm sorry I showed you that picture without any warning. I wanted to get your gut reaction, and it turned out to be a very interesting one. Still, I hope I didn't upset you."

"It's okay. I'm fine," Libby said. She was fine mostly because Clare's hand was still on her arm, warm through the fabric of her shirt. She was also thankful to have seen the photo, in a strange way. She had felt detached about the murder—he really hadn't been someone close to her—and she had been sort of cavalier about wanting to help Clare and play at being a detective. She had needed a push to feel the gravity of what had happened in this place.

Clare moved her hand, and they started walking up the steps leading to the library doors. "Which one was he most like, of the three concepts?"

"Not Inspiration," Libby said with certainty. "I team-taught seminars with him a few times, and I've heard comments from his students, and he wasn't inspiring the way I think a teacher ought to be. Thought seems to imply a more contemplative nature than I ever saw in him, although I didn't know him well enough to judge. I suppose Mastery would be my choice. He was like talking to a living architecture textbook. He had an encyclopedic knowledge of the subject."

Her comments weren't the most flattering, but they were true, and she figured if Clare was going to solve this case, she needed to hear truth more than empty praise.

CHAPTER EIGHT

Clare carefully watched Libby as they approached the place where Turnbow's body had been found. She hoped she hadn't upset her by springing the photo on her like she had, but the element of surprise was often one of Clare's best investigative tactics. The expression on a person's face could tell more accurate stories than the ones that came out of their mouths. In this case, Libby's reaction to the placement of the body was what intrigued Clare the most.

She had never handled a murder case in which the position of the victim had felt so integral to the crime. Granted, she had only been part of a handful of homicide investigations during her short time in the unit, but she had studied dozens of cases at school and had read plenty of reports while with Seattle PD, studying investigative techniques and protocols. The Turnbow case seemed to have subtext that Clare didn't always see and didn't fully understand. This detail in the murder was more in Libby's wheelhouse, and Clare was glad to have her help. And her company, but Clare was trying to ignore those feelings. This was a hobby to Libby, and once the excitement and novelty wore off, so would her interest in Clare.

She had felt comfortable talking to Libby when they were alone in her office. She liked it when Libby's playful and flirty side came out, especially since she sensed it wasn't a side of herself that she often showed—Libby usually seemed surprised by her own comments whenever her words had a more suggestive meaning.

Clare had enjoyed those moments, but once they were outside of the private space and surrounded by the college crowds, Clare had mentally resumed her position as an outsider, while Libby seemed perfectly at ease. Of course she was. The university was her home, while it was merely Clare's workplace. She had timed her visit with Libby to coincide with the end of her office hours, and she hadn't considered that the top of the hour was also a time when classes would be ending, spilling their students and professors into the halls and walkways around campus. Her mind still refused to adapt to an academic timetable, and she was usually caught unawares when she found herself swarmed by people during those in-between times.

Libby walked past the place where Turnbow's body had been found. She glanced at it indirectly, as if wanting to see the location they had just been discussing but not wanting to gawk and be disrespectful. Her expression and body language held the awkwardness of an innocent person—not the forced nonchalance of someone guilty of murder.

Cappy's voice annoyingly intruded into her thoughts, telling Clare she was thinking with other parts of her body besides her brain, because how the hell could she determine Libby's innocence based solely on the way she looked at the murder site? Clare mentally told Cappy to shut the fuck up.

Libby raised her head and looked up at the statue of Inspiration, mirroring the sculpture's upturned face as she did. "Everything about Gothic architecture is meant to elevate us," she said, as if aware that she was mimicking the terra cotta figure. "Our eyes, our minds, our hearts. Sweeping arches, columns and pillars, sculptures of accomplished figures or concepts of great consequence. We're supposed to be lifted out of the mundane world, which is part of the reason why so many universities and colleges embrace this style in their buildings."

Clare stared at Libby. Her voice was soft, and she obviously felt a connection to this building, this style. Would she kill someone who didn't follow her sense of ideals? Someone who was promoted over her without necessarily deserving the honor?

And what if he wasn't just a mediocre teacher, but one who was possibly also using the power inherent in his position to compromise his students, dragging them down into the dirtiest and most mundane sphere of life?

Clare wasn't sure. She doubted Libby's distaste or anger would move her to such a violent physical act, but she was basing her conclusion on a mere two occasions of talking to her.

"Are we going in?" Libby asked her, snapping Clare out of her unusually pensive mood and bringing her back to the present. "I can introduce you to Jazz. Jasmine Harald, I mean. She's the director of the library."

"Oh, sure," Clare answered, not really certain how a librarian was going to help them, but willing to give it a try. She followed Libby through the front doors and came to a halt when she got inside. She had assumed the part of the building with the high arched windows was two or three separate stories, but instead the entire room was a massive open space with vaulted ceilings. Soft sunlight shone through the stained glass, giving the space a warm, yellowish glow. Rows of long wooden tables filled the room, and the edges were lined with bookcases. Low hooded lights over each of the tables provided modern brightness for reading, while not detracting from the room's general feeling of an ancient cathedral.

Clare had never spent much time in libraries since most of her past experiences in them weren't positive, but this had to be one of the most beautiful places she had ever been. She wanted to sit at one of the tables and just…think.

"Your first time inside the building?" Libby asked, her voice pitched low. This room demanded nothing louder than a hushed, awed whisper.

Clare nodded. "I've been past it lots of times, but I never came in. I can see what you mean about the architecture of the place being meant to elevate us. It's stunning."

"It's a work of art. This is the Reading Room. I can show you the other…Oh, here comes Jazz."

Clare turned and saw a tall woman striding toward them. Her straight blond hair was pulled into a tight, high ponytail, and she was wearing a pair of maroon glasses. She was dressed completely in black—a simple pair of slacks and a thin, ribbed sweater that managed to scream high quality. The outfit was unadorned on the outside, but Clare had no doubt the labels were designer and most likely had the words *cashmere* or *silk* on them.

"Oh, good, Libby. You brought a cop. Come with me."

She walked briskly away, and Clare and Libby hurried to keep up with her. They went up an enormous stone staircase, and Clare would have liked to stop and admire the beautifully carved railing, but she sensed that Jazz wasn't someone who would want to be kept waiting if Clare dawdled. She led them up the stairs, through a Staff Only door, and down a long hallway as if she was marching them toward a prison cell.

"Are we in trouble?" she whispered to Libby when they seemed to be nearing the end of the corridor.

"No, of course not," Libby said with a forced-sounding laugh. "Well, maybe. You never can tell with Jazz."

"That's comforting, thank you."

The hallway containing staff offices was obviously more of a modern, utilitarian design than the section they had first entered, but Jazz's office took them another step back in time. Clare had anticipated a clean-lined, minimalist type of space, all black and white and glossy. Over the years as a police officer, she had developed pretty good instincts about people and was usually spot-on when she imagined what their homes or other personal spaces would look like. With Jazz, she had been dead wrong. A massive burl walnut desk took up three-quarters of the small office. It was scuffed and worn and gave the impression that it had been here forever, and the rest of the library had been built around it. Clare had no idea how else they could have gotten the behemoth into the room. The walls were lined with shelves, mostly stacked in a mix of books with old leather covers and others that were sleek new editions. Sharing space with the books was a collection of what appeared to Clare to be Viking artifacts, including a dangerous-looking elaborately carved axe.

She wasn't even going to bother seriously considering Jazz as a suspect in Turnbow's murder—she probably would have taken his head clean off with that thing rather than waste her time cutting at him with a little knife.

Jazz rummaged through the papers and books on her desk before extracting a bright blue file folder. She handed it to Clare.

"What is this?" she asked, barely glancing at the printout inside.

"My books. The ones Jimmy Turnbow borrowed from the library and never returned. I'll need them back, please."

Her *please* managed to convey the sense of *So get your ass over to his house and find them. Now.*

"I'll look into this," Clare said, tucking the folder under her arm. "I can't promise I'll get them back to you right away, since some of his items at home and in his office can't be removed yet, but any material belonging to the library will eventually be returned."

Jazz was silent for a moment, and then nodded. "Fair enough," she said. "Very professional."

Libby was standing close to Clare's side, and she gave a small sigh and seemed to relax. Clare doubted she was truly nervous around her friend and wondered if Libby had been anxious about whether Clare and Jazz would get along. Curious.

"Was he in the library often?" she asked Jazz, shifting her position slightly and feeling her arm brush against Libby's. She was closer than Clare had realized, probably because there wasn't much room for the three of them to stand in the office with the monster of a desk taking up most of the floor space. For the same reason, Clare didn't pull away.

Jazz rested her hip against the corner of the desk and crossed her arms. "He was, but not an unusual amount. We're the graduate library, so most professors who are doing research will spend a lot of time here. The architecture halls have their own collections, but ours is superior."

"I'm sure it is," Clare agreed. She had no idea, actually, but it seemed the right thing to say. "When he was here, did he spend time talking to anyone in particular? Did he ever seem to be, say, meeting someone here?"

"Are you asking who his friends were, or are you asking if he was conducting an affair in my library?"

"An affair?" Libby asked with surprise in her voice. "You didn't tell me he was having an affair. With whom?"

Clare closed her eyes and exhaled slowly. She opened them again and looked at Libby, who was now facing Clare with her hands on her hips. "First of all, I never said he was. I'm just trying to learn about his habits and routines, remember? Second, you're basically here to be a campus tour guide, so I'm not going to share all the details of the case with you."

"Freelance expert," Libby said, somewhat haughtily. "And it seems like something I should have known."

"No, you really shouldn't."

Jazz watched their interchange in silence. Once they finished, she continued, "To answer your question, Officer…"

"Sawyer," Clare and Libby said in unison.

Jazz narrowed her eyes at the two of them. "No, I never noticed him meeting anyone in particular. Sex in a library is a more common turn-on than most people realize, but not all of us have keys that give us access to the building after hours. Trust me, if he had tried to have sex in here, I would have found out. He never did. He would sometimes sit and talk with colleagues, and he also liked to stop by study carrels and visit with students he knew."

"Were these welcomed visits, with all his students?"

Jazz gave her a tight smile of understanding. "Awkward visits, with female students."

Clare nodded, ignoring Libby's strangled gasp. Jazz was a shrewd one. Clare probably should have asked to speak with her without Libby in the room, since this conversation was doubtless going to engender an uncomfortable conversation once they left the library.

Clare handed Jazz one of her business cards. "If you think of anything else that might be informative, let me know."

"Or you can let me know, and I'll pass it along to her," Libby offered.

"No, don't do that," said Clare, putting an arm in front of Libby as if to shield her from more details about Turnbow. Libby pushed her arm away.

"How else am I supposed to find out about anything if you're not going to tell me?"

Jazz cleared her throat, and they both turned toward her. "You're one of my best friends, Libby, but I'd still better not catch the two of you making out in here."

"I'd never...we wouldn't..." Libby sputtered for a moment before falling silent. Clare decided to get the two of them out of there before Jazz figured out that, as a campus police officer, Clare could access any of the buildings at any time. She didn't want to get on Jazz's bad side by telling her that a library was probably one of the last places on earth that Clare would choose for sex. Although that Reading Room was certainly gorgeous, and echoey.

"It was...interesting meeting you," she said, gently pushing Libby out of the office. "Just one more question. Where were you Monday morning between two and four a.m.?"

Jazz gave her an enigmatic half smile. "I couldn't get in my library for hours after Jimmy's body was found because you police naturally—and annoyingly—blocked off the crime scene. If I had been the one to kill him, I would have left him over at Odegaard. Let them deal with it."

Okay, then. If Jazz needed to be interviewed at a later date, she was going to let Cappy deal with her. That would be something to witness.

Libby walked back through the library and out the front doors without speaking, leading Clare over to one of the stone benches built on to the low wall in front of the building. Clare sat next to her, the green metal of the ramp's handrail just above their heads and the area where Turnbow had been hit from behind mere yards away.

"I can't be your campus expert anymore if you're not going to keep me updated on what's going on with the case," Libby said.

Clare shrugged and started to rise. "Okay, then. It was nice knowing you."

"Oh, sit down." Libby laughed and grabbed her sleeve, pulling her back down. "I was bluffing."

Clare assumed an exaggerated expression of shock. "No! I never would have guessed. And on a completely unrelated topic, do you happen to play poker? I was thinking of getting a game together and would love you to join."

"I would clean you out," Libby assured her. "But, really, an affair?"

Clare shook her head. "We want to know what Professor Turnbow was doing on campus so late on a Sunday. There are any number of reasons, and we're exploring all avenues of possibility."

True, although the number of plausible reasons for a professor to be skulking around in the shadows of a library in the middle of the night was quite small. Sex and buying drugs were the top contenders, although Clare admitted to herself that he really could have been on campus to grade papers.

"Hey," Clare said, suddenly remembering the first day of class at college. "He'd have a syllabus for every course, wouldn't he? Is there a way I could find them?"

"Sure. You can find most of them by searching on the university's website, but I can get copies for you from the program assistant."

"Are you offering to get them so you can check them for clues before handing them over?"

"Maybe," Libby said with a grin. "I'll accept that you won't tell me everything, but you have to accept that I'll try to find out whatever I can. It's who I am."

"Have at it, then," Clare said. She only wanted to check and see if Turnbow's classes had even been assigned papers worthy of all-night grading sessions this early in the quarter. Scouring them for real clues would be a time-consuming and fruitless distraction for Libby.

She was about to suggest they go get the syllabuses right now when her phone chimed. "I'll be right back," she said to Libby, getting up and walking to the bottom of the ramp, out of earshot in case the message was something Libby didn't need to hear. The spot really was a quiet, out of the way place, even with the bustling activity of a university day taking place on the other side of the shrubs. She tapped her phone and Kent's voice came through. She was obviously angry, even though she only spoke four words.

"Get back here, now."

Clare put the phone back in her pocket. *Here* must mean the police station. Clare had told Cappy where she would be, so no one should be mad at her for doing her job. She had no idea what she could have done to make Kent angry, but she'd better get over there and find out before it got any worse. She walked back to Libby.

"I've got to get to HQ," she said. "Do you have any time tomorrow to meet? I was hoping you could walk me through Turnbow's schedule—where his classes were held, where he might have parked or ate. That sort of thing."

"Sure. I have time after classes. Should we meet outside Denny Hall around two? I'll get the syllabuses before then."

"Thank you. And that'll give you a whole night to spend searching for clues in them. I'll expect you to have solved the case by tomorrow."

CHAPTER NINE

Clare hurried off campus and across Fifteenth to the police headquarters. When she got to Kent's office, the door was ajar, and she could hear the mumble of Cappy's voice. She tapped on the door and started to push it open when something slammed into it. She hesitated on the threshold, her gaze moving from Cappy—who was giving her a sort of grimace and gesturing for Clare to come over to her—to Kent's face, tight with anger, to the cracked in-box and scattered papers on the floor at her feet.

"Oh, come in, Sawyer," Kent snapped. "I wasn't throwing it at you."

Clare walked over to Cappy's side, ready to duck in case the old coffee mug still on Kent's desk came at her next.

"What happened?" she asked, relieved that the sergeant's fury didn't seem to be directed at her personally.

"You tell her," Kent said to Cappy. "I'm too mad to speak."

She shut the door and crouched down and started picking up her papers.

"Sergeant Kent sent some of Turnbow's clothes from his house to the forensics lab. They found six—"

"Six!" Kent slammed a handful of papers onto her desk.

"Six different DNA samples," Cappy continued in a steady voice, as if she hadn't been interrupted. "They've found matches to three so far. They're all undergraduate students here at the university, in the architecture department."

"Women?" Clare asked, although she had already guessed the answer.

"Yes." Kent and Cappy's voices answered at the same time, one furious, the other deliberately calm.

Kent threw another stack of papers onto the desk with such vehemence that they slid right off the other side. She stood up and glared at Clare and Cappy.

"I want to know how this happened on my campus, without even a whiff of a formal complaint against him. What century is this, anyhow? You two need to find out what was going on, and why no one reported anything. Figure out exactly what he was up to, and with whom, so we can get them the support they need. And once you're done, bring him back to life so I can make him pay for this."

"Yes, Sergeant," Clare said, echoed by Cappy. They scooted out of the office, shutting the sounds of Kent's violent tidying behind the door.

"In here," Cappy said, grabbing Clare's arm and pulling her into one of the smaller meeting rooms.

They stared at each other for a moment before Clare spoke.

"I think we should work independently on this. I'll find out about the DNA matches, and you can work on resuscitating the dead guy."

"Hilarious."

Clare shrugged. "It was worth a try. You do realize that there could be an innocent explanation for why he had their DNA, don't you?" There were possible explanations, but she doubted any of them were true. Still, they needed to remain as objective as possible. Kent's burst of anger—as keenly as Clare wanted to react the same way—didn't belong in an investigation.

"Of course. He might have bumped into them in a crowded hallway, although one or two would be more likely than six. And that was in a small sample of work clothes, not his entire wardrobe. These are just the items that hadn't been washed or dry-cleaned recently."

Good. Logic. Clare was relieved that Cappy was remaining in control of her reactions, because it would help Clare do the same.

Some people around here were very territorial about this university. It was Jazz's library, Kent's campus. Clare didn't feel nearly the same sense of proprietary attachment to the buildings or people here, but she felt a fierce sense of protectiveness in this case. She didn't think it was different in intensity from what she'd feel in any situation where innocent people were potentially being victimized, but she wasn't sure. This was a professor they were talking about. Just like police officers and other people in powerful positions, they were held to a higher standard of conduct. No matter whether or not the women in question had consented to shed their DNA on his clothing, if they were students, wrong was wrong.

"What about the suit he was wearing when he was killed?"

"Nothing aside from his wife and sons."

Alicia Turnbow—another possible explanation. "She could have planted the evidence, hoping to incriminate someone else in the murder."

"That should come out when we question them. *No, I never touched Professor Turnbow, but his wife came on campus and pulled out some of my hair the other day.*"

Clare walked over to the conference table and lifted herself onto it. "These women are likely to jump toward the top of the suspect list after we talk to them, you know. Even if he did something wrong, even if they have good reason to hate him or want to make him pay for it, they won't be justified in committing homicide."

"I know that, Sawyer," Cappy said with an annoyed expression. She paused, then added, "But you might want to remind Kent about it if the time comes."

Clare was only going to do so if she was allowed to check out a full suit of riot gear first. "I met the chief librarian at Suzzallo today. Her opinion of Turnbow was very interesting, given this new evidence."

She told Cappy what Jazz had said about Turnbow's interactions with students in the library.

"What did you think of her?" Cappy asked. "Maybe she knew he was behaving inappropriately and decided to take him out to protect the students with a little vigilante justice."

Clare bit her lip, uncertain how much to share about Jazz. Her axe? Her comment about leaving the body in front of the undergraduate library?

"I really don't see her for this murder. But it might not hurt to keep her name on a list somewhere, just in case something else comes up in the future."

Cappy frowned. "What kind of list?"

"You know, in the movies when they say to round up the usual suspects? One of those lists. Oh, and she gave me an inventory of library books Turnbow checked out and didn't return. She wants them back."

"She sounds charming," Cappy said dryly. "What about your girlfriend?" She held up her hands, palms out, to stop Clare before she could protest. "Sorry, I meant tour guide. Did she have anything else to share today?"

Clare told her about the statues and Libby's comments about Suzzallo and the general intentions behind its architectural style. But when she mentioned showing her the photo of the crime scene, Cappy's expression shifted immediately from interested to pissed.

"The picture's online," Clare said, her usual defensiveness kicking in just as quickly as Cappy's mood change had done. The photos had shown up on social media just before the person who found the body called it in to the police. Even though the police had tried to shield the entryway once they arrived on the scene, spectators had managed to get some more shots, partially obscured but still graphic enough to be disturbing. Department officials were scrambling to track them down and remove them, but the damage had been done. "I didn't show her anything she couldn't have found herself."

"I know. I'm not mad at *you*, Sawyer, but at the insensitive creep who posted them in the first place. Who does that? Find a body, snap a couple selfies, then call the cops. It's sick. Anyway, what did she say about it?"

Clare told her about Libby's take on the crime scene. She could tell that Cappy was impressed by the reasoning behind Libby's observation, and she felt strangely proud of her. She had no reason to be—she barely knew Libby, and her intelligence had nothing to do with Clare. Still, though, she admired the way Libby pieced together information and came up with insightful observations, and she liked that Cappy seemed to agree.

"Interesting," Cappy said when Clare had finished. "The idea of a sacrifice makes sense, if we consider the likely trail this DNA is going to take us on. We might need her help, once we get the names of these students and call them in to talk."

"I was thinking the same thing," Clare said, glad she hadn't needed to be the first to bring up the possibility of having Libby be part of their interviews with the DNA-identified students. "I saw her interact with one of her students, and she seems to care about being an inspiring type of teacher. If these women really were being taken advantage of in some way, and they didn't come forward and tell anyone, they might not be willing to talk to us."

"And having someone they trust in the room might make the difference between silence and confession, especially if they've had her as a professor, too."

Clare nodded in agreement, feeling slightly nauseated at the thought of telling Libby about this. Her enthusiasm about being included more fully in the investigation would surely be tempered by the circumstances. They were both silent for a few minutes. Clare hadn't really felt as if she was part of this team of officers yet, and the sting of Cappy's initial rejection of her as a partner hadn't faded completely, but she, Sergeant Kent, and Cappy were all united at this moment. They were angry at what might have happened to some of the students they were meant to protect, and they were afraid of what truths their investigation might uncover.

"Let's wait and see," she said. "If there seems to be more to this than suspicions and circumstantial evidence, I'll ask her to help."

❖

Clare stayed at work for another four hours after Cappy left. They were both still pulling some patrol duty alongside their investigation, with only a small overlap of hours since Cappy was coming in early, and Clare was staying for part of the swing shift. Clare didn't mind the respite from the case, while she and Vance Dayton wandered along the section of the Burke-Gilman Trail cutting through the east side of campus. The paved path was beautiful, giving city-dwellers the feeling of being out in nature even though civilization was near at hand. Busy Montlake Boulevard ran parallel to the trail here, and across that road were Husky Stadium and the other sports complexes owned by the university. They caught occasional glimpses of Mount Rainier and Lake Washington through the trees lining the trail.

The route was peaceful, but Clare and Vance weren't out there to get exercise or commune with the birds and plants. The isolated nature of the trail made it potentially dangerous, and the campus police sent regular patrols out there. At least the duty was mindless enough to allow Clare's thoughts to wander back to the homicide case in between her and Vance's occasional comments to each other. They had worked together on Clare's first day on patrol, and she was usually glad to get assigned with him. At first she had thought his quiet demeanor and infrequent talk meant he didn't particularly like her, but she had seen him act the same way with almost everyone else in the department. Now, she welcomed his introspective company, especially on days like today when she had too much else going on in her mind to devote much of herself to in-depth conversations.

Clare appreciated the trail duty for another reason, too. Ever since leaving Libby by Suzzallo and returning to the station, she had been tempted to go back and find her. To check at her office, or to lurk outside her room when her class was about to finish. She didn't have a good excuse to need to see her. They had plans to meet the next day, and the news Clare had learned from Kent wasn't something they were ready to share with Libby. She just wanted to see her again. To talk with her. Even to get a lecture on another of UW's buildings.

Her attraction to Libby was dangerous because once the case was finished, they would return to their separate worlds. They'd probably see each other on campus, but casual hellos as they passed would be painful if Clare let herself get too accustomed to more now. She needed to see Libby only when their tenuous connection through this case required her help. She also needed to stop thinking about her as often as she did.

Clare spent the rest of her workday reminding herself every five minutes or so to stop thinking about Libby. It wasn't going well. When her shift was finally over, Clare drove north on I-5 and then headed west to her Greenwood apartment. She parked in front of her building and sat in her car for a few moments, toying with her phone before giving in and calling Libby. So much for her resolve to be sensible and keep their relationship on a professional level and not attempt to push it toward friendship. Oh well. Nothing she had done since quitting her old job could be considered sensible—why start now?

"Hey," she said when Libby answered the phone. She struggled to come up with an excuse for contacting her, wishing she had taken a few minutes to do so before actually placing the call. "I just... um...wanted to confirm our meeting tomorrow."

There was a pause before Libby spoke, and Clare could hear the amusement in her voice. "Really? You're calling to confirm the appointment we made just a few hours ago?"

Clare smiled. She should have expected Libby to see through such a flimsy excuse. "Yes. It's protocol, from page twenty-three of the campus police handbook. We must obtain verbal confirmation of all appointments with civilians."

"Can I get a copy of that handbook? As an expert witness, I should be well-versed in police procedures."

"As a professor who is doing nothing more than showing me around a building tomorrow, you really don't need to know much beyond that one rule."

"Hmph. And I suppose you're also not going to tell me why you had to rush back to the station today. Was there a big break in the case?"

Clare closed her eyes and leaned her head back against the seat. "No." At least she hoped not. She hoped that the new evidence would prove to have an innocent explanation and that she could shield Libby from it forever. She doubted her wishes were going to come true, though.

"Liar," Libby said, reading Clare more correctly than she probably realized. "Don't worry. I'll keep asking until you give in and tell me everything. Where are you?"

"Greenwood. In front of my apartment building." Clare got out of her car and walked along the uneven path to her door, stepping automatically over the segments of pavement that were sunken and heavily cracked. "I'm sure this lovely structure would appeal to you, as an admirer of fine architecture. I don't know the proper term for it, but the bottom half is covered with fake bricks, and the upper part is kind of yellowish stucco with dark wood beams crisscrossing it, like it's trying to be a Tudor-style home. Trying, and failing miserably."

"Ah, yes. We architectural historians refer to that as Mid-Seventies Debacle. Also known as Post-Modernist Make-Libby-Weep style."

Clare laughed at the way Libby's voice deepened, as if she was lecturing about the grandest of cathedrals. "Yes, and I can see how its eclectic elements are designed to drag the eye downward, to the mundanity of its patchy lawn and weedy flower beds."

Clare's breath caught when Libby joined in her laughter. They weren't even in the same place, but just picturing her smile was enough to make Clare's chest grow tight. Damn. She should have taken a hammer to her phone rather than trying to rely on her own willpower to keep from contacting Libby. She was treading in dangerous waters here.

"Poor old building," Libby continued. "We shouldn't tease it."

"You're right. It might not be glamorous, but it does its job and keeps the rain off me. Mostly. We can't all aspire to be Suzzallo, after all," Clare agreed, letting herself into the apartment. Libby's presence on the phone somehow made the empty rooms seem a little warmer than normal. Definitely dangerous.

"No, we—ouch!"

Clare heard a series of thumps and a muffled curse before Libby came back on the line.

"Sorry about that. I dropped my phone."

Clare unclipped her duty belt and sank onto the sofa. "Did a book fall on you?"

"As a matter of fact, yes. How did you know? Some sort of cop instincts?"

"Just playing the odds." Clare started unbuttoning her top, then stopped and refastened it. She didn't need to make the call feel any more intimate than it already did. Something about having Libby's voice in her ear while she was lounging on her couch seemed very homey and comforting, and she needed the heavy layers of her uniform to keep her from getting carried away by those feelings. "Is everything okay?"

"Yes. Some of the pages are bent, but no real damage."

"I meant you, not the book," Clare said.

"I'm fine. It missed my head."

Clare smiled at Libby's quirky priorities, but then her grin faded as she let the silence grow between them. She had indulged herself for a few moments, but now it was time to stop, before she lost the ability to do so. Libby was far too appealing.

"Well," she said, trying to keep her reluctance out of her voice by injecting a false-sounding breeziness. "I suppose you have to prepare for classes, so I should let you go. I'll see you tomorrow?"

Libby paused before answering. "Oh, of course. Yes, see you tomorrow."

They said good-bye, and Clare ended the call. She sat for a while, thinking about Libby's pause and wondering if she was just imagining an echo within it of her own reluctance to end the conversation. Eventually she sighed and got up to change clothes and make her dinner.

CHAPTER TEN

L ibby pushed Tig's partially open door with her foot and stepped inside. "Hey," she said, walking in the office when she saw that Tig was alone. "You busy?"

"Always," Tig said with a surprised smile on her face. "But not too busy to visit with you. I didn't expect to see you today."

"I've thrown my schedule out the window. I'm a whole new person," Libby said, handing Tig one of the large paper cups of tea she had been carrying. The statement wasn't exactly true. Libby always had an English Breakfast tea on Thursday afternoons, she just usually didn't come by Tig's office on that day. She had put her visits with her friends on a rotating schedule, so she still had the predictability she liked, and they would think she had randomized her days enough to get them off her back. They'd eventually notice the new pattern, which repeated every three weeks, but she had some breathing room until they did.

"Yes, you're unrecognizable," Tig said wryly, taking a sip of her tea. "Am I to assume that this complete overhaul of our Libby is due to your new girlfriend? Jazz told me you're dating a cop."

"Not dating," Libby said firmly, both to herself and to Tig. She had taken to repeating the phrase sternly in her mind every time she thought about seeing Clare again, fighting against the sense of anticipation that had nothing to do with Clare's investigation. Last night's unexpected phone call hadn't helped. Ten minutes of light conversation certainly didn't constitute a date, but it had felt like something close. Like a step forward, somehow. "I'm showing her around and answering some questions about the university. That's all." At least that was all Libby was prepared to admit.

Tig just gave her a skeptical look and didn't bother to argue. "Jazz likes her," she said instead.

"Really?" Libby felt her smile was too wide, since obviously she wasn't dating Clare and didn't care if her friends liked her. And she wouldn't need Jazz's approval anyway. She drew her eyebrows together in a frown, hoping it would cancel out her grin and make her expression neutral. "That's good to hear. Maybe I should set them up."

"Yeah, you do that," Tig said with a laugh. "So, is she your new hobby?"

I wish, Libby thought, somehow managing not to say it out loud. "Not her specifically, but helping her." Libby toyed with the sleeve on her cup. "Officer Sawyer questioned me about Jimmy Turnbow's death on Monday because a few years ago he got the tenure-track position I applied for, and now tenure. She thought I might have killed him for it, which seems like an overly dramatic reaction, not to mention a fruitless one. Anyway, I offered to give her an insider's perspective on university life and what we do day-to-day. At first, I was treating it like a lark, something interesting and challenging to break up my routine, but I wasn't taking it seriously enough. Now, I feel like I might actually be useful and do something important."

Tig shook her head. "You do important work every day, Libby. You're an amazing and inspiring teacher. Don't sell yourself short."

Libby had a mental flash of Clark's Inspiration statue. "Thank you, Tig. I'm proud of what I do, but this has a different kind of importance. Teaching matters, but so does the work Clare does. She's amazing."

"I'm sure she is. She seems to have gone from Officer Sawyer to Clare very quickly."

Libby refused to be embarrassed. Much. "I like her. Not *like* her like her"—oh my God, how old was she?—"but I like being with her. I'm more confident when I'm with her. More…forward, I guess, or direct."

"It sounds like you're more yourself with her," Tig said. She set her tea on the desk and leaned toward Libby. "You've retreated into yourself over the past year. We've all seen it, and that's why we were worried enough to confront you. You had lost some of your glow, I guess. If she brings your vibrancy back out of you, then by all means, spend as much time with her as you can. But don't give her credit for turning you into someone new, because that would be untrue, and not fair to you."

Libby was quiet, thinking about Tig's comments. She had been struggling to keep Alternate Libby under control, but maybe that was because dimming herself had become a habit. She wasn't sure why she had started to do so in the first place, but she probably wouldn't have noticed—or would have taken much longer to notice—if her friends hadn't pointed it out to her. And she would have had more trouble breaking free from Bored, Stuck in a Rut Libby if it hadn't been for Clare. She had felt more awake this week than she had for a long time, and she was grateful to all of them for giving her the push she needed. She would have wasted a lot of time without their help.

"What were you working on when I came in?" she asked, determined to get the conversation off her and onto another topic. She had plenty to think about after this talk with Tig, and she'd take time later to process it. "You looked pretty intense."

"Subtle redirection," Tig said with a smile. She picked up her tea and settled back in her chair again. "But I'll accept it. Lukas has to take a leave of absence. His husband is sick—the prognosis is good, so don't worry—but Lukas will need time off to be with him. I can take one of his classes, and Deb can cover another, but I'm looking for a replacement to teach the other three. I've got some good applicants, and it might be kind of exciting to get some fresh blood in the department, but his courses this quarter require a specific set of specialties. I'd really like to find someone who's an expert in Roman legal systems for his graduate seminar, and that narrows down the field significantly."

They chatted about some of the CVs for another fifteen minutes, until Libby glanced at the clock and started to gather her things together. "Sorry to go, but I have to get to my meeting," she said as she stood up.

"Ah, yes. The Island of Misfit Students awaits," she said, using her and Jazz's nickname for Libby's informal chat session on Denny's steps. "You take open-door policy to a new level. Maybe the university should just give you a section of those steps to use as your full-time office."

"I'd love it, but my books would get wet," Libby said, stepping around the desk to give Tig a kiss on the cheek. "Thank you for talking to me about Clare, and let me know if you want to go over more of these prospects."

"I will, thanks. See you tomorrow at the movies. Oh, and next Tuesday when you come visit me again."

Damn. How had Tig cracked her new visitation schedule's code so quickly? Her friends must be comparing notes. She just shook her head without responding and left, jogging down the marble corridor and staircase, careful not to spill her tea. She pushed through the front doors of Denny Hall and saw about a dozen of her students already waiting for her. Most were grouped in small pockets, talking and laughing together. A few, like Angela and two of Libby's new freshman students, were sitting alone and reading while they waited for her. Apart but part was the way she thought of them. They'd get there.

"Hi, everyone," she said, handing out papers as she walked among the group. "I wanted to start today with a discussion of the Muses, and how they're depicted in art and architecture."

She sat down on the edge of the group and was glad to see Angela and the other outliers scoot closer. The circle of students easily expanded and made room for them. "These packets have a few examples of paintings and sculptures of incarnate Muses, but I'd also like to talk about the *idea* of a muse. Why did the Greeks create characters to embody this concept? How do modern artists, writers, and architects relate to the abstract idea of a muse? I've also included a reference section in here with links to articles you can find in the library databases, as well as a reprint from the *American Journal of Philology*. Let's start, though, with one of the most well-known examples of the Muses in painting, by Tintoretto."

Thank goodness she hadn't gotten rid of the journal article she was using today in yesterday's purge—not that anything had actually been purged, of course. If she hadn't gone through all those issues, though, she wouldn't have stumbled upon the article she had added to these packets. She had been prepared to discuss a different topic today, but after yesterday's visit to the crime scene, her mind had grasped on to this idea instead, even disturbing her sleep with odd dreams of her, Clare, and Turnbow being chased by Clark's Inspiration sculpture come to life. The confusing thoughts of inspiring others, being inspired, and being sacrificed to inspiration had turned into today's theme, because Libby hoped that thinking about the topic and preparing for the meeting would help her mind settle and stop circling through the images from yesterday. It hadn't worked.

As usual, though, the students gradually took charge of the direction of the meeting, and the conversation followed tangents Libby never could have predicted. This wasn't a lecture, with a defined purpose and specific knowledge to impart. It was a discussion, and for many of her students who had recently come to the university, it was the first time they were able to truly talk about a subject that interested them, as opposed to being *talked to* by teachers. When she had initially started this group, which had sprung from a casual and impromptu chat between classes and had now become a weekly ritual, she had struggled to let go of control over the route they took. She had begun to realize that the discussions had nothing to do with her and what she wanted to teach. They belonged to the students and needed to be directed by them.

She eventually became aware of a feeling that attention was focused on her, and she turned to see Clare leaning against the wide concrete railing on the opposite side of the steps. Clare's legs were stretched in front of her, and casually crossed, with her hip resting on the railing. Her black uniform set her apart from the students around her, as did something in her expression, and Libby sensed a gulf between them, wider even than the massive set of steps. At the same time, she longed to pull Clare all the way into her world.

She smiled at her, and then turned her attention back to the group. As soon as there was a lull in the discussion, she stood up.

"I need to go, but I hope the rest of you stay and keep talking. Come by my office if you want more information on the Muses, but otherwise I'll see you either in class or here next week."

"You can stay if you need to," Clare said when Libby got close. She pushed herself off the railing and smiled at Libby. "It looked like you were having a good conversation, and I hate to interrupt. We can do this another time."

"I rarely stay longer than an hour," Libby said. Well, sometimes she did, but as soon as she had seen Clare she was ready to go. "I'm more of a catalyst, and my goal with these sessions is to get the students talking to each other, not relying on me to guide their discussions."

All of it was true, but her eagerness to be closer to Clare had been why she had jumped out of her seat and hurried across the steps toward her. Libby kept that part private.

"Your students seem to really admire you," Clare said as they walked around Denny and toward the University District. "Why else would they voluntarily come to an extra lecture?"

"I think they like being part of something larger than themselves, part of a discussion about big ideas and universal themes. I could be replaced by almost any other professor, and the benefits would be the same."

"Doubtful," Clare said, bumping gently into Libby with her shoulder. "Even if they were willing to volunteer their time like you do, I hardly think the results would be the same. Your students seem devoted to…hey, wait." Clare stopped and tugged on Libby's arm, bringing her to a halt as well. "This isn't some sort of secret society, is it? Nothing I need to worry about?"

Libby laughed. "A secret society that meets Thursday afternoons on the steps of a public building?"

Clare thought for a moment and then her face brightened. "Maybe these are recruiting sessions. The actual meetings might be held at midnight on the full moon or something."

Libby started walking again, and Clare hurried to catch up with her. "You watch too many movies. No, I'm not the leader of a secret club." She shrugged and grinned at Clare. "Although if I was, I'd still say no, wouldn't I? I mean, I took a blood oath to protect this secret murder club, so of course I'm not going to admit it to the first person who asks me about it."

"I might need to get you back to the station for more questioning."

"Good luck with that. I take my made-up blood oaths to fictitious societies very seriously." Libby pushed the button for the walk signal at Fifteenth. "I really don't think anyone on this campus has some sort of underground society, where they dress all in black, conduct violent rituals, and plot to take control of the entire university."

The signal chimed, and they started walking across the avenue. "I think you just described Jazz," Clare said.

"Did not," Libby said with as much indignation as she could inject into her voice. It wasn't easy, since her thoughts had immediately gone to Jazz, too, before she had even completed her sentence. It was the axe, Libby decided. It seemed made for some sort of creepy ritual. "And don't you dare bring up my name if you decide to confront her about this topic. Besides, I don't think she'd keep it a secret if she was trying to take over the university—she'd just barge in and do it. Well, here's the building."

They were directly across from the police station, standing where Libby had been the first day she had met Clare. Back when she'd had no idea in what a strange and unexpected way their paths were going to cross. She felt as in the dark now, with no clue how their relationship would progress. They seemed to be becoming friends, even though they had shared very little personal information with each other. All she knew for certain was that she wanted to learn more about Clare.

Clare looked at her expectantly. "What, no two-hour lecture on the architectural magnificence of the building?"

"It's a cement and glass box," Libby said, which wasn't exactly fair. It had some interesting design elements, such as the smaller metal and glass box attached to its side like a tumor. "It's not my style. I try not to look directly at it."

"Let's get inside, then," Clare said, heading through the entrance. She came to a halt at the edge of the interior court of the building and looked around. "I suppose this part doesn't appeal to you, either?"

"Not really." The central area of Gould was open all the way to the large, industrial-style skylights. Tiered concrete staircases and straight walkways snaked across the room. Everything was sharp angles and lines, and the only natural-looking building materials were the slatted wood panels covering sections of the lower-level walls and the hardwood floors.

"So, this is the home of the College of Built Environments," Libby continued, gesturing at the active space in front of them. She felt transported back to her grad school days, when she had taken any job she could find in order to support her addiction to getting degrees. Leading tours for prospective students had been one of her favorites because she could talk for hours about UC Berkeley's buildings. The people on her tours had often been much more interested in what was going on inside those buildings than in their style and history, but that hadn't stopped her from trying to teach them something new. "Architecture is just one of the departments within the school, along with others like construction management, landscape design, urban planning. The Architecture main office is here, as well as the dean's office. Jimmy taught one class here, and three others in Architecture Hall, where the professors' offices are. His is in a separate wing from mine, and I can take you there after this, if you need to see it."

"Not right now. We wouldn't be able to get in, anyway. The forensics team from Seattle PD is still doing work in there."

"Really? What do they hope to find in his office?"

"Can you show me where his class was held?" Clare asked, completely ignoring Libby's question, which of course made her want to continue to push for an answer.

She squinted at Clare, trying to read her expression, but Clare's return gaze was calm and neutral. Yep. Definitely hiding something.

"We'll circle back around to that topic in a bit," she said, balancing her bag on one of the black plastic chairs while she hunted for Jimmy's syllabuses. "Aha, here they are. I picked these up for you this morning."

She shuffled through them, finding the course sheet for his special topic seminar and checking the room number. "Oh, it's down in the basement. Be prepared, things only get worse from here."

"Well?" Clare asked when Libby handed her the sheaf of papers. "Did you figure out the clues and solve the case?"

Libby was about to protest that she hadn't even glanced at them, but she doubted she could sell it. "I didn't find anything. I had an elaborate theory about a connection between the class numbers and the date he was, um, found, but I couldn't make Arch 532 fit. Are you going to tell me what I missed?"

"I just wanted to know what homework he had assigned so far this quarter," Clare said. She glanced through the syllabuses, then folded the stack and tucked it into her pocket. "Lead on, to the basement."

What did his assignments have to do with his murder? Libby wanted to take the pages back and see what connections she might be able to see, now that she knew where to focus her attention, but Clare didn't look prepared to let her have them again. Oh well. Luckily, she had copies in her office. She would just have to look at them later.

CHAPTER ELEVEN

Clare followed Libby down the stairs leading to the basement, ready to defend herself in case Libby turned on her and tried to wrestle the sheaf of paper away from her. She had seen Libby's attention drop to Clare's pocket once she told her what she had wanted to learn from the class schedules. She would have liked to imagine that Libby was staring at her breasts, but she was sadly aware that the contents of her pocket were the big draw at the moment. Libby would know soon enough what they had been learning about Turnbow, whether because the information became public, or because Clare and Cappy would need to ask her to help talk to the possible victims. Clare wanted to keep the details from her as long as possible, mainly to fend off the sadness and outrage she was certain Libby would experience.

For now, though, Clare would just follow in Turnbow's footprints, with Libby as her guide, observing how he had spent his days and trying to find any possible clues about who had hated him enough to murder him.

Their steps rang with a metallic echo as they walked down the flights of stairs. The walls were cinderblock, giving the stairwell an unfinished, bare look. Something about the cleanliness of the building appealed to Clare. It hadn't struck her with awe the way Suzzallo had, but it had a transparency she appreciated. Suzzallo whispered that it had secrets hidden in shadowy corridors and concealed rooms. Gould's open court and glass walls shouted that it wouldn't allow anything to be hidden, that its wisdom was available to all.

Clare shook her head. She had never had these romantic notions about buildings before she had met Libby. Or was it the university itself that had been affecting her thoughts since she had started working here?

Libby led her over to a large metal door and peeked through the window. "Good, it's empty," she said, tugging the door open and going inside. "This is the Mad Lab. The Materials and Daylighting Lab. Jimmy taught an advanced graduate seminar in here on the historical development of structural foundations. It was a really interesting theme, combining history and geography alongside practical applications. It wasn't the type of class he usually taught, and the general assumption is that he only proposed such a unique seminar to impress the tenure committee."

Clare walked the perimeter of the room, staring at the metal shelves full of bins and tools, sheets of wood and other materials, and miniature models of all sorts of structures. She kept her hands clasped behind her back to keep from giving in to the temptation to touch everything within reach, and to scale the shelves to get to those out of reach.

"What was your opinion?" she asked, unable to resist the urge to reach toward a mock-up of a three-story building, using one finger to swing a tiny door open and shut on its perfect miniature hinges. "Do you believe that's why he came up with the concept?"

Libby turned a crank next to one of the models, raising the two sections of a drawbridge. Clare wanted to take some of these things home. Or better yet, to figure out how to make some of her own.

"I believe it was inconsistent with his usual choices, and not particularly suited to his teaching style."

"Diplomatic," Clare said. "And inconsistent with your usual way of speaking."

Libby laughed, her eyes crinkling the way they did when she was surprised by something funny. Clare hadn't known her long, but she had come to look forward to the times when she brought this expression out in Libby.

"Well, then, yes—I thought he only came up with it because he thought it sounded impressive. But if that's what it took to inspire him to expand his teaching methods and open his mind to more interdisciplinary ideas, then I can't criticize him for it. Maybe he was only doing it for personal gain, but his students were the ones who would benefit."

Clare reached out and gave Libby's shoulder a gentle squeeze. The temptation to touch her was even more difficult to fight than anything else in this fascinating room. She had such a pure approach to teaching, willing to forgive other professors their shortcomings and selfishness as long as the end results were beneficial to their students. If she found out Turnbow had been taking advantage of some of the women in his classes, she would never be able to...

Clare's internal musings stuttered to a stop. She turned away from Libby, pretending to study another building model while she doggedly followed her new train of thought, refusing to ignore it merely because she hated the direction it was taking. What if Libby already knew? What if one of their mutual students had come to her, sharing what had happened to her? Would Libby be enraged enough to kill him? To symbolically sacrifice him to Inspiration—the one quality she had repeatedly claimed he didn't possess? She had briefly considered this at their first interview, but now she saw more clearly how devoted Libby was to her values. They defined who she was and how she lived her life on campus.

Everything in her shouted *No!* The very idea of Libby dragging his body around, messily slitting his throat...it was insane. Unbelievable. Still, though, Clare had easily been able to imagine Alicia Turnbow or one of his potential victims committing the same deed. Her unwillingness to see Libby as anything but innocent was based solely on her personal bias. She liked Libby. Was attracted to her. She looked forward to her company. None of those were reasons to believe she wasn't as capable of murder as the wronged wife or the silent victim if sufficiently provoked.

She felt gentle fingers tugging on her sleeve, and she turned around to face Libby, whose forehead was creased in a worried expression. "Clare, what is it? What's wrong?"

Clare cupped Libby's cheek in her palm, looking directly into her eyes and doing her best to ignore how vibrant they seemed in this muted concrete and metal environment. "Did you kill him?"

Libby laughed, then faltered to a stop. "Wait, you're serious, aren't you?" She covered Clare's hand with hers. "No, I didn't."

Clare dropped her hand and took a step back. Every instinct she had said Libby was innocent. Trouble was, she wasn't sure she could trust herself anymore where Libby was concerned.

"Come on," said Libby, heading toward the door. "Let's go to the station. You can hook me up to a lie detector and ask me that question again."

Clare stayed in place until Libby came back to her. "That's not how it works. Besides, we don't have one."

"Then go buy one. I'll wait."

Clare tried not to laugh but couldn't stop it. "Okay, I'll just pop down to Home Depot and get one. I hear they're on special this week."

Libby gave a relieved-sounding sigh and smiled at her. "That's better. You looked so serious for a moment, it was scary. I mean it, though. Search my apartment, do whatever it takes to believe I'm not guilty. How can I help you solve the case if you don't trust me?"

"I do trust you," Clare said, meaning it with her whole heart. Unfortunately, her heart wasn't infallible. "And you're not helping me solve the case. You're showing me around the architecture department."

"Same thing. And now I'm going to show you the Greek restaurant on the Ave. where Jimmy ate lunch at least once a week, according to the receptionist who gave me his syllabuses. The least you can do after accusing me of murder is buy me lunch."

"I'm sorry I—" Clare started, but Libby waved her off.

"You're doing your job," she said as they walked up the stairs toward the ground floor. "Besides, it was an informative discussion for me. I could tell you've been hiding something about Jimmy from me, and now I know it's bad enough to make you think I'd possibly be willing to kill him if I knew what it was. That narrows it down quite a bit."

Clare stopped in the middle of the flight of stairs. "Can you please rephrase that?"

Libby stopped as well, turning to face her. "That narrows it down completely, to nothing at all, because nothing would ever make me be willing to kill him. Is that better?"

Clare sighed. "A little, but not much. And I'm not hiding things from you. I'm not allowed to talk about certain aspects of the case with a civilian."

"With a civilian, or with a suspect?"

Clare shrugged. Honesty was her only option. "Both."

❖

Ten minutes later, she was sitting down for lunch with her civilian-slash-suspect. The short walk from Gould around the corner to the Greek restaurant had felt like an architectural tour, as Libby pointed out features on the buildings they passed. Clare wasn't accustomed to looking up while she walked—her attention was usually focused on the people around her and the direction she was going. She hadn't even been fully aware of the world of balconies and decorative cornices hovering overhead. She doubted she'd ever walk down a street the same way again, without at least glancing up now and then to see the world as Libby did.

They ordered their food soon after they sat down, and Clare opted for dolmades, her standard choice when she ate at Mediterranean restaurants. The diner was narrow and dingy, more like a hallway than a dining room. Faded photos of white buildings and turquoise blue seas hung on the walls, covered with a film of grease. The table was clean, though, and the service friendly. The smell of frying herby food coming from the kitchen made her willing to overlook the sketchy decor in the hope of getting a great meal.

"What first drew you to architecture?" she asked, buttering a piece of fresh bread.

"I had a history teacher in high school who once said that you could tell a people's gods by the temples they built. He was talking about more than religion—he meant that you could see what really mattered to a culture or a nation by looking at the structures within it. Chapels, football stadiums, shopping centers. Buildings illustrate values and priorities." Libby rested her elbow on the table and propped her chin in her palm. "I was interested in a lot of different subjects at school—Classical history, Medieval and Renaissance art, the role of women in different time periods and different cultures. His phrase stuck with me, though, and I always seemed to find architecture at the heart of every subject I studied. It was my first postgrad degree, and all my other academic work always related back to it."

Clare took another piece of bread. It was warm and fresh, and she didn't care if she spoiled her appetite by eating it. Hooray for being a grown-up. "So, what gods does Gould Hall serve? You've told me why *you* don't favor that type of architecture, but it must have meaning to the people who designed it, and to at least some of the people who work there."

Libby stopped in the middle of squeezing the juice from a lemon wedge into her water. "You're right," she said after a pause. "I sometimes focus on the negatives of buildings that don't have the historical significance I prefer, or ones that don't convey grandeur and that seem too modern. I see what's missing from them, instead of looking at what's there." She dropped the lemon wedge into her water and poked at it with her straw in a distracted way. "I guess Gould could be seen as a place where function rules over aesthetics. It's a clean vessel that highlights the creativity inside, without masking it at all."

Clare told her what she had been thinking in the stairwell, knowing Libby wouldn't criticize her for being overly sentimental about a building.

"Interesting," Libby said, reaching into her bag and pulling out a notebook and pen. "It's designed not for its own sake, but for the purpose of revealing what's inside. Walls that are meant to be as invisible as possible. Oh, and the green spaces—I should have shown you the garden in back. Those same walls let the outside in. Just a second, I need to write this down. It'll be an interesting comparison to use in Friday's lecture on cathedrals, and I think I can bring it into my other classes, too."

Clare smiled as she watched Libby frantically spill her thoughts onto paper. She helped move their waters and the bread aside to give their waiter space to put Libby's plate since her notebook was covering her placemat.

"Whew, thank you," Libby said, setting her notebook to one side and pulling her hummus plate in front of her. "I might be able to actually look at the building now, instead of shielding my eyes as I walk past." She piled a pita triangle with some hummus, an olive, and a chunk of tomato. "What about you? What did you study in school?"

Clare hesitated, preferring to talk about Libby's experiences in school—which she clearly loved, whether as a student or a teacher—rather than her own struggle to get through those four years.

"I went to WSU. They have a good criminal justice program, and I'd always wanted to be a police officer." She was prepared to stop there and change the subject, but Libby was listening quietly, obviously expecting more to her answer.

"I would have applied to the force directly after high school, or maybe a two-year degree, but college was very important to my parents. I don't think they really expected me to succeed in academia, but I guess I wanted to please them. Or maybe prove they were wrong and that I could do it." Okay, time to shut up. Clare took a bite of her lunch to give her mouth something to do besides talking.

Libby nodded, a small frown on her face as she scooped up more hummus. "Well, you're obviously smart, so I don't see why anyone wouldn't believe in you. I understand that it's more challenging when you're dyslexic, since our traditional school systems aren't always as accommodating as they should be, but there are so many resources available now."

Clare carefully, deliberately set her fork down on her plate. A small, detached part of her brain applauded her for not dropping it hard enough to shatter the ceramic. "What?" she asked in a quiet voice.

Libby looked up from her plate and seemed startled by the expression on Clare's face. "Oh, I'm so sorry. Was I wrong? I just thought..."

Clare took a deep breath. Here's where it changed. Libby would look at her differently now. She'd treat her differently. And why wouldn't she? She lived for school—for books and reading and learning. Clare was nothing like her. Yes, she liked those things as well, but she'd never experience them with the same facility and effortless ease as Libby did.

"How did you know?" she asked.

"I…well, I noticed the way you wrote at my interview. You remember that—it was the *first* time you accused me of murder." She gave a forced laugh at her own joke, then sighed and continued. "You were using a brush pen, and you weighted the bottom of your letters. You changed the curve and height of them, too, so they look more distinct, like the curve of *n*'s and *h*'s, or the height of *t*'s and *h*'s. You tend to use your phone to record notes rather than write them down, probably because it's quicker for you to do it that way. You also ordered food here without looking at the menu, but I wouldn't necessarily have noticed that one without having seen the others."

"How did you…" Clare realized she was repeating her question and faded to a stop, but Libby seemed to understand what she was asking this time.

"I worked in the student resource center at school and did a lot of tutoring. It was my job to help new students discover the kinds of accommodations they needed to help them succeed at college. I just recognized some of the coping skills as ones I'd share with them. Plus, I've had plenty of dyslexic students since I started teaching. These days, most of them have been diagnosed early and are aware of what they need from me in order to get the most out of my classes, but it's important for me to be aware of signs in case they've slipped through the cracks in our educational system and need more guidance from me." She picked up another pita triangle, then set it down again, as if she wasn't sure if it was all right to start eating again. "I hadn't thought of using a brush pen, though. That's a pretty cool idea."

Clare wasn't sure what to say. She silently pulled her pen out of the pocket of her uniform and handed it to Libby. She had tried all sorts of brush pens from art supply stores, finally discovering one that had a fine enough tip to let her write reasonably small letters, rather than the larger and softer tips used most often in calligraphy.

Libby took it with an eager smile and uncapped it. Libby didn't seem to have changed in the way she was talking to her now, but maybe she was just trying to be polite and get through the meal. Then she'd make an excuse not to have to see her anymore.

Clare's family would have loved Libby—she was everything they were. Smart, studious, enamored with the very idea of college and higher learning. They hadn't meant to hurt Clare with their teasing—or so they said whenever she would get upset by it—but their jokes about her being the stupid one in the family hurt because she knew they believed there was truth behind it.

Would Libby be the same now that she knew Clare's secret? Would her jokes have a bitter sting to them, instead of the playful teasing they had shared since the first time they met?

The full meaning of Libby's words slowly penetrated her mind as she watched Libby try out her pen on the paper placemat. Libby *had* known since the first time they met. The schedule she had written for Clare at the interview—carefully and clearly printed on the legal pad, although Clare had just seen the sloppy scrawl she used in her notebook. Turnbow's syllabuses Libby had given her, printed in a larger sans serif font with extra spaces between the lines. Tricks she had used since she had approached one of her professors in college and asked—for the first time—for help. He had given her some pointers, encouraged her to record his lectures, and had directed her to the resource center where she had met some people like Libby.

"You don't care," she said, a sense of wonder spreading through her at the thought. The truth about her, which had been at times a source of shame, of frustration, and of pride as she learned how to cope with it, was no big deal to Libby, in the best way possible.

"Care? Why should I? You see words and letters differently, that's all. It's part of you, so it's good. You see the world differently, too, like the way you just got me to look at Gould with a whole new perspective." She started covering another pita with hummus, seemingly relieved that they were past those tense moments. "Now I just need to take you through Padelford Hall sometime. If you can get me to appreciate that lump of awfulness, you'll be a miracle worker."

Chapter Twelve

L ibby sat in her office on Friday morning with lecture notes for her classes spread across the desk in front of her. She had been adding comments in the margins inspired by her talk with Clare the day before, but remembering their conversation only managed to make her think about Clare herself.

Their tour of Gould and lunch together had been more complicated than Libby had expected. She enjoyed Clare's company and wanted to get to know her better, and she was also interested in solving the puzzle of Turnbow's murder, so she had thought their afternoon would be simple and fun. She continued to underestimate the emotions and strange energy the crime brought into every interaction related to it.

Libby tapped her pen against her thigh. Clare had come right out and asked her if she had killed Turnbow. She had vaguely wondered if she should be feeling offended by the accusation when Clare had first voiced it, but the absolutely stricken look on Clare's face had washed away any anger or indignation Libby might have felt. Something had clearly triggered a real concern in Clare's mind that Libby was some sort of crazed vigilante murderer. Even more apparent was Clare's fear that her suspicion was true. She didn't want Libby to be the guilty party even more than she wanted to solve the case. They hadn't spent much time with each other yet, but the expression on Clare's face had let Libby know she was starting to matter to Clare. She felt the same, already feeling the ache of Clare's absence even after a short time apart. She was getting accustomed to her company.

Besides, Libby knew she was innocent, so obviously everything would be cleared up once Clare solved the crime. Clare needed to explore every possibility, and Libby happened to be one of them.

Questioning the waitstaff at the restaurant had turned up nothing more intriguing than the confirmation that Jimmy had gone there quite often, usually in the company of Avery or a couple other professors from the department. They were friends and colleagues, and the restaurant was right around the corner from their workplace. The news that they ate there together was certainly nothing earthshaking. To be honest, Libby had mentioned going there because she wanted to spend time with Clare, not because she thought the diner was going to provide the key clue to crack the case. Of course, they hadn't gone back into the kitchen. Maybe there had been a bloody knife lying on the counter with the murderer's initials carved in the handle.

Libby mentally went down that path for a while, imagining the hostess as Jimmy's spurned lover and picturing a dramatic argument over a plate of spanakopita the day before the murder. It seemed unlikely to have occurred in real life, so she would refrain from spinning the tale for Clare.

The spurned lover part might be a factor, though. Based on the conversation Clare and Jazz had in Suzzallo, Libby had come to the conclusion that Jimmy had been having an affair. Clare seemed to truly believe Libby might be capable of murder if she knew the truth about him, but why would she care about his marital issues? She would feel a passing sympathy for his wife, but otherwise her life would be untouched by any infidelity on Jimmy's part. She was very aware that she was avoiding following this reasoning to its logical conclusion—the things Jimmy might have done that would be offensive enough in her mind for her to consider murdering him. Even though she badgered Clare for inside information every chance she got, she was secretly—well, not so much secretly as *consciously*—relieved that Clare wasn't able to talk with her about this subject just yet.

She had learned how to block out the pain and loneliness of real life by focusing on her courses, both as a teacher and student. She was content to do so now. She would face it when she had to, but beyond occasionally fishing for information she knew wasn't forthcoming, she wasn't going to go out of her way to confront reality.

Libby sighed. Her intro to architectural history class would be starting soon, so she skimmed through her notes again, making sure she was prepared. She thought adding Gould Hall to her theme was inspired—inspired by Clare, who had helped her look at the building she cringed away from every day with a new attitude. The other structures she had already been planning to discuss today used beautiful architectural elements to elevate the minds of the people seeing and entering them. The determined lack of ornate beauty in Gould Hall was meant to elevate minds as well, giving them open space and freedom to expand and create. Even if the building didn't make her heart sing, it was a source of inspiration and admiration to others. She was excited about the lecture, but even more so at the prospect of the potential conversations she and her students would have after. She gathered her books and papers together and headed toward her classroom.

❖

A little over an hour later, Libby was sliding her notes back into her satchel while her class stuffed texts and laptops into backpacks. Their discussion had been stimulating, and if some of her students hadn't needed to get to their next classes, she was sure they would still be talking. Over half of her regular attendees on the steps of Denny Hall were in this class, and she would definitely revisit some of the topics they had covered today during their next informal session.

"Professor Hart."

Libby turned and saw Tig standing in the doorway, addressing her in an unusually formal way since the room was still full of students.

"I wanted to introduce you to Professor Abraham's replacement for the rest of the quarter."

Libby was surprised by the news. Just yesterday, Tig had been evaluating applicant packets. She must have found a particularly qualified one as she continued to read through the stack of them to have made such a quick decision. Tig grinned at her and stepped back, letting Libby see who was standing behind her.

"Laura!" Libby exclaimed, throwing formality out the window and hurrying forward to hug the new arrival. She stepped back, her hands on Laura's shoulders. "It's great to see you again."

"You, too, Professor Hart."

"It'll have to be Libby now," she said with a laugh. "Since it seems we're going to be colleagues."

They stepped out of the way as the students filed out of the room. Tig and Laura stood to one side as Libby said good-bye to her class. "The room's empty this period," she said once the three were alone. "Do you two have time to sit for a minute?"

"We do," Tig said, sitting at one of the student desks. "Laura is going to observe Lukas's seminar today, but it's not until afternoon. We'll need to get to the admin building before that."

"We'll have all quarter to catch up. For now, tell me about grad school. You went to U Penn, right?"

"Yes. I loved it, but I'm glad to be back in Washington." Laura went on to talk about her experience in graduate school, prompted by questions from Libby and interrupted by Tig when she wanted to elaborate on one of Laura's accomplishments or exclaim about her familiarity with Roman law.

Libby happily listened to Laura talk. Laura Hughes had been one of those students who was a favorite with all her teachers, brilliant and unpretentious, hard-working and an avid listener in class. She definitely hadn't been one of Libby's special cases but instead had come to the university with the confidence needed to make friends and get involved in a variety of campus activities. Libby didn't often get to see her students after they graduated, aside from the ones who stayed for graduate school or who lived in the area and remained involved with the school. For the most part, once her students left, they disappeared from her life. It was a rare luxury to get to reconnect with a former student, especially one who had continued her studies in graduate school.

When it was finally time for them to go, she reminded Tig about the movie they were going to see with Ariella that night. "You should come, Laura. It's a midnight showing on the Ave. of the new Daphne du Maurier film *The King's General*."

"Ariella's forcing us to see it," Tig said with a gloomy expression. "It sounds depressing."

Libby laughed. "Really? And this is coming from the woman who spends most of her days reading and teaching Greek tragedies?"

"Yes, but those are fascinating and layered with complexity. This is gothic. They're not the same at all."

"You're just worried that you're going to cry in front of all the students who will be there." She turned to Laura. "I found her sobbing in her office the other day after she had watched some YouTube video about a dog and a parakeet who are friends."

"I was not sobbing. I was mildly touched by the interspecies bond between such disparate creatures."

"Sobbing like a little kid who had just lost their dolly."

This devolved into a childish *I was not, You were too* argument as Libby walked with them to the top of the staircase.

Libby waved them off, then returned to her office to grab what she'd need for her next class, which was in the Art Building. She slung her heavy bag over her shoulder and headed past Suzzallo and over to the Quad. This was her favorite nonstructure feature on campus. In the spring, the grassy rectangle would be a mass of blush-pink flowering cherry trees. Even in the nonblooming months, the space was gorgeous, and a popular area for students and sometimes staff to sit and read or study or talk. The stately buildings surrounding it blended well with each other, all collegiate Gothic, brick and cream-colored stone.

As she walked, Libby took out her phone at least four times, wanting to call or text Clare and invite her to the movie. Each time, she stopped herself. It wasn't that she thought Clare wouldn't enjoy the film—she was as likely to as Libby and her friends, although probably not as much as Ariella, who specialized in gothic literature. More accurately, she *lived* for gothic literature. Libby also was confident that Clare would get along with her friends. She had handled her first encounter with Jazz remarkably well. The others would be no problem in comparison.

The reason she kept returning her phone to her pocket—texts unsent and numbers not dialed—was because asking Clare to the movies felt too close to asking her on a date. Although they had eaten lunch together, their conversation had stayed close to the topic of Clare's case. Libby had shared some of her past, her reasons for studying architecture, and she had inadvertently forced Clare to talk about herself and her challenges in school. Hardly a deep getting-to-know-you session.

Libby sighed and zipped her phone into an interior pocket in her bag, hoping that would deter her from taking it out again. She was trying to fool herself by minimizing what she and Clare had shared. No, she couldn't say how many siblings Clare had or where she had grown up. But what she had learned about her was much more intimate than those general trivia facts that so often formed the basis of a first date. She knew Clare was smart and resourceful. That she had overcome challenges and defied those who insisted that she couldn't succeed. That she had a playful sense of humor and an unwavering sense of justice and fair play.

Libby pushed through the doors of the Art Building. Soon enough, she'd be in class, and the option of taking out her phone again would no longer be available, which was good because even though a large part of her wanted to contact Clare, a tiny and fearful part of her did not. Her growing familiarity with Clare went beyond her surface attractiveness and the quantifiable details such as her birthday or the first concert she had ever seen. And going beyond the surface of someone was a good way to get hurt.

She'd be much safer keeping her relationship with Clare confined to tours of Jimmy Turnbow's old haunts and to discussions about the buildings on campus. Anything more was too risky to consider.

❖

The September nights were getting chilly even though the days had continued to be unseasonably warm. Libby put on a dark cranberry turtleneck and navy wool slacks. She was just buttoning a thin-knit gray cardigan over the top when she heard a knock at her apartment door. She opened it to find Ariella in the hall, impatiently bouncing from toes to heels and back again. Where Libby's style tended toward classic and understated, Ariella went the opposite way, with an old-fashioned glamour infusing all her outfits. Tonight she was wearing a bright navy top made of what looked like crushed silk. The deep V of the neckline was edged with elaborate lace, and a wide heavy lace neckband made it look as if she was wearing an ornate necklace. The top was longer in the back, shading to a lighter blue. With it she was wearing jeans and tennis shoes, in her usual manner of wearing one statement piece and keeping everything else nondescript.

"Are you ready to go? We can't be late and miss the beginning."

"We have an hour to make a ten-minute walk. I doubt we'll be delayed by heavy traffic on the way." Libby pulled the door shut behind her. "But, yes, I'm ready. Let's go."

"I've heard the film stays quite close to the book," Ariella said, tucking her short, curly hair behind her ears as they went downstairs and out into the night. She pulled on a navy pea coat and continued talking about the reviews she had read. Ariella talked about du Maurier's works with the same fervor Libby felt when she talked about buildings. A flush of excitement colored her normally pale cheeks, and she chattered away as they walked, even though she was normally the least talkative one in their group.

They met Tig and Laura at the theater, and Libby slowly made her way inside, stopping often as she ran into students and some colleagues from her various departments and introducing Laura to them. When they got inside, she dropped into a red velvet seat next to Laura. She was going to fit in well with Libby's friends—she was already joking with Tig and talking to Ariella about favorite books. Her years away in grad school had matured her, making it easier to think of having her as a friend instead of being teacher and student.

Libby missed their banter once the lights dimmed and the movie started because their conversation had distracted her, but once the theater was dark, she had more trouble keeping her mind on the film and off Clare. She was relieved when it ended, and they returned to teasing and laughing. Tig and Laura left soon after they got outside, heading in opposite directions. Libby and Ariella remained for another half hour, leaning against the building and dissecting the movie—well, Ariella dissected, while Libby listened and added an occasional sound of agreement. The street was dark and empty once the other moviegoers had dispersed, and Libby realized with a start—catching herself in a yawn—that it was almost three in the morning.

They said good night, and Libby was almost back to her place when she got the text from Laura. *Lawn behind Gould. Please come.* Weird. Libby frowned, hesitating, unsure what to do. If she hadn't just traded numbers with Laura, she wouldn't have believed this had really come from her, but it seemed to be legit. It also sounded urgent, and she didn't want to waste time trying to decipher why Laura might need to see her.

Libby started walking back toward the U District, letting her thoughts wander on the way. She considered calling Clare, or even 911, but didn't want to jump to conclusions if there was no real danger. Maybe Laura just needed to talk. She might be nervous about taking over classes when she was so fresh out of grad school. Or she lost her keys, or forgot where she parked.

Libby hurried down the street, trying to keep from obsessively checking the empty sidewalks behind her. The enfolding darkness that had seemed peaceful only minutes earlier now felt sinister. She kept out of the streetlights as much as possible, preferring to hide in the shadows.

She reached Gould Hall, which no longer held any of the appeal it had when she had been there with Clare. Now, it was just a scary block of a building, hiding a secret she couldn't figure out. She slipped around the side, not wanting to call out until she saw Laura and could determine what exactly was going on.

She lost her nerve halfway along the side of the building, before she reached the far corner, and called Clare. Even if nothing was wrong here, she'd at least have some company on the phone while she found out.

The phone rang several times. Libby suddenly realized that some other woman might be there with Clare, might answer her phone. At least that disturbing thought was enough to get Libby's mind momentarily off the creepy shadows around her.

She paused by a wooden bench at the narrow end of the long rectangle of lawn behind Gould. A cement walkway lined one side, edging the inset lower floor, which was basically a long bank of windows. The upper floors jutted out over the walkway, making an open-sided tunnel along the grass.

Finally, Clare answered her phone in a sleepy voice. "Libby? What's wrong? Where are you?"

Libby whispered what had happened, peering all the while along the green space, hoping to see Laura sitting out there, just wanting to chat about something ordinary like how to fill out grading reports or how to get copies of the textbooks she'd need.

"Fuck," said Clare once Libby had finished her story. Her voice was no longer sleepy sounding. "Get the hell out of there, Libby. Walk across the street to the police station. Now. I'll be right there—I just need to put on some clothes and…Ouch! Damn it. Are you on your way to the station?"

Libby had just noticed a figure sitting against the lower floor windows. She recognized Laura's long ponytail, and the black sweater she had been wearing at the film.

"Wait, Clare. I see her. Let me just ask if she's okay." She raised her voice slightly. "Laura? Laura!"

Libby continued to walk toward her, not quite sure when she recognized that something was terribly wrong with the slumped figure, but unable to stop her approach. The windows were black, reflecting Laura's face, her bloody neck. Libby held her arms at her sides, her phone loosely held in her hand. She could hear Clare's voice dimly but wouldn't have been able to recognize words even if she had been holding it to her ear. She tripped as she stepped onto the concrete walkway, dropping her phone with a loud crack. She knelt on the path, a few yards away from Laura, and froze in place.

She wondered vaguely why she wasn't screaming, but instead she felt herself melt into the silence of the place.

CHAPTER THIRTEEN

Clare raced through the nearly empty streets from Green-wood to the U District, skidding around corners and taking every shortcut she could remember. In her mind, she replayed her short conversation with Libby, always getting stuck on the part where Libby was calling her friend's name, her gasp, and the loud clunk before their connection was broken. She would blame herself for this, no matter what had happened after Libby's phone went dead, because she had brought Libby into her dangerous world. Later, though. Now she had to get to Libby, to help her or rescue her. Self-focus and self-blame had to be secondary to finding her.

There was a chance none of this was related to the Turnbow case and Libby's peripheral involvement with it, but Gould Hall? A missing person who had been with Libby earlier in the evening? The connections felt too strong to be coincidence. Whatever was going on tonight, Clare had brought it to Libby's doorstep when she had walked into her office and agreed to her offer of help with the investigation.

The roads were lined with shadows and darkened businesses until Clare turned the corner and reached Gould Hall. Several patrol cars were parked along the curb, their lights flashing in eerie silence. The police station—usually dimly lit with a skeleton crew during the night—was bright as day, with silhouettes passing the windows in greater numbers than normal for the time.

Clare parked behind one of the police vehicles, her car skipping onto the curb and thudding back to the pavement because she had taken the corner too hot. She jumped out and ran toward Gould, not even pausing long enough to shut her car door. As she came around the building, she could see the overlapping circles made by the portable spotlights.

Images hit her mind and were flung away as she searched for the only one that mattered. The forensics team. Cappy, kneeling near the building. A body, propped unnaturally against the glass— no, not Libby. Long hair, a different shape. Cappy stiffened slightly and then turned to look over her shoulder. She rose and came over to Clare, her eyes rapidly skimming over Clare's face.

"She's fine, Sawyer. She's in the station and has a friend with her."

Clare nodded, fighting back the pang of tears and holding herself upright out of sheer willpower when every muscle seemed to sag with relief. Libby was okay. There was another dead body. Clare needed to get to work, do her job. She cleared her throat, trying to formulate the right questions to get up to speed with what had happened tonight.

"Um…" She took a deep breath and was about to start again when Cappy interrupted her.

"Go see her. See for yourself that she's all right. You're no use out here until you do."

Clare wanted to protest. She was a professional with a job to do. Cappy didn't need to baby her. She could push through this. There was no sign of annoyance or contempt in Cappy's expression, though. Clare only saw understanding. She nodded.

"I'll be right back."

She jogged over to the station, and the man at the desk— someone she thought she had met before but couldn't place now— gestured with his head toward the interview rooms without bothering to ask what she needed. She came to the first half-open door and pushed against it, hesitating in the doorway when she saw Libby huddled in a chair against the wall with a blanket wrapped around her. Alive. Safe.

Libby looked up at her, and then was out of her chair and hurrying across the room in the next heartbeat. Clare met her halfway, wrapping her arms around Libby's waist and pulling her close. Libby's hand fisted in her hair, the other clutching the shoulder of her sweatshirt as if she never wanted to let go. Everything else seemed to drop away—the sounds of the busy station, the lights of patrol cars shining through the front windows and playing across the door to this room, the mental picture of a crumpled young woman with Libby's broken phone lying next to her. Clare gave herself these brief minutes to simply hold Libby and let the world disappear.

Eventually, she eased away from Libby, leading her back to the chair and draping the blanket over her shoulders again. She was reeling slightly, both from the sensation of Libby's body against hers and the dump of adrenaline in her system. Words fought to the surface, clamoring to break free and shout at Libby about how foolish it had been to walk behind that building alone. To demand to know why she hadn't called Clare the very second she got that suspicious text. Sometime soon, she would let those words come. Not to yell at Libby, but to lecture her on safety and common sense and why she needed to stop pretending to be a detective. Right now, though, Libby looked far too fragile to withstand the full force of words fueled by the terror Clare had felt on her drive here.

Libby curled her legs underneath her, and Clare crouched next to her chair. "I was terrified," she said, careful to keep accusation out of her voice, only wanting Libby to know she cared.

"Me, too," Libby said with the shadow of a smile. "I can't believe she's…" Libby paused, seeming to swallow a sob. "What happened? Why her?"

Clare shook her head. "I don't know, Libby. I need to get out there, to find out more. Will you be okay in here until I get back?"

"Yes. Ariella Romero's here, so I'm not alone." Libby nodded toward the other person in the room. Clare had dimly registered another presence when she had come in, but it could have been Jazz standing there with a bloody axe for all she knew. Now she stood up and faced Libby's friend. She was shorter than Clare, and pretty in a delicate sort of way, emphasized by the lacy collar at her neck. Ariella looked at Libby, then met Clare's eyes with an expression Clare couldn't interpret in any other way than fierce protectiveness. She had no doubt Libby would be safe with this woman.

"Ariella," she said with a nod, as a way of acknowledging her. *Nice to meet you* sounded way out of place in this situation. She turned back to Libby, resting a hand on her shoulder. "I'll be back as soon as I can. Until then—"

"Don't leave the country?" Libby suggested, reminding Clare of her parting words after their first interview.

Clare smiled. "Forget the country. Don't leave the station."

She reluctantly left the room, but once she had managed to break free from Libby's gravitational pull—something she had been feeling from her since they met, although it was stronger than ever tonight—she hurried across the street and back to the crime scene.

Cappy had been right about Clare needing to see Libby before she came back here. Her first impression of the area behind Gould had been blurred around the edges because she had only been focused on finding Libby, but now she saw details in sharp relief. She joined Cappy where she was crouched a short way from the corpse, shining her flashlight along the edge of the pavement.

"If it's the same killer, it looks like their knife skills are improving," Clare said, nodding toward the body. One deep gash opened her throat. "Was she struck from behind, too?"

"Yes, but only twice. Hard. It seems likely that the second blow killed her instead of knocking her unconscious like Turnbow." Cappy waved the beam of her flashlight toward the northeast corner of the green space. "It most likely happened back there. Luckily, Libby entered this lawn area from the side of the building, and all the cops from the station who came pouring in here after you called entered from the front, the same way you came. See where the grass over there is flattened? The dirt behind that shrub is packed down, as well, so it looks like the tarp or something like it made another appearance."

Clare walked over to the far wall, carefully skirting the markings in the grass. She could see where the dirt and a few stray dried leaves had been dragged onto the lawn, which was pristine everywhere else. The green space was as full of lines and angles as the rest of Gould Hall—everything clean and sharp and unobtrusive. The mussed-up grass and dead body really didn't match the design team's aesthetic. This was a secluded spot, and probably a peaceful place to visit to get away from the busy campus when there wasn't a killer lurking in the shadows.

She turned and looked at the spot where the body had been posed, the young woman's face reflected in the dark glass. Laura, Libby had called her. She couldn't see any obvious reason for hauling her over there, rather than leaving her where she must have dropped after being struck, but she felt certain there must have been one, at least in the killer's mind. No statues or other obvious forms of iconography to give meaning to the murder. Suzzallo was full of those symbolic opportunities. Gould refused to offer any—at least none that Clare could easily identify.

She returned to the body, staying well out of the range of blood spatter, and Cappy joined her there. Everything about Turnbow's wounds had spoken of panic and inexperience. Laura's were more determined, appearing unhesitating.

"We might be dealing with a separate killer, someone stronger than Turnbow's, but if it's the same one, this murder feels more personal," she said. "Vengeful."

"I know. I just have no idea why." Cappy sounded angry at herself about that. She sighed audibly. "We'll find out, though. You've been careful not to ask whether Libby is a suspect."

Clare didn't meet Cappy's gaze. She had avoided getting Cappy's opinion on the matter, even though she couldn't believe Libby was capable of this. Sloppily killing Turnbow to protect her students? Maybe. But not this one. "Do *you* think she's a suspect?"

"No. In fact, we're fairly sure she's not. She was supposedly standing in front of the theater talking to her friend—the one in the station with her—at the estimated time of death. The manager and an usher also confirmed seeing them there when they locked up for the night. Even if the forensics team is off in the time, she would have had to rush over here, murder her, change clothes, and hide the weapons. She's too clean. And the officers got here too quickly for her to have done more than shove a tarp full of bloody crap into the bushes, which we would have found by now. She just didn't have time to stage everything the way it is."

Clare breathed a sigh of relief. She hadn't needed Cappy's reasoning to convince her, but she had been afraid that everyone else would see Libby as the most likely suspect.

"On the phone, when she called…" Clare paused, caught again in the net of fear that had trapped her when she had heard Libby's whispered story. She took a deep breath and continued. "Libby said she was a former student and had just today come back to fill in for another professor. She thought that's why Laura texted and wanted to talk to her, because she was nervous about it. Do we know anything else about her?"

Cappy shook her head. "Kent's pulling her records now, so we'll be able to find out if she was ever in a class with Turnbow, or if she got into any trouble while she was here at school. Libby might be able to tell us more now. She was in a pretty bad state of shock when the officers got here, so they just got her to the station and secured the scene. I got here right before you did and didn't want to talk to her without you."

Clare nodded her thanks. She took a few steps backward, wanting to get back inside and see Libby again. "I'll go talk to her now, if you want to—"

"No." Cappy's voice was sharp. She took hold of Clare's arm and led her around the corner of Gould, so they stood between the building and the station, out of hearing range of the forensics team and the officers who were guarding the perimeter of the scene.

"*We* will talk to her. The rules have just changed, and you're not calling the shots anymore. No more of this divide and conquer bullshit—from now on, we work together."

Clare pulled her arm out of Cappy's grip. When they had started working together on Turnbow's case, she had wanted to work alone for very different reasons. Now she wanted to protect Libby. "She just found a friend murdered. She'll probably feel more comfortable if I'm talking to her since she knows me."

"She was the first on the scene of a homicide. This isn't a counseling session."

"I know that," Clare snapped, although Cappy was right about Clare wanting to handle it like one.

"I don't think you do. Listen, Sawyer, this is a bad situation. This is two homicides in a week, same MO. This isn't just a targeted attack on some jerk professor or unfaithful husband. Now we have the corpse of a young woman lying over there. And now someone is targeting your girlfriend."

"She's not my…" Clare started to protest, but the words died on her tongue when Cappy's sentence fully penetrated her mind.

"All right, then, someone is targeting the one woman who had the ability to get you racing here in the middle of the night, all stupid and frantic with worry. And don't even try to deny it."

Clare couldn't. She had watched for pedestrians, but everything else had been fair game. Curbs, traffic signals. She felt sick to her stomach, wishing Cappy would stop harping on the idea of Libby being personally targeted by the killer.

Cappy shook her head, as if reading Clare's mind. "I don't mean they're after her. Hasn't it occurred to you that she might have been used to get to *you*? You've been nosing around—we both have—and maybe you somehow got too close to the killer and haven't realized it yet. If someone has seen you around with her, they might have figured out a way to get to you. Maybe by framing her, or maybe by drawing you here without backup. We don't know what might have happened tonight if she hadn't decided to call you, or if you hadn't called the station as fast as you did. Both Laura and Libby might have been bait to get you here."

Clare rubbed her temple. She had already been feeling guilty about getting Libby involved in the case. Now, Cappy was telling her that she might have inadvertently drawn Libby into danger by getting too close to the key to solve the case—even though she had no fucking idea what it might be.

"I let it slide, the whole *You go your way, I'll go mine* shit," Cappy continued, apparently determined to continue this lecture until Clare's head exploded. "I know you have something to prove here, and you wanted the leeway to investigate on your own, maybe solve the case by yourself and get credit. It's why I didn't want to work with you in the first place, because it seemed like you were only looking out for yourself. Tonight, I guess I realized that you aren't completely. Anyway, I let it happen for a while, but no more. We can do this the easy way or the hard way, but we're going to work together from now on."

Clare had started this investigation wanting to prove herself. She needed to. Somehow, though, her focus on getting ahead in her career had been in the forefront of her thoughts less often lately. Maybe because of being with Libby, or maybe having the chance to do the type of detective work she valued and wanted to get better at doing. And tonight, she would have willingly traded every future promotion to ensure Libby's safety. She wasn't sure how she was going to feel about this tomorrow, when the cold hard facts of her life here on campus and her growing attachment to Libby hit her, but right now she was feeling weak. No, not weak. Tangled, not just with Libby, but with Cappy, too, even though they barely knew each other and hadn't really worked together yet.

"I have a headache, so just tell me what the easy way is."

"We go to the gym, and I beat the crap out of you," Cappy said. Clare normally wouldn't doubt her ability in a fight, but Cappy had a crazed look in her eyes. Clare might have been acting without thinking when she had driven herself here, but now her mind was clearer, and she wasn't about to agree to fight someone who was looking at her like that.

"Then what's the hard way?"

"We sit down with a cup of tea and spend the next five hours hashing this out, talking about our feelings until we're besties and willing to work together." Cappy gave her a wicked grin. "What'll it be, Sawyer?"

"What if I just say okay, and we skip the rest?" Clare couldn't deny that Cappy's arguments made sense. When this had been an isolated homicide, unrelated to her or anyone close to her, the decision to try her hand at solving the case solo had been tempting. If Libby was in danger now, then Clare would do whatever it took to keep her safe. She wanted Cappy on her side.

"I accept," Cappy said. "We're in this together. Real partners. Agreed?"

"Agreed." They started walking toward the station. "So. If we're real partners, maybe I should know your real name. I've asked around, but no one would tell me." Probably because they'd be threatened with an ass-kicking if they did.

Cappy grimaced, looking directly ahead and not at Clare. "Caprice."

Clare wasn't sure what to say. Cappy was the least capricious person she had ever met. She wasn't about to say so, though, especially since Cappy was fully armed while Clare hadn't managed to change out of her plaid pajama pants before driving here, let alone put on her duty belt.

Cappy stopped and faced her. "What? You've got a problem with my name?"

"No, no, of course not. It's…unique. Interesting?"

"It's a ridiculous name," Cappy said, turning back toward the station but not quickly enough to hide her flash of a smile from Clare. "I think I would have had more respect for you if you'd said so."

Clare smiled a little, too, a welcome moment of levity in a dark night.

"Caprice, I think this is the start of the most annoying partnership ever."

CHAPTER FOURTEEN

L ibby lifted her head, surprised at the amount of effort it took, when Clare and another police officer entered the room. She was starting to get some feeling back in her limbs after spending the past two hours shivering under heavy blankets. Her mind was starting to thaw, as well, which was horribly painful. The dull, distant sensation caused by the shock of finding Laura in the garden was giving way to acutely painful thoughts. She was relieved to see Clare again, but she felt a difference in her. She was here now as a detective. The difficult part of the ordeal was about to happen, when she was going to have to relive the moments behind Gould before the officers had come and gently led her away from the scene. The Clare who had come in here earlier had been someone else, someone only thankful to find Libby safe and alive, uninterested in any other part of the night. This Clare obviously was still happy to see her—even in her numbed state, Libby could see those emotions behind her carefully controlled, professional mask—but she also had more serious matters on her mind.

"Libby, Ariella, this is my partner Cappy Flannery." She pulled a chair closer to Libby and sat down. "We need to ask you some questions about tonight, so we'll ask Ariella to step outside while we talk."

"I should stay," Ariella protested. "Does she need a lawyer?"

"Are you a lawyer?" Cappy asked her.

Ariella paused for a moment. "No, I'm an English lit professor," she admitted, but her body language seemed to indicate that she wasn't about to back down about staying in the room, law degree or no.

Clare glanced over her shoulder at the two women who were now glaring at each other. "We have to get Libby's statement as a witness to a homicide. She's not under arrest, and we're not accusing her of anything. Please, we need you to wait outside."

"I'll scream if I need you," Libby said, trying to be helpful, although given the way Clare was now rubbing her forehead, she might not have appreciated Libby's assistance.

Ariella seemed to be appeased, though. "Good. I'll be right outside the door. Are these things soundproof?"

"Of course not," said Cappy. "It's a meeting room, not a torture chamber." She ushered Ariella out and shut the door. "See? It's not soundproof," she said loudly.

"Good. Thanks!" Ariella called back, her voice only slightly muffled.

"There. No need to yell." Cappy brought another chair over to Libby's side of the room, seating herself to the side and farther from Libby than Clare.

"I like the new uniform," Libby said. She hadn't noticed what Clare was wearing until now. "It's much more stylish than the old one."

Clare looked down at her blue and gray flannel pants and sweatshirt with frayed collar and sleeves. She smiled a little, and Libby loved that there was no self-consciousness or embarrassment in her expression. "I grabbed what was closest to me. I was so worried about you that I'm grateful that I didn't just run out the door naked."

"Yes, we're all grateful for that," Cappy said wryly. "Libby, can you walk us through the events of the night?"

Libby stumbled through the beginning of her story. She was dazed and sad, but part of her couldn't keep from responding to Clare's tousled hair and her outfit that seemed intimate, somehow, even though the loose-fitting shirt and pants were even less revealing than her full uniform. The word *naked* hadn't helped either. She tried to focus on the timeline even as the details kept slipping from her mind, replaced sometimes by the tantalizing thought of Clare in bed with nothing on and other times by the snapshot of Laura huddled against the building.

The jolting swing between the completely opposite emotions those two images produced in her was upsetting. Clare and Cappy listened patiently, though, with Cappy writing notes and Clare recording her like she had done before. Cappy prompted her to repeat something once or twice, and she had to backtrack at one point and fill them in on Laura's recent arrival at the university and what had brought her here. Libby paused now and then when Clare seemed about to interject—such as when Libby said she had considered calling her when she got the text, but had instead headed to Gould alone—but Clare controlled what Libby could see was an obvious desire to lecture her. The occasional kick in the ankle from Cappy seemed to help her self-control, too.

Libby faltered to a stop when she got to the part about finding Laura's body. Luckily, they didn't ask her to describe the scene aside from making sure she hadn't touched or moved anything, and that they had seen exactly what she did. She wondered at the way the night seemed far away at times, as if the events had happened long ago and to someone else, but at other times, it felt close enough to punch her in the gut. She was still herself, but now she was someone who had seen the body of a violently murdered friend. She was having trouble reconciling the two parts of her.

"Can you describe your relationship with the victim?" Cappy asked. Clare seemed agitated by the question, but Libby wasn't sure why.

"She was one of my students. I haven't seen her since she graduated, and we reconnected today. I already told you that."

"Yes, but what was the nature of the relationship," Cappy repeated. "Were you friends? More than friends?"

"Oh," Libby said, finally understanding the question. She had no idea why Cappy was asking it, but she answered with emphasis. "She is…was engaged to a man she met in her junior year here. He's still in Philadelphia but was planning to move back here next month. As far as her relationship with me, we were professor and student. Not friends. I enjoyed having her in my classes because she was very engaged and focused, but we never spent time together outside of the classroom or activities within the Classics department. She seemed to get along with my group when we were at the movies tonight, and I was thinking that we would probably become friends now that she's a colleague, but I have...*had* no interest in anything more, even if she hadn't been involved with someone else." She leaned toward Clare. "And she wasn't in my secret murder society."

"What?" Cappy interjected.

Clare shook her head at Cappy. "Most of her jokes sound like confessions. You'll get used to it. Maybe." She turned back to Libby, seeming more settled than she had been at the start of this line of questioning. "What about Professor Turnbow? Was Laura one of his students, too?"

Libby frowned. "Possibly, but I can't say yes or no for sure. Laura was in the Classics department, not architecture. She took two courses on Roman architecture from me because they were connected to her major. Jimmy never taught any classes on the ancient world, but she might have taken a different subject from him as an elective. I'd be surprised if she had, though. She had already decided on her major when she came to university, and if she took classes outside the department, I'd bet they were either basic prerequisites or were related to Greece and Rome somehow."

Laura had been as tightly focused as Libby was wide-ranging in her course choices. Laura's dedication had earned her scholarships, a place in a prestigious grad school, and now a great teaching opportunity here at UW. Libby couldn't stand thinking about how such a promising young life had been brutally ended. She blinked, as if to clear tears from her eyes, but they were dry. The sense of sadness and the shock were still too overwhelming, and she had gone past the point of crying. She tried to concentrate on Laura's death as being part of an investigation, not as something personal. "I was trying to figure out why her. Why the two of them. If they were killed by...I mean, it looked like the same..."

Clare put her hand on Libby's knee, and she felt the comforting weight of her through the thick blankets. "There are similarities, so they might be connected. We don't know yet. Do you know of any people who would have known her when she was a student here? Friends who are still around and might be able to tell us if she had been having a relationship with someone besides her fiancé?"

Libby's mind slowly absorbed the question and made the leap to what Clare and Cappy really wanted to find out. Her brain was sluggish, but not completely out of commission. "If she was…Do you mean Jimmy? An affair? No way. I can't even…" She shook her head, as if to emphasize her denial of the very idea of the two of them together.

"You made it sound as if he was having an affair when you talked to Jazz," she continued. "Do you think his wife killed him for it, then went after Laura because she thought she was his girlfriend?"

Clare and Cappy exchanged a series of glances and gestures that seemed to convey an argument. Libby couldn't figure out what they were trying to say to each other, but Clare seemed to have lost because she crossed her arms over her chest and leaned back in her chair with a huffing kind of sigh.

Cappy rolled her eyes, then leaned toward Libby, resting her elbows on her knees. "We sent some of Turnbow's clothes to the lab, and they discovered DNA from six different people on them. Three are students here, and the others haven't yet been identified. Now, there are numerous possible explanations for this, from the innocent to the other extreme. He might have brushed by them in the hallway, and a hair was transferred to his suit jacket. Or he might have been close to them in a more intimate way. My partner doesn't want me telling you this because she believes it will upset you, but we need to find out what was going on with him. If he was having inappropriate relationships with students recently, then he could have been doing the same thing when Laura was a student."

Libby shook her head. She had guessed at something like this from Clare's comments and mysterious omissions but she—like Clare—had wanted to keep the details from her conscious mind. She couldn't hide any longer. "I can't believe Laura would have let anything happen without telling one of her professors or her dean. At the very least, she would have told her fiancé. She was too confident, too sure of herself. And if she told someone, they would…Hey!" She turned to Clare. "Is this why you accused me of murdering him when we were in Gould the other day? Because you thought one of my students had come to me, and I decided to get revenge?"

"She accused you of killing him?" Cappy asked. She turned to Clare. "You didn't tell me you saw her as a viable suspect."

"I don't," Clare said, then amended her statement before Libby could jump in and contradict her. "Okay, I did, but it was for a very brief time. Seconds, really. But I'm convinced you would have reported him, not taken matters into your own hands."

"Well, good," Libby said, strangely proud that Clare had thought she would be so protective of her students that she would kill for them. She wouldn't, of course, but she liked that Clare understood how important they were to her. "I can help find out what really happened. If you give me their names, I can talk to them. If they were afraid to speak up before, then maybe they'll be willing to talk now."

Cappy nodded. "We were going to ask for your help. Not on your own, but to be with us when we question them."

"Were," Clare said. "Past tense. Now we're not letting you anywhere near this investigation until the case is solved."

"I want to help," Libby said.

"She wants to help," Cappy echoed.

"No, Libby," Clare said, ignoring her partner. "I've put you in enough danger already. As of now, your involvement in this case is limited to talking to us about the events from tonight, and then you're done. Don't you understand? The killer texted you, brought you to the crime scene. Who knows what would have happened if…"

She stopped and ran a hand through her already mussed hair, as if unable to even say the words. Libby froze inside, replaying the events of the night. She had called Clare, and the police had arrived seconds later. What if she hadn't called? Was someone hiding nearby, ready to kill her, too? She tucked her shaking hands deeper into the folds of her blanket, wishing she could be holding Clare instead. She looked like she needed comfort as much as Libby did.

"Why me?" she asked.

Clare made an impatient gesture toward Cappy, as if giving her permission to share their suspicions. "We don't understand the link between the two crimes yet, if there even is one. You might be connected, too, somehow. More likely is the idea that the killer was trying to get to Clare through you. Either to lure her to Gould and attack her, or to punish her by hurting you. We've both been talking to a lot of people on campus over the past week, and it's possible Clare has spooked the killer into thinking we're close to discovering their identity."

Libby ran through the scenarios in her mind. Honestly, they sounded like stories she would have concocted, and not like possible truths. She thought back to the text, and to the sound of her phone hitting the paved walkway when she had dropped it.

"There's a simpler explanation for why I got the text," she said, latching on to the least frightening option. "Maybe the killer wanted the body to be discovered and sent the message to the last person to text Laura. When we were at the movies, I texted her with my number because I told her I'd take her to the bookstore and show her what to do if she needed to order specialized books for her classes. We're assuming someone scrolled through her contacts to find me specifically, when it might have been a fluke from hitting reply."

Clare and Cappy exchanged another of their loaded glances. From the way Clare's shoulders dropped and the crease between her eyes softened, Libby guessed they hadn't even considered such a benign reason for the text from Laura's phone to her.

"So, I can keep helping with the case?" Libby asked. She had wanted to solve the crime before, when it seemed like an important way to contribute to her community, but now she had more personal motivation for assisting Clare.

"Still no," Clare said. "Your explanation makes sense, but ours do, too. I would like to ask you one more question about what you saw tonight, though. We talked before about Turnbow being posed like a sacrifice, and the symbolism in where he was placed. The person who murdered Laura seemed to have intentionally moved her into the position where you found her. What do you make of it?"

Libby hadn't anticipated the question, and it inspired a sudden recall of the scene and a gut reaction, in the same way that showing her the photo of Jimmy had done. She let the impressions move from visual images to words without filtering them or making judgments. Clare obviously wanted her instinctive response to the scene, not a carefully prepared essay.

"The windows were opaque. She was meant to be seen at night, not when it was light outside, because the dark made the glass more reflective. She's an outsider, coming back here where she doesn't belong anymore. Her palm was on the window, as if trying to get in, but her death means she's forever on the outside. We talked about the glass making the interior of the building and the knowledge inside visible and accessible to everyone, but tonight it was the opposite. The way her hand was placed also reminds me of gestures of supplication I've seen in paintings and sculptures—I can print out copies of some, if you'd like. But the pose suggests she's subservient in a way. Jimmy was abased, on the ground, but she was begging. She was at someone else's mercy, and mercy was denied. So were inclusion and acceptance."

Cappy frowned at Clare. "Are we sure she didn't do it? She seems to understand this positioning business far too well."

Clare shook her head. "She didn't do it. She just sounds like she did. Come back in, Ariella," she added, raising her voice slightly.

Ariella opened the door, having obviously been staked out right outside it the entire time. "Are you finished?"

"For now," Cappy said. "We'll probably have more questions once we've been able to examine the evidence in more detail. We'll also get your phone back to you as soon as we can."

Libby grimaced. She wouldn't be able to keep using the phone after it had been used to receive a text from the person who had murdered Laura. "Keep it," she said. "I'm getting a new one."

Clare walked over to her and rested a hand on her shoulder. "I'll take you home," she said. "You need to try to get some sleep."

"I'll take her home," Ariella corrected her. "She'll be safe with me."

Libby felt Clare's hand tighten slightly. "And she wouldn't be safe with me? I'm the cop."

Ariella snorted. "You're in your jammies."

Cappy laughed. "It's awesome, isn't it? She hasn't noticed, but I've been taking pictures for the department newsletter."

"I don't care what I'm wearing. I'm going to take her home and check her place—"

"I'm perfectly capable of looking under the bed and in the closets."

Libby decided she'd had enough of their bickering. Yes, she was feeling emotionally fragile right now—who wouldn't be in this situation?—but she hadn't regressed to childhood. "It's my decision whether—"

"What are you going to do if someone's hiding there?" Clare continued. "Read poetry at them until they expire from boredom?"

Insulting poetry in front of Ariella was a dangerous move. Libby reached up and tugged on Clare's sleeve in an attempt to warn her.

Ariella ignored the literary slight, though. "You know perfectly well why I should be the one to take her home and stay there with her. She's been through a horrifying experience. She'll turn to you for comfort, and if she does that while she's not in her right mind, she might regret it. You both might, if it ruins what you're starting to have together."

What they were starting to have together. Libby liked the sound of that, but the rest of it was rather rude. "I'm in my right mind," she said, but they ignored her.

"I understand trauma," Clare said. "I would never take advantage of her in this state, no matter what she tried."

"Excuse me. I'm right here. I'm not about to throw myself at you, Clare, no matter how sexy you look in those flannel pants, so both of you can quit discussing this like I'm not here."

"She's right," Cappy said. "And while this little interchange has been entertaining, I'm going to take Libby home now. Her delicate virtue will be safe with me, so stop glaring, the two of you. You look exhausted, Ariella, so you need to take care of yourself and get home for some rest. And Clare, I'm better equipped for checking her place for intruders than you are right now. What were you planning to do, anyway? Throw your bunny slippers at them? Come on, Libby."

Libby hugged Ariella. "Thank you for staying here with me," she whispered. "I'll call you tomorrow, okay?"

She hesitated, then stepped toward Clare, who opened her arms and pulled Libby close. They didn't speak, but just the moment of standing there, pressed against each other, said more than Libby could have articulated. She sighed, feeling the movement of her breath deepen the contact between them. Maybe someday she'd admit to Ariella that her concerns had been valid. If she and Clare were alone in her apartment, Libby would definitely have done her best to seduce her. She smiled. Clare wouldn't have stood a chance—not that Libby believed she really would have tried too hard to resist. She allowed herself another long moment with Clare in her arms, and then she pulled away and followed Cappy outside.

CHAPTER FIFTEEN

C lare pushed the stack of papers off to one side and wearily rubbed her eyes. Cappy had done more than her share of the reading today, as they had plowed through every record they could find on Laura. Clare had long since suspected that the rest of the department was aware of the reason why she had been given oral and recorded entrance exams when she had applied. She didn't believe Sergeant Kent would have blabbed about her dyslexia at a shift meeting, but this type of information always managed to spread through departments and became common knowledge. She had come to her first day on the job ready to defend herself against anyone who accused her of cheating or of using her reading challenge as a way to get sympathy from the hiring committee, and her anticipatory antagonistic stance combined with her desperate need to validate this job change had made her push Cappy and everyone else away. Her experience with Libby—realizing she had known about Clare's reading ability all along and hadn't seen it as a big deal—had made her revisit the memories of her past few weeks with the campus police. When she looked for positive signs instead of negative ones, she saw how sergeants had read handouts out loud during meetings, and how everyone had made sure to send her voice recordings of important memos and bulletins. No one had treated her as if she was stupid or like she *couldn't* read, but they had made the effort to ease the way for her as much as they were able.

After hours of squinting through pages of tiny fonts on blotchy faxes and photocopies, Clare was more than happy to let Cappy do most of the reading. In her first week on the job, she would probably have seen her effort to shoulder most of the burden as a condescending act, or one designed to make her look bad. Now, she saw it as a simple matter of logistics. They needed to get through the information as quickly and as thoroughly as possible, and Cappy was faster. Clare was growing more comfortable with the awareness that she had her own strengths to share, and it wasn't a sign of weakness to accept Cappy's help in this area.

"She was perfect," Cappy said, tossing another transcript onto the pile. "Excellent grades, volunteer work, active in campus government. Maybe the killer murdered her because she made them feel bad about themselves."

"So, low self-esteem is our motive?" Clare sighed and picked up the application packet Libby's friend had sent over, tapping the pages into a neat pile. "You're right about her, though. She might have had some less-than-ideal personal traits—like maybe she snored or flossed her teeth in public—but on paper she's a dream. Maybe it really was an opportunistic murder. The killer saw her with Libby and decided to use her as bait."

"I hate bad luck as a motive even more than low self-esteem," Cappy said, scowling at the table full of Laura's life, reduced to one-dimensional sentences. "But I can't see any way to connect her with Turnbow. She never took a course from him, and if he was using his position to take advantage of students, then he'd need to have some power over them. Grades, letters of recommendation, whatever. If she wasn't in his classes or even his department, what could he do to her?"

"Well, if we're looking at the wife or a jealous lover as a suspect, then she didn't actually have to be connected to him. The killer just needed to think she was, for some reason."

"Oh, goody," Cappy said, with her usual ill-concealed sarcasm. "Mistaken identity. That sucks as a motive, too, you know. I want this to make sense, not to be random."

"So do I. But we might not get what we want." Cappy's desire for the murders to have a reasonable explanation seemed to come from a general longing for the world to follow predictable and fair rules. Clare's need for there to be a clear and understandable explanation for the homicides was more personal. She couldn't protect Libby if she didn't understand what was going on. How could she keep her safe if she didn't know who was behind the danger, and why, and where they might strike next?

Cappy sighed. "Let's call it a night. None of this seems to be helping us with the case, and if I have to read much more, I'm going to develop an inferiority complex. Nothing like being jealous of a dead woman to ruin your night."

Clare agreed. "Maybe tomorrow will be more productive. We should get the ME's report, plus we have the interview in the afternoon."

"Yeah, I'm sure we'll have the case wrapped up by dinnertime."

They said good night, and then Clare walked several blocks to get to her car. She had spent most of the night and morning at the station, going over the crime scene with Cappy one blade of grass at a time. She had run home for a short nap, but she had been too restless to sleep and had given up and come back to the station, at least in uniform this time. Arriving later than usual meant traffic in the U District was at its peak, and finding a parking spot had been a pain. When she was on a regular schedule again, she was going to switch to public transportation.

Once she got in her car, she sat for a few moments and considered her options. She could go to Libby's and check on her. Or she could go home, then drive herself right back here and check on her. Either way, she wasn't going to do the sensible thing and leave Libby alone. She wanted to keep her out of the investigation— and out of the way of the killer—but that didn't mean she couldn't make sure Libby was okay after last night.

She drove the short distance to Libby's neighborhood, which was just on the outskirts of the main campus, and parked two blocks away. There were open spots closer to Libby's, but Clare didn't want to leave her car right out in front of the apartment. No need to advertise that she was here to anyone who might be watching one or the other of them. She walked a roundabout route to get to the correct address and entered the foyer of the large Craftsman style home. Judging by the number of mailboxes near the front door, the house had been divided into four apartments. Of course, Libby had her name displayed on her box, along with her apartment number. Clare sighed, mentally rehearsing her lecture on basic safety protocols. Even without a murderer on the loose, Libby was too trusting of other humans. Clare doubted she'd win the argument for being more cautious, but she was going to give it her best shot.

The interior of the house was clean and plain, with faded yellow wallpaper and sage-green carpets. Clare climbed the steep stairs and knocked on the darker green door with the number three on it. She was tempted to try the doorknob, just to make sure Libby locked herself inside when she was at home, but Libby opened the door before she had a chance to check. Libby grinned when she saw her, and Clare's breath caught at her welcoming smile. She wasn't going to lose her focus on safety, though, no matter how much she wanted to forget about the rest of the world and just concentrate on Libby's face.

"Really?" she asked, fighting to look stern. "Some unknown person knocks, and you just fling the door open without checking to see who it is?"

"You're not unknown. You're Clare," Libby said, still smiling and seeming unperturbed by Clare's firm tone. While Clare was glad that Libby was feeling more like her playful self than she had last night, she wasn't about to be deterred from her goal of keeping Libby alive.

"Next time, please ask who's there before you answer the door." She put her hand on the doorframe. This was designed as an interior opening, so it wasn't as sturdy as she would have liked. "Do you need permission from the apartment's owner to install a peephole and a dead bolt?"

"I'll check. But for now, I think I'll stick with pushing my dresser in front of the door every time I come home." She stepped back. "Are you coming in, or have you posted yourself on guard duty out there?"

"I can guard from inside." Clare took a step forward, but Libby put her palm against Clare's breastbone, stopping her.

"I'd like to see some ID first," she said.

Clare covered Libby's hand with her own and held it against her chest for several heartbeats. Then she lifted it to her mouth and kissed Libby's open palm before letting go.

Libby sighed, her gaze flickering from the place where her hand had been touching Clare up to her mouth, then her eyes. "I was thinking more of a driver's license or your police ID card, but that'll work, too."

Clare felt the memory of Libby's skin against her lips as they curved into a smile. She walked past Libby and into her front room.

"Oh, this is beautiful," she said, looking around. Most of the furnishings were dark in tone, from browns to rich burgundies to deep navies, but the pieces were eclectic, giving the impression that Libby bought furniture and decorative things because she liked them, not because they were part of a set. There were two tall bookcases in the room, and piles of books were stacked on every surface. A sofa and two chairs—all looking invitingly soft and squishy, with blankets arrayed across them—were grouped around the unlit fireplace, and several candles were placed on the mantel and side tables. Clare had no trouble picturing Libby here in the evening, curled under a blanket and absorbed in a book, the glow of firelight playing across her cheekbones. Surprisingly, since she had never considered decorating any of her apartments as if they were antique bookstores, Clare easily imagined herself next to Libby on the couch. The sense of coming home was startling to her. It was only because Libby had made this into such a cozy and welcoming space—anyone walking inside would feel at home.

She'd do her best to fool herself into thinking it was the apartment, and not Libby herself, that felt like home.

"Thank you," Libby said. "I like it here. Let me show you the rest."

The tiny dining area was adjacent to the living room, and the oval oak table was covered with papers. Clare guessed that Libby used this as a desk and ate elsewhere. The setup seemed too permanent to be moved at every meal. Connected to this room was a galley kitchen, which, aside from the coffeepot near the sink and a tea kettle on the stove, appeared to be unused.

"Do you cook here or just make things to drink?" she asked, wanting to be nosy and open the fridge, sure she would find takeout containers and creamer and little else.

Libby laughed. "I mainly eat on campus or pick up something in the U District on my way home. How can you tell?"

Clare shrugged. "Just a feeling. If this kitchen was an item of clothing, I'd look to see if it still had the tag hanging on it."

Libby took her hand. "I want to show you something in the den. You'll appreciate this."

Clare didn't care what she was about to see, as long as Libby didn't let go of her. She let herself be pulled down a short hall and into a room full of—unsurprisingly—books.

And a gargoyle. A life-sized, ugly, sneering gargoyle with small bat-like wings, pointy ears, and a gaping mouth with several chunky teeth. A gray cat was curled on the lap formed by its crouched pose, and Clare wasn't sure if it was real or part of the stone statue until it raised its head and yawned at her, showing its pink gums and tiny fangs.

"Am I supposed to be appreciating the cat or the statue?"

"Well, Boots is adorable, but I was talking about the gargoyle. His name is Pierre. You're so obsessed with keeping me safe, I thought you'd be happy to see him here. He can protect me from burglars."

Clare walked closer and put her hand on the cold stone. "How? Are you hoping they'll trip over him?"

"No, although that would help, too. If someone tries to come in the window, they'll see him and panic, thinking he's a real person. So they'll leave."

Clare scratched the cat on its chin and was rewarded with a raspy purr. "It's brilliant. No one would ever think it wasn't a real person. In fact, when I came in the room, I thought it was Ariella. On an unrelated topic, when you're asking for permission to fix the front door, see if it's okay for us to install an alarm system in here. Just in case the burglars have relatively normal vision and can tell a human from a hunk of stone. How did you get it in here, anyway?"

"Piano movers. They didn't seem too pleased with the job after they'd been at it for two hours, though, so I'll probably have to hire a different company if I move again."

"Unless you're now on some sort of piano mover watch list, and no one will take you as a client."

Libby gave her a playful push, and they walked back to the living room. Clare noticed that the bedroom hadn't been on the tour. Perhaps one day, she might be able to arrange for a private showing.

They sat down on the sofa, and Clare rested her arm along the back of it, where a knobbly fleece blanket had been draped. Libby sat sideways, facing Clare, with her legs tucked under her.

"I'm not going to tell Ariella you compared her to Pierre. I want my friends to like you."

Clare laughed. Petite, delicate Ariella was about as far as one could get from the hulking stone gargoyle. Physically, at least. Clare sensed a will as hard as stone inside her. "So do I," she said, surprised by how true the statement was. She and Libby were still getting to know each other, at the stage in her relationships when Clare usually wanted to learn about the person she was dating but didn't want to get too deeply involved in her world—whether it was with friends or family—just in case things didn't work out. Which they apparently never had, since she was still single. Things were different with Libby. Clare wanted to know everything about her. She wanted to have a drink with her friends and hear them tell funny stories and share happy memories about Libby. She wanted to take Libby to meet Zeke and Erin because she was sure they'd love her. They had a few embarrassing stories to tell about Clare, though, so she'd have to steer the conversation clear of those.

She looked around the room, trying to find photos of Libby's family. She had some beautifully framed photos and prints of buildings, alongside postcards and posters of paintings, Roman temples, and aqueducts that had merely been tacked onto the wall. The mix seemed very Libby-esque to Clare. She would want to be surrounded by images that spoke to her and inspired her but wouldn't care how fancy or perfectly framed they were.

The mantel and the end table beside Libby also had a few small photos of her and her friends—Jazz and Ariella and the woman who had brought Laura's application packet to the station today. Cappy had talked to her, and Clare didn't know her name. No snapshots of family, though.

"What are you thinking?" Libby asked. "You have your detective face on, like you did in the kitchen. Something insightful to share?"

"I don't see any pictures of your family," Clare said, without pausing to consider her answer. She cringed inside, wishing she had filtered her words a bit more. "I hope I'm not bringing up something sad or distressing. I was just wondering."

Libby shrugged in a nonchalant way. Clare was relieved when she didn't seem to be upset by the mention of family, but neither did she seem fully at ease. "They're alive and well," she said. "Parents, two brothers, and one sister. I love them, of course, because they're my family. We're just not the types to document things much, so I don't have a lot of pictures of them."

Clare made a sound of neutral acknowledgment—somewhere between *ah* and *hmm*—and gave Libby some space in case she wanted to elaborate. Clare wouldn't pressure her, but she wanted to understand her better, and something about this subject seemed key to who Libby was.

Libby sighed, shifting her position and bringing her hips closer to Clare. "I was a surprise baby." She gave a humorless laugh. "My parents never used the word *mistake* around me, but my brothers and sister did when they'd get mad at me. Typical sibling insults, but I'm assuming they associated the word with me because they'd heard my parents say it when I wasn't around."

Clare tentatively reached out and rubbed her knuckles along Libby's leg, just a gentle caress against the soft material of her sweatpants. Comforting her. And come on, her thighs were *right there*.

Libby leaned into the slight pressure instead of pulling away. "Whatever word was used, I was clearly born at an inconvenient time. My mom had stayed home while the other kids were young, but she had gone back to work by the time I came along. She and my dad were focused on their careers, so I was left with my brothers and sister as babysitters most of the time. They were more than ten years older and didn't want their little sister underfoot, so their supervision mainly consisted of them telling me to be quiet and stay out of their rooms."

"But as you got older...I mean, what parents wouldn't be proud of having a daughter like you? You're intelligent and caring and... well, wonderful."

Libby laced her fingers with Clare's and held their hands against her leg. "Thank you. The thing is, they had already been the proud parents of smart, high-achieving kids. They'd done the trips to Disneyland and Friday night dinners at their favorite restaurant. All the typical family-bonding activities were over. You know the stage—the kids are getting ready for college, and the parents are excited to be empty nesters with the chance to travel and redecorate the teenagers' old rooms."

"So you turned to books for company," Clare guessed.

"Yes. It was a quiet, self-contained activity, and I loved the stories and characters I discovered once I learned to read. Everyone was happy with my hobby. When I started school, I was already ahead of my classmates, so I spent more of my time sitting up front and helping my teachers during recess." She laughed and gave Clare's hand a squeeze. "Looking back, it's easy to see that I was searching for parental figures in my life. I didn't have a lot of friends growing up because of that, but once I got to college, everything changed. I found other students who were interested in the same subjects as I was, and I was sort of forced into contact with my peers in the dorms. It took almost the full four years to do it, but I really transformed during that time."

Clare thought back to the shy student who had been in Libby's office when Clare visited. She'd also seen her on the steps at Denny Hall. "And now you look for students who are like you were, and you've found a way to connect them with each other. That's really an amazing thing to do, Libby."

Libby shrugged, but her smile showed how much she cared about the work she did beyond what was required. Her parents might not look her way long enough to feel the pride in her that they should, but Clare felt more than enough for an entire family. And she understood far too well what it was like to be overlooked in that way.

She curved her hand around Libby's thighs and gently tugged until Libby's legs were resting across her lap. "My parents used to tell their friends they were glad I was pretty since Jane, my sister, had gotten all the brains in the family," she admitted. "They thought it was funny, but I believed it for far longer than I should have. I refused to ask for any accommodations or help in school because I thought it made me seem weak, so classes were always a struggle. It took until college before I decided they were wrong—not just because their teasing was hurtful, but also because what they were saying wasn't true. Once I got the tools I needed to cope with the way I read, I did just fine in classes and even enjoyed the ones that really interested me."

Libby brushed her fingers against Clare's cheek. "It's ridiculous that anyone wouldn't realize how intelligent you are. I guess the hurt from words we hear as children—or the loneliness caused by the lack of them—can linger far too long, even when we think we should be over them."

Clare leaned forward and rested her forehead against Libby's, her arm holding Libby's legs against her until she felt the pressure of them against her thighs and hips. "It helps to talk about them, though. Especially with someone who understands that we don't deserve to feel broken or unwanted for even a second."

Libby nodded in agreement, the friction of skin against skin causing Clare to feel a warmth start in her belly and radiate outward. She kissed Libby then, and the curve of her lips, the softness of them felt as good as she had imagined they would. Libby pressed into her, flicking her tongue across Clare's lower lip until she opened her mouth and deepened their kiss. Libby scooted closer, responding to the tightening of Clare's arm as she gathered Libby to her. She pulled back for a moment, hesitantly watching Libby's expression. Libby smiled—a slow, contented grin that let Clare know the kiss had nothing to do with Libby being upset after last night, desperate to find solace from any available source, and everything to do with the connection that had been gradually building between them, even after such a short time of being together. Clare returned the smile before their mouths met in another kiss.

Chapter Sixteen

L ibby sat at the table in the same station meeting room where she had met Clare nearly a week ago. She couldn't believe they had only known each other such a short time—the events and emotions Libby had experienced since Jimmy's death were more intense than anything from her past—both good and bad—and they had been compressed into such a brief span of days. Well, her friends had been hoping she would shake up her life and try some new things—she had certainly done that and more. This amount of newness ought to keep them satisfied for the next twenty years or so.

It seemed strange to her that in the midst of tragedy and crime, she had also had one of the most wonderful things occur. Meeting Clare. Their growing relationship seemed to provide a sharp contrast to the external events happening around them. Where the murders had been sudden and frequent, the attraction between her and Clare seemed as if it was slowly blossoming into the promise of something momentous. Where the crimes and the ensuing investigation seemed harsh and arduous, their interactions seemed comfortable and easy.

She really hoped she wasn't about to blow it with Clare today and lose what they had only just begun to develop.

She jiggled her knee nervously against the table leg. Last night had been beautiful. Kissing Clare was obviously the highlight, but it hadn't taken over the evening. They had spent hours talking, delving deeper into their childhoods and school years, their past relationships and future plans. While sitting on the floor of her living room and eating pizza by the fireplace, she had finally learned what was behind the calm and collected mask Clare usually wore to conceal her true self, a habit Libby thought was the result of years of being bullied by her parents and her peers in school. And Clare had learned about her, too, about the loneliness that could persist even in a life filled with friends, students, and books.

There had been more kisses, of course, but they had never moved beyond the innocent intimacy of the first one. Every time they seemed to be pushing past it, one or the other of them would pull back, just enough to slow them down again. The night before had been too overwhelming, too sad. Libby didn't want their relationship to become tangled in the memory, permanently connected to the tragedy, and she sensed that Clare felt the same way. Without needing to say it out loud, they naturally worked together to keep control. Some day soon, though, Libby hoped they would abandon that control completely. And then she would—

"I have a gun, you know," said Cappy, her voice sounding irritable. "I might use it if you keep banging your leg against the table."

"Are you threatening to shoot me?" Libby asked, gesturing with her head toward the camera near the ceiling.

"I didn't say I was going to shoot you," was all Cappy said, not bothering to elaborate about what she *would* do.

"Well, I'm nervous. I don't want her to hate me for this."

"Yeah, well, she's going to kill me. No threats, she'll just do it. God, here she comes."

Clare walked into the room and jerked to a halt when she saw Libby. "No," she said simply and calmly, even though Libby could see tension in the way her eyes narrowed, and her lips thinned into a tight line. She also thought she saw a flash of hurt, of betrayal when she made eye contact with Libby.

Her stomach clenched with anxiety, but she wasn't going to back down. She couldn't. "Clare, please, just listen—"

"No," Clare repeated. "Cappy, can I speak to you in the hall?"

"I'd rather stay here, where I can upend this table and hide behind it if you attack me."

Clare rolled her eyes. "I'm not going to attack you. I'm going to reason with you. But how could you go behind my back like this?" she asked, her voice rising slightly in pitch. "You knew I didn't want her here, and you knew the reasons why. You're supposed to be my partner, to support me."

"I do support you. She came to me and said she wanted to be here, not the other way around."

"Hey!" Libby protested, kicking the table just hard enough to bump it into Cappy. "It's true," she admitted to Clare before glaring at Cappy again. "But you didn't have to use me as a human shield. Besides, you're the one who told me you were doing this interview today."

Clare crossed her arms over her chest. "I can recognize a conspiracy when I see one. I just don't know which of you I'm most pissed at right now."

Libby and Cappy pointed at each other at the same time, and Libby lightly slapped Cappy's hand away. "Give us a minute, would you?"

"Fine." Cappy got up and sidled past Clare, shutting the door behind her with more of a bang than necessary.

Clare stood in place, now not quite meeting Libby's eyes. "Please, sit down," Libby said, indicating the chair next to her. Clare exhaled with a huff, then sat next to Libby.

"You understand why I don't want you to be part of this investigation anymore, don't you? You understand the danger you could be in if you don't stay far away from all this?"

Libby nodded. "Of course I do. I saw what happened to Laura, and believe me, I've imagined over and over what could have occurred next if I hadn't called you or if you hadn't gotten the police there right away. I can't make the images stop. But this isn't about me. This is about one of my students, and if I can help her by being here, then I don't really have a choice."

"You have a great choice. Go home."

Libby shook her head. "You know me, Clare. At least, I hope you do. You know what matters to me, and how I have to defend what does."

Clare nodded, staring at the table with a defeated expression on her face. She reached out her hand, and Libby grabbed hold of it, grateful for the gesture.

"You do, too," Libby said. Clare looked at her with a question in her eyes, and Libby elaborated. "You matter to me. More than I thought possible, for someone I only met days ago."

Clare squeezed her hand. "I feel the same about you," she said. Unnecessarily, Libby thought, since every way Clare tried to protect her was proof of how much Libby mattered to her.

Cappy opened the door a crack and poked her head in. "She's here. What's it going to be, Sawyer?"

Clare sighed and let go of Libby's hand. "She can stay. Go ahead and bring her in." She turned to Libby. "I'm assuming Cappy already talked to you about how this is going to go?"

Libby nodded, although Cappy's explanation had been full of ifs and maybes. Her job was mainly to sit there and be supportive. She could do that.

Cappy ushered Miriam into the room. The tall junior had been in a couple of Libby's classes but had never come to the Denny Hall sessions even though Libby always extended invitations to all her students. She seemed to put a lot of effort into her coursework but had struggled anyway, tending to settle in the middle of the pack in terms of grades.

She looked terrified as she walked in—understandably so, Libby thought, since how many twenty-year-olds got called into police stations regularly enough for it to seem normal?—but her expression changed the moment she saw Libby.

"Professor Hart," she said, beelining toward her with relief apparent in the way her face and shoulders relaxed a fraction.

"Hello, Miriam," Libby said. She stood up and Miriam hugged her.

"I'm so scared," she whispered in Libby's ear.

"I know, but it's all right," Libby said as she broke contact and gestured toward a chair for Miriam to sit. "You're not in trouble. The officers just need to ask you a few questions."

Uh-oh. Libby was pretty sure Cappy was meant to say that part. Judging by the looks the two officers were giving her, she wasn't correctly performing her role of silent supporter. She made a face at them from behind Miriam's back and sat next to her. She hadn't really expected that she'd be able to refrain from speaking during this, so they might as well get used to it. It was too late to throw her out. Maybe.

"Professor Hart is correct," Clare said, stepping in smoothly. "We're investigating Professor Turnbow's death, and we wanted to ask you a few questions about him. Are you willing to talk to us?"

Miriam hesitated, glancing at Libby, then she nodded.

"You've taken two classes from him, correct? One when you were a freshman, and one this quarter?"

Another nod. When Clare let the silence after her question lengthen, Miriam finally spoke up. "It was, um, an intro to architectural drawing class in my second quarter here. I was taking Architecture and Theory this term, but now Professor Johnson is teaching us, since..."

"Architecture and Theory," Cappy repeated when Miriam seemed to run out of things to say. "That sounds like a hard class."

Miriam nodded, her earnestness replacing some of her earlier fear. "It was. My uncle's an architect, and he was so proud when I told him I was majoring in it, too. At family holidays, he likes to say how he'll hire me at his firm as soon as I graduate, but I'm going to be a disappointment to him. I'm not really good at any of it, except the drawing part."

Libby opened her mouth, about to tell Miriam she should explore other options that might be better matches for her, and that her uncle would surely understand. Clare nudged her leg under the table and shook her head slightly, so Libby closed her mouth again. This wasn't a career counseling session, but as soon as she had a chance, she was going to talk to Miriam about those things.

Cappy flicked through some papers on the table in front of her, as if checking on some detail in her notes. "Did Professor Turnbow ever offer to help you with your grades or your classwork? Maybe in exchange for some favor?"

Miriam's sudden jolt into stiffness was unmistakable. "He...I... nothing ever happened. I didn't mean to do..."

She faltered to a stop and looked at Libby. *Don't say it*, Libby wanted to beg her. "It's going to be all right now," she said instead. "You can tell us what happened, and no one's going to get in trouble."

Miriam bit her lip, eyes downcast, then started to talk, fumbling over her words at first, until they started to flow from her as if she had been fighting to keep them inside and had finally let go. "About a month ago...he said, well, he asked me to stay after class. He had my quiz we had taken, and, well, he said I was between a C and a B, but he'd help me if I...He just liked to talk, mostly. About what he was like in school, or what he would have done if he hadn't become a professor. He liked to hug me sometimes, but nothing more. He said I shouldn't tell...that nothing was wrong with us talking, but no one else would understand. I was so afraid he'd fail me, or I'd get expelled. I didn't know what to do."

Cappy's pen snapped in half, the sound echoing through the room in the silence that followed Miriam's monologue. "Sorry," she mumbled, staring at the broken pieces in her hand as if unsure how they had gotten there.

Clare took over the questioning, her voice still even and neutral even though her leg was pressed tightly against Libby's. Libby wasn't sure if she was seeking comfort from their connection, or if she was trying to keep either Libby or herself from exploding in outrage. Libby needed Clare's touch for both reasons.

"Did you ever meet him outside of his office, or late at night?" Clare asked.

"No, never," Miriam said, shaking her head.

"Did he have other students he was...helping with their grades?"

"I don't know. I would never have asked."

Clare nodded, then glanced up at the camera. Moments later the door opened, and an officer Libby hadn't met yet came into the room. She was wearing civilian clothes and her smile seemed friendly, though slightly tense. Libby had a feeling she had been listening in on the conversation.

"Miriam, this is Officer Raven Montgomery. She's the department liaison to the university's administration. She's going to get you set up with someone to talk to about this, someone to help make sure nothing like this ever happens to you again."

Miriam looked from the officer to Libby. "Am I going to be kicked out of school?"

"No," Libby said firmly, probably overstepping her bounds again, but not caring if she was. "We're on your side, Miriam. All of us, okay?"

Miriam nodded and left with the officer, who began speaking to her in an earnest, low voice before they had even left the room. Libby stared at the door after it shut, until Clare's quiet voice caught her attention.

"Cappy? Are you all right?" Clare was looking at her partner with concern. Cappy's face was pale, and her expression—usually openly sarcastic—was shuttered.

"I'm fine," she snapped. She sighed and nudged Clare with her elbow. "I'm fine," she repeated more calmly. "I should go check on Kent. She's probably tearing apart the observation room about now."

She went out, leaving Clare and Libby alone. Clare rubbed her eyes wearily, then reached over and put her hand over Libby's. "I'm glad you were here. I think this was much easier on her than it would have been without you in the room. Still, I'm sorry you had to hear all that."

"So am I," Libby said. She felt angry and sad and incredibly tired all at the same time. Clare looked as if she was going through a similar range of emotions. "But I wouldn't have stayed away even if I'd known what she was going to say. I hate that he got away with this. Or that he was getting away with it, I guess. Who knows how long it's been going on?"

"We'll probably never know. At least now we'll have a chance to help the ones we can identify. And Miriam won't have to go through this alone anymore. That's something."

Clare sounded as if she was trying to convince herself that easing one person's pain was enough, when Libby knew Clare was the type of person who would want to save the entire world if she could.

"You don't think she killed him, do you?" The interview had been very short, and the questions Clare and Cappy had asked hadn't seemed to indicate that they saw her as a suspect. Clare hadn't hesitated to come right out and ask Libby if she'd killed Jimmy—she doubted she would have held back today if she'd thought Miriam was a murderer.

Clare shook her head. "No, but we needed her testimony on record for the case. We already checked her alibi, and she has three roommates who are willing to confirm that she was at home both nights. Besides, she doesn't quite fit the physical description we've gotten from forensics."

"How so?" Libby asked, curious to find out what the killer was supposed to look like. She was already looking at everyone she came across on campus with the awareness that any one of them could be the person who had murdered Laura and Jimmy. It would be helpful to her peace of mind to be able to rule out at least some of them. Clare wasn't about to share her information, though, and merely shook her head without saying anything else. Libby figured she'd try again once they were away from the station and its cameras. She wanted to ask if Clare thought Cappy was all right, but she didn't know if she was within earshot of the recording devices. Another question for later. Clare was going to have a busy night either answering them all or pretending she hadn't heard them.

Clare sighed. "I'll be finishing up here in about an hour, and then I was supposed to meet some friends from my old department for dinner. Do you want to come out with us?"

"Yes," Libby said without needing to stop and consider.

"Good." Clare smiled and stood up. "I'll come by and pick you up around five."

"And I'll demand that you identify yourself and shove three letters of recommendation under the door before I let you in."

❖

Both the station and campus were relatively quiet on a Sunday afternoon. Libby was relieved to be out of the room where she had listened to Miriam's sad story, but the nausea she had felt while hearing it lingered. She did her best to identify and support those of her students who didn't seem able to fit in and thrive at college because she wanted them to develop confidence and to have a great experience while at school. She understood how lonely it was to feel isolated from classmates, unsure how to make friends. Now, she had even more reason to seek out those students and give them opportunities to connect with their peers, since being on the outskirts apparently made some students more susceptible to manipulation and abuse. She had always known those problems existed, of course, but she hadn't had much direct experience with them until now.

A few days ago, Clare had asked—in a semi-joking way—if she was involved in some sort of secret society. Libby wanted to create the complete opposite, a place where everyone who wanted to come felt welcome. No hiding, no secret shame. She wanted to find a way to do something more than her hour a week on the steps of Denny Hall.

"Have they given you a job with campus police? You seem to be at the station a lot."

Libby turned to find Ariella walking up behind her. "Hi," she said, giving her a hug. "I was just helping Clare with…giving her some information about the architecture department."

It wasn't really a lie, Libby told herself. She wasn't about to share personal information about Miriam, even with another professor and a friend, and she wasn't supposed to talk about even the little bit of information she had on the murders. "What brings you to campus on a Sunday?"

Ariella held up her shopping bag, with the logo from a local used bookstore printed on it. "I needed some books," she said.

Libby smiled. Ariella needed more books just as much as Libby did. What she really needed was an entire extra house in which to store the books she already had.

"Do you have time to grab a coffee?"

"Yes, although I'll need to get home before five. I'm going out with Clare...well, not really going out...I'm going to show her..." Libby stuttered to a stop, not quite sure what to say.

"You're going to show her..." Ariella prompted, "Your blueprints? Your floor plan? Are either of those the euphemism architects use?"

Libby laughed. "We're just going to dinner with some of her cop friends."

"Ah, meeting the friends. Come on, we'll get a quick cup of coffee, and you can fill me in on this new hobby of yours. I'll bet you're glad you took our advice and are trying someone...I mean *something* new."

CHAPTER SEVENTEEN

"Who is it?" Libby called through the door after Clare had knocked.

"It's Clare. Thank you for checking."

"Clare? Clare who?" Libby leaned her shoulder against the doorframe. She wouldn't be able to hear it from this side, but she could picture Clare sighing before she responded.

"Clare Sawyer. I'd push my ID badge under the door to prove who I am, but I'm afraid you wouldn't give it back and would use it to impersonate a police officer and try to solve crimes."

Libby opened the door. "Oh, *that* Clare," she said. "I recognized you by your blatant mistrust of my motives."

Clare shook her head, but with a smile, as she came into the room. She shut the door behind herself and locked it—they were just going back out again in a few minutes, for goodness' sake—before brushing her hand up Libby's arm and then cupping her cheek. She hesitated, a question clearly in her expression, and Libby answered it by stepping closer and meeting her halfway for a kiss. She understood Clare's tentativeness, since she was feeling a little oversensitive about the issue of consent today, too. She had no doubt, though, about their utter willingness to be as close as possible to each other.

Clare broke off the kiss and wrapped Libby in her arms, holding her close. Libby slid her arms around Clare's waist. She had changed into civilian clothes—jeans and an oversized black sweatshirt—and Libby's hands moved over her, unencumbered by Clare's duty belt. Oh, except for the gun resting against her lower back. Libby pulled away from it instinctively, mainly because she was afraid she'd jostle it and accidentally shoot Clare in the ass. That would be a real shame.

"I'm not going out unarmed when there's a killer on the loose who might have a personal vendetta against me. Especially if I'm with you."

"Do you think I should—"

"No! I mean, no," Clare repeated, less forcefully the second time. "Not without a lot of training, and a lot more thought than five seconds' worth."

"That sounds like smart advice," Libby said, running her forefinger down Clare's breastbone. "We can wait and talk about it next time I help you with one of your investigations. That'll give me time to think it through."

"Excellent idea. As soon as I let you assist on a case again, we'll definitely have that conversation."

Clare looked pleased at the result of their bargain, and Libby assumed she wasn't anticipating them ever having a reason to talk more on this subject. She was underestimating Libby's ability to find a loophole, though.

"And if someone ever, say, starts spending nights over here, and happens to have a gun, then it would only be prudent for me to be able to use it if I had to."

Clare looked decidedly less enthusiastic about Libby's counterargument. "It would be prudent, yes. Although I'd be afraid that you might accidentally shoot Pierre while on your way to the bathroom in the middle of the night sometime because you mistook him for an intruder."

Libby laughed, allowing the humor to help them gloss over the suggestion she had just made about a potential future for them. One Clare had accepted without running away, or even flinching a bit. Instead, she took hold of Libby's hand after they went out into the hall and she locked her door. Libby was thinking about how much she enjoyed the grounding feeling of their entwined fingers when they got to the front door of the apartment building and Clare let go of her.

"Okay, when you go outside, turn right and walk two blocks, then go east for one."

"East?" Libby repeated, wondering if she'd somehow misunderstood Clare's invitation this afternoon.

"That way," Clare said, pointing behind them.

Libby rolled her eyes. "I know which direction is east. I've seen a sunrise before. I just thought we were going together."

"We are. Once we get to the car, that is. I'll go the opposite way and meet you there. My car is green. Really green. Look for the greenest thing around you, and that'll be it."

"Can I walk on the sidewalk, or should I fling myself from shrub to shrub?"

Clare seemed to take her question seriously. "Sidewalk is fine. Just keep alert."

Libby frowned and headed out the door, turning in her assigned direction. She thought Clare was exaggerating the danger of their situation, but her sense of urgency made Libby more aware of her surroundings. She noticed which parked cars had people sitting in them, and where the pedestrians who passed her were heading. She thought back to two nights earlier, when she had been walking home and got the text from Laura's phone. She hadn't noticed anything except a general sense of creepiness caused by the shadows and the mysterious text. The killer could have been standing in a doorway she passed, or behind a bush right next to the sidewalk, and she wouldn't have noticed. They were very likely close to her when she got to Gould and found Laura's body. This wasn't a paranoid reaction on Clare's part, but a very reasonable one when they had a murderer who had made what seemed to be deliberately threatening moves toward them.

She startled a bit when she got to Clare's car and found her already waiting in the driver's seat. Libby shook her head. After all Clare's precautions, she was driving what was possibly the least unobtrusive vehicle in the city.

She got in the passenger seat and shut the door. It took her three tries before she got it to close properly.

"Do I need to help pedal, or are you good?" she asked.

"Very funny. I can drive by myself, thank you," Clare said. "Although I might need you to open the door and drag your foot on the pavement when we have to stop."

Clare drove them out of the U District and took an overpass over I-5, zigzagging along side streets as she headed toward the Ballard neighborhood.

"Are you going to tell me what kind of description you have for the killer?" Libby asked as they drove through Wallingford and continued west. "I'll be safer if I know because then I'll be on alert if I see someone following me who is a match."

"If you see anyone following you, call 911 immediately. No, first call me, then call 911." Clare passed the Ballard Locks and pulled into the parking lot of a small pub. She parked and turned off the engine before facing Libby. "All we really have right now is an estimated height based on the angle of the blows to the backs of both victims' heads. It's not definite because there are a lot of variables involved, but it seems likely that we're looking for someone around five four or five five. At that height, the killer is statistically more likely to be a woman, but none of the physical evidence gives a clear indication of gender."

"A woman makes more sense when you consider Jimmy's behavior with his students."

"Maybe," Clare said. "But an angry boyfriend or family member wouldn't surprise me, either."

Libby frowned. "How does Laura fit in either of those cases?"

Clare fidgeted with her key chain. "She doesn't, and that bothers me. There's got to be a connection somewhere, but I'm missing it. Either that or her murderer is a copycat, which doesn't seem right to me. Some of the details from Turnbow's murder aren't widely known, but they were repeated with Laura. And no, I'm not going to tell you what they are. I only shared the guess we have for height because I can't keep information from you if it can directly protect you. Come on, let's go inside."

"Can I walk with you, or should I take the route around those trees and through the back door?"

Clare took her hand, her fingers warm and strong as they wrapped around Libby's. "We can walk together this time. I took so many side streets, I'd have noticed if we were being followed."

Ah, that was why she had gone such a roundabout way, when the drive from the university to Ballard was a fairly direct route. Libby had thought she was keeping off the main roads to avoid traffic. She still had a lot to learn about being a detective. Actually, she had just about everything to learn about it.

Once they were inside the crowded and stuffy little pub, Clare waved at two people who were leaning against the bar.

"Oh wow," Libby said as they got closer. "I was about to look over my shoulder for the photographer. They look like they're models on a shoot."

"Right? They're gorgeous," Clare said, with zero envy in her voice. Which was as it should be, Libby decided, since even as good-looking as the two of them were, neither was anywhere near Clare's league.

They looked close in age to her and Clare. Zeke was a tall Black man, and he was leaning one elbow on the bar with the other hand holding a leather jacket hitched over his shoulder. He had friendly brown eyes, and some of the longest lashes Libby had ever seen. Erin wasn't about to be outshined by him. Her brown hair was caught in a simple ponytail, and her peaches and cream complexion seemed untouched by makeup, but she managed to convey a sense of glamour with her high cheekbones and dancer's build. She even moved with a ballerina's grace as she rose from where she sat with one hip perched on a barstool and came over to meet them halfway across the room.

They hugged Clare, and then she introduced Libby to them. They greeted her warmly, somehow already feeling like old friends to Libby, maybe because they interacted in similar ways with Clare as her own friends did with her. She wondered if it had been hard for Clare to leave them behind when she took her new job with the campus police.

When they got to their booth, Clare sat next to Libby, close enough for their bodies to be touching from hip to knee, and Libby melted into the contact. The night before with Laura and today's disturbing talk with Miriam seemed to hide in the shadows of her mind, springing out at unexpected moments and making her feel queasy. When she was close to Clare, though, she felt a comfort in her presence. She felt grounded with her, even as the pressure from her thigh made Libby's stomach tingle with a spreading warmth.

Erin leaned across the table toward her. "Clare told us your friend was murdered, and that you found her," she said, as if reading on her face where Libby's thoughts had been traveling. "I'm very sorry, Libby. I understand what a shock it must be for you. If you ever want someone to talk to, we're here for you. The chaotic mix of emotions you're probably feeling can be overwhelming."

"Yeah, and it's not always easy to talk about it to people who haven't been there," Zeke added. "People can be disturbed by the details and not want to hear them, so you have to carefully censor what you say, and then it feels more stifling to talk than to keep silent. You need people who won't be upset by what you have to share. You have Clare, and now you have us, too."

Libby thanked them, fighting back the tears suddenly pricking at the back of her eyes, probably due to the memory of seeing Laura's body combined with the kindness of these people. Thankfully, they shifted their attention away from her while she pulled herself back together, talking about the menu options and what everyone was having to drink. She wondered if this was part of the reason Clare had wanted the four of them to get together tonight, to give her a chance to connect with some other people who had seen death and would give her the space to talk about her experience if she needed to. Somehow, just knowing she could if she wanted to made a lot of the tension in her neck and shoulders ease. She hadn't even realized how tightly wound she had been until now.

They ordered food and drinks—three IPAs and one Coke for Clare, who said she was perpetually on call. Clare was holding Libby's hand in hers again, resting them on her lap under the table, but not in a surreptitious way, while they talked about Libby's job, and then she learned about their families and positions on the Seattle force. Once their meals were served, Libby reluctantly let go of Clare, and Zeke nodded toward their hands as they separated.

"Looks like your move to the campus department wasn't as huge a mistake as you thought, Clare. It's good to see that you're settling in there."

Libby looked at Clare. "What was a mistake? I thought you came to the campus department on purpose, for the opportunities it offered."

Clare grimaced and shook her head in Zeke's direction. "I did. I just made the decision to leave Seattle more hastily than I should have." She sighed, swirling her fork through the mashed potato topping of her shepherd's pie. "I had been a detective for a little over two years when I got a chance to fill in for someone in homicide. Instead of letting me keep the job, a guy with less seniority—"

"And less brains," Erin interjected. Zeke nodded in agreement.

"As I was saying, he was moved into the position permanently, and I was sent back to my old unit. I got angry and quit. Then my high-maintenance morals and I had to find another position. I'd heard good things about UW's police department, so I applied and got the job."

"So they're not as open-minded as you expected?"

"Oh, they are," Clare said. "But they're also small, with fewer openings available for promotions. I regretted my decision right away, but then it was too late to either go back or go forward to somewhere else. I knew I had to take advantage of any chance to prove myself, or I'd be stuck in the same place for years." She traced her forefinger along Libby's jawline, then used it to turn her head until she met Clare's eyes. "I'd make the same decision to quit again in a heartbeat because if I hadn't, we wouldn't have met." She cupped Libby's cheek, then dropped her hand, addressing the three of them again. "And it hasn't been all bad there. I'm slowly getting on more friendly terms with my new partner and the other officers. And I actually had a chance to work a homicide case much quicker than I expected."

She paused, exhaling softly. Libby saw Erin and Zeke exchange worried looking glances.

"Trouble is," Clare continued, "I'm not as good at being a homicide detective as I imagined I'd be. If I'd been able to solve the case more quickly, Libby wouldn't be in danger, and Laura would still be alive. I know the Seattle detectives are ready to step in if Cappy and I can't resolve this soon, and I'm starting to think it will be better if they took over."

Libby looked across the table at Zeke and Erin, hoping they would say something to make Clare feel better. She wasn't a failure—she was doing good work, but just hadn't found the missing clue yet. But she would, Libby was sure of it. She doubted her words would make a difference to Clare, though, since her real-life experience in these matters was limited to hovering on the edges of this single case.

She raised her hand to her cheek, where Clare had touched her. She still felt the line of heat where Clare's finger had moved, but the sensation was less soothing now. It was a fleeting touch, there and gone. As tenuous as the way they had chanced upon each other on campus. So many small events had taken place to ensure they would meet, and sadly, Clare regretted them all. Libby believed her when she said she'd go through it all again just to meet Libby, but if Libby had the chance to change them, she would have to choose Clare's happiness over their meeting.

Zeke and Erin banded together and gently nudged the four of them onto lighter topics, eventually settling on the tried-and-true tension breaker of telling embarrassing old stories about each other. Libby soon found herself laughing along with them, without force or pretense.

Even as she interacted with them, part of her was still focused on Clare's words, and the defeat in her voice because she hadn't solved the case yet. It finally made sense to Libby why Clare had easily believed that she might kill for a promotion. To Libby, her multidepartmental work—even though it made her one of the least likely to advance at the university—was worth doing even without tenure or other accolades. Clare wanted the chance for promotion, and since the campus department wasn't likely to offer her the ease of movement she wanted, she would eventually decide to leave. Libby leaned into her, wanting to keep her close as long as she could.

Clare seemed distracted as they left the pub. The evening had been fun, and everyone had done their best to make the night a good one, but Clare obviously had things on her mind and needed space to think them through. Libby had originally imagined the night ending with Clare staying at her place, but now she was revising her vision for the end of their date. Not only because Clare needed time, but because she did, too. The cathartic effect of laughter, good company, and a lot of food had broken her free from the more visceral responses her body had gone through while finding Laura and hearing Miriam. Now she was too tired to move and was seriously considering taking a nap in the foyer before she tackled the flight of stairs.

Clare parked just around the corner, but even though they walked back to the apartment together, she was acutely alert, seeming to notice every car or dark corner where someone could be hiding and watching them. Libby looked around a little, too, but mainly she let the professional handle the surveillance. Once inside, Clare moved from room to room, checking every window and closet. Boots followed Clare around, her tail weaving in the air as she joined in this fun new game of hide-and-seek.

Finally, Clare came back to her. She wordlessly gathered Libby to her, seeming to bypass her skin and move directly to her soul. Clare pulled back a little and kissed her with enough urgency and pressure to let Libby know she wasn't alone in her feelings, but not enough to suggest they go beyond this kiss tonight. She ended the kiss but stayed close, twirling a lock of Libby's hair around her finger before tucking it behind her ear.

"Thank you for bringing me tonight," Libby said. "I liked your friends."

Clare smiled. "I'd like them a lot better if they stopped telling those stories about me."

"I thought that was their most endearing quality," Libby said with a laugh.

"Wait until they get to know you well enough to share your most embarrassing moments. It's not so endearing then." She kissed Libby again, lingering in the contact. "I'll see you tomorrow, okay?" she said when they broke apart. "Be sure to lock the door behind me."

She reached down and picked up Boots, who was sitting on her foot, and handed her to Libby. She gave her another quick kiss on the mouth, and then was gone. Libby locked the door, then started toward her bedroom. She only made it to the couch, though, where she collapsed onto the soft cushions, barely pulling a blanket over herself before she fell into a deep sleep.

CHAPTER EIGHTEEN

Clare struggled out of her slouched position and arched her back, stretching her muscles before settling into a more upright posture. Cappy was across from her, her feet on the table and legs crossed at the ankles. They had been here for almost an hour, digging through the notes and reports strewn on the table and having a variation of the same conversation they had had nearly every day since Turnbow's murder. Clare pinched the bridge of her nose. They would continue to have this conversation—speculating, cycling through the facts of the case, going over the same arguments for and against every possible solution—until they either got fresh information or suddenly saw an overlooked clue in a new light.

"I still like the wife as a suspect," Cappy said, tossing a folder onto the table.

"His five foot nine wife?"

"Yes. She seems awfully happy to have him gone. Maybe she was crouching down a little when she hit them, just to throw us off track."

They had been to the Turnbow's Mercer Island home again today, and Cappy was right—Alicia Turnbow was one of the most cheerful grieving widows Clare had ever met. She looked a good five years younger than she had a week ago, and she had spent most of her time today telling them about a dinner party she was planning and how she was prepping her garden for winter.

"You'd think she'd at least pretend to be devastated about her loss, at least when we're around. She's not even trying."

"Yeah," Cappy agreed, leaning her head back and staring at the ceiling. "But if she didn't do it, I'll bet she sends a thank-you card and box of chocolates to whoever did, once we figure it out."

Clare nodded. *"If* we figure it out."

"You're such a pessimist, Sawyer. We're right on track with this."

"Are we?"

Cappy shrugged. "I have no idea. You're the expert here."

Clare gave a snort of disdain. She felt about as far from being an expert as possible. Where before she had felt pressure to shine on this first case with the campus police, now she felt near panic because as long as the crime went unsolved, Libby was in danger. And the other innocents on campus, too—if she had been quicker to solve Turnbow's murder, then Laura might still be alive. If she wasn't fast enough now, someone else's body might be their next discovery.

Among the reasons why someone would want to kill Turnbow was one that also applied to Laura, but she couldn't see it yet. They could be random crimes, with an opportunistic killer, but the body positioning and text to Libby seemed to refute that idea. She felt certain there was a pattern or consistent motive, and she hated how far she felt from knowing what it was.

Her motives had changed. Partly—well mostly—because Libby had become far more important to her than Clare would have imagined after so short a time, but also because she felt an obligation to this new community of hers. She hadn't realized how much the locus of her universe had shifted until last night, when she and Libby had gone out with Erin and Zeke. She had fallen back into the usual self-centered litany of regrets over career mishaps while talking about her campus job, but partway through she had realized how little she cared about them anymore. The Angry Quit, the lack of research into her next job. She had been focusing on those out of habit, but now they seemed far enough from her list of concerns as to be insignificant. She didn't need to be the hero here, or to impress everyone enough that they would create a fancy new position in the department just to promote her to it. She wanted the case solved, and she didn't care if Cappy or another officer or some random eyewitness off the street managed to do it.

"What are the two of you doing in here—having a tea party? Is this what I'm paying you for?" Sergeant Kent was standing in the doorway with her hands on her hips, which put them uncomfortably close to her gun. She had been storming around the building ever since she had received the analysis from Turnbow's clothes, and yesterday's interview with Miriam had only made her expression more thunderous. Clare was surprised she still had words coming out when she opened her mouth, and not a nonverbal, primeval roar. She knew Kent's anger was only indirectly coming at her, but still… She was scaring the shit out of the entire department.

Cappy snapped her legs off the table too quickly, catching the edge of it with her foot hard enough to jostle half their papers onto the floor.

"Who wants overtime?" Kent asked, ignoring the paper landslide. "Simpson called in sick, and Dayton's on the graveyard shift."

"I'll do it," Clare volunteered hastily. Not because she was intimidated by Kent—well, not really—but because a late shift on campus might help her get some perspective. She hadn't spent much time here in the dead of night since she had taken this case, and getting back into the eerie, out-of-real-time atmosphere she had experienced on the night of Turnbow's murder might help clear her head of the overanalyzed details she and Cappy rehashed every day. Cappy sent her a grateful look. She had already been here since four in the morning, while Clare had come in at noon, only expecting to stay until midnight.

"Good," Kent said. She was halfway out the door when she turned back. "Well? Are you going to pick up those papers, or are you going to leave that mess on my floor?"

Clare and Cappy hastily started to gather their notes off the floor. "We'd better solve this soon or she's going to implode," Clare said in a low voice. "We're going to come here someday and just see a crater where the station used to be."

❖

Clare had an hour between the time when Cappy went home and when she was supposed to meet Dayton for their shift. She hurried across the street to the university and just managed to make it to Architecture Hall as some afternoon classes were ending. She spotted Libby near the doorway, talking to some students, and she hovered on the edge of the crowd until their conversation was finished. She tried to look as though she was there in a professional capacity, patrolling the campus and keeping everyone safe, and not a stalker. Still, her eyes were only on Libby, and she was relieved to see her looking more rested. Last night, she had been getting a bit gray around the edges toward the end of their evening together. Libby had experienced a lot in two days, more than she should be expected to process without a lot of time and support. Unexpectedly coming across a dead body was a jolt to the system, especially the first time—well, even the hundredth time—and even more so when it was the corpse of a friend. The revelations about Turnbow, while not entirely unexpected, were disturbing, as well. Add the speculation that the murderer might have been after Libby or herself, and therefore close to Libby when she was behind Gould Hall, and Clare was surprised Libby was still functioning, let alone coping with everything as calmly as she was. She was very strong. Add that to the list of things Clare adored about her.

Clare had worked very few homicide cases so far in her career as a detective. Investigating the crime while, at the same time, navigating the early stages of what had already become the most promising relationship she had ever had was proving to be a challenge, made even more difficult because Libby had gotten entwined in the case. First as a potential suspect, then as an outside expert from the architecture department, and now as someone who had gotten the attention of the killer, for some reason. Maybe coincidentally, as the most expedient person to text from Laura's phone, or maybe for a more specific reason, like drawing out Clare.

Protecting Libby had to take priority over developing a relationship with her. More accurately, it had to override the relationship, because the more involved Clare got with Libby, the more likely she was to be in danger.

Still, as if drawn by an irresistible magnet, she set off at an angle and intercepted Libby on the path toward the Quad.

"Hi," she said, falling into step beside Libby. "You look better today."

Libby gave her a smile—it wasn't as bright and carefree as the ones she had shared with Clare when the investigation had first started and she had seen it as an interesting game, but it still had enough spark to it to put Clare at ease. "I feel better. Most of the time, at least."

Clare nodded, shifting slightly to brush her shoulder quickly against Libby's before moving away again. "There are unexpected triggers, aren't there. It's normal to feel a little shaky or tense when something reminds you of what you went through."

Libby sighed. "Exactly. I came out of my classroom a few minutes ago, and I realized I was standing where Tig and Laura and I had been laughing and joking around. I couldn't move or breathe, and everyone was walking past me like nothing momentous had happened."

"It'll ease," Clare assured her, wishing she could erase the memories from Libby's mind. Better yet, wishing she could go back in time and do a better job of catching the fucking murderer before they had gotten to Laura. She took a deep breath, trying to calm the sudden rush of anger she felt. Anger at whoever had done this, but also at herself. Apparently she had some triggers of her own. She decided both she and Libby could do with a change in subject.

"I'd offer to carry your books for you, but my hands are full," she said, nodding toward the stack of hardcovers she had in her arms. "Plus, I know how heavy that bag of yours is."

Libby grinned and shrugged the satchel's strap onto her other shoulder. "I need to get something with wheels. Are you planning to do some gardening?"

"These are the books Turnbow had checked out," Clare said, glancing at the stack of thick guides to Northwest plants and architectural landscaping she was holding. "I'm on my way to return them to Jazz. Maybe I can sneak a library cart out of there for you. It would make it easier to haul all those books back and forth from your apartment."

Libby laughed, leading Clare out of the flow of traffic on the walkway and onto the grass near the path leading to Suzzallo. "Careful," she said. "I'm pretty sure Jazz has installed tracking devices on all her carts."

"Maybe I'll just buy you a skateboard instead. You can set your bag on it and pull it along." Clare paused to return a greeting from another professor—she and Cappy had given him a jump start a few nights ago when his car died in one of the staff parking lots—then turned back to see Libby looking at her with a scrutinizing expression. "What?"

Libby shrugged, but a smile was teasing at the corners of her mouth. "You're different here, you know. On campus. When we first met, you seemed to hold yourself at a distance when you were around other people, but now you seem more comfortable, I guess. Like you belong."

Clare waited for the instinctive wince she should feel at those words. Her? *Belong* at a university? But as ridiculous as the notion would have been to her even a week ago, she could feel some of the truth of it settling inside her. She might not fully belong here, but she couldn't deny her growing need to protect the people on campus, and to protect Libby, above all. This should be a place of learning, of growth and idealism and practical knowledge. Not murder and abuse and fear.

"I'm getting used to it, I guess," she said, shrugging off the fury she felt when she thought of those negative things intruding on the campus. On Libby's life. She could let Kent and Cappy get more emotionally involved with the university and its people. She needed to remain detached and level-headed if she was going to solve this case. Looking at Libby now, though, made her feel anything but detached.

She cleared her throat. "Well, I should get these back to Jazz."

"And I should get to class," Libby said. She brushed close to Clare as she turned toward her building. "See you around."

Clare watched Libby walk away before she went into Suzzallo and climbed the marvelous stone staircase, carefully balancing her stack of library books. She went through the Staff Only door, only halfway expecting to be zapped with an electric charge because she wasn't really library staff, and walked down the hallway to Jazz's office.

Her door was open, and she was sitting at her mammoth desk, immersed in some paperwork.

"Hi, Jazz," Clare said from the doorway since she didn't have a hand free to knock, and kicking at the door with her foot didn't seem to be a wise choice in this situation, unless she was prepared to lose it.

Jazz looked up and smiled at the sight of Clare. "Officer Sawyer. Come in. Are those my books?"

"Yes. We picked them up this morning." She set them on the desk.

"Have a seat." Jazz indicated the chair across from her as she came out from behind her desk and flipped through each of the books. She'd probably fine the department if Turnbow had dog-eared any of the pages, Clare decided as she sat on the uncomfortable folding chair. Jazz's chair matched the scope of her desk and looked far softer.

"Sorry about that," Jazz said, correctly reading Clare's thoughts about the chair. "I don't want any of the board members feeling too cozy in here."

"It's fine," Clare lied, watching as Jazz pulled a piece of paper from between the pages of one of the books. Clare had shaken all of them, to see if anything loose fell out, but this sheet must have been tucked in tight.

Jazz unfolded it and started to read. "If I'm dead, and you find this note, my murderer is…Huh, that's all there is." She laughed and handed the page to Clare. "Just kidding. It's blank, probably just something he used to mark his page."

"You've got a sick sense of humor," Clare said, shaking her head as she held the paper to the light and then put it in her pocket. It could just as easily have been left by a previous library patron and remained inside the book, unnoticed when it was next checked out. Unless it really had contained the testimonial Jazz had made up, even a clear fingerprint on it would be useless evidence.

Jazz, satisfied with the condition of the books, sat down again. "It's a shame about the dead girl," she said. She rested her elbows on the arms of the chair—Clare's seat didn't have arms—and steepled her fingers. "Let's see. You're going to ask if I knew her. I looked her up in a yearbook after Tig told me what happened, and I recognize her face, but that's about it. I rarely get to know the students as well as the others do, since I only teach the occasional seminar for the Information School—that's Library and Information Sciences. Next, you'll ask if I ever noticed her and Jimmy Turnbow together. I'm sorry, but I couldn't say for sure. As I said, he was quite the social butterfly and liked to talk to a lot of young women."

She paused and got an envelope out of her top drawer. She handed it across the desk to Clare. "Copies of my plane tickets for Chicago, where I spent the weekend at a library conference, and the names and numbers of three people who saw me in the hotel's gym at five Central on Sunday morning. I assume your last question was going to be my whereabouts at the time of the murder."

"Easiest interview I ever had," Clare said. She pulled out the envelope's contents and flipped through them, amused that Jazz really had printed out copies of her tickets. Clare put them back into the envelope and added it to her pocket. "You do realize you were never a suspect, don't you?"

"I like to be prepared. Now, it's my turn. How is Libby handling all this?"

Her question, and the obvious concern behind it, surprised Clare. She had been expecting something along the lines of *What are your intentions toward my friend?* or *I'll let you rot in the library's dungeon if you hurt her.*

She told Jazz briefly about Libby's experience—leaving out details about their suspicion that Libby had been used as bait to get to Clare, as well as Miriam's interview—and reiterated how well she seemed to be coping with everything. Even with her omissions, the events Libby had faced sounded daunting.

"She needs her friends," Clare said.

"She needs *you*," Jazz countered.

"I'm here for her. She knows that. But my job is to protect her. Providing emotional support is secondary to keeping her safe, and if it comes down to a choice between the two, I'll pick the latter every time."

Jazz nodded. "It sounds as if she might need her friends' support while dealing with more than just the events that happened to her this weekend. Well, you're an honest one, I'll give you that."

"I try," Clare said. She stood up and tapped her pocket. "And now I'm going to go contact these so-called witnesses who saw you in the gym. They sound like made-up names to me."

"Oh, get out of here," Jazz said, but her laughter followed Clare as she walked back down the hall.

Clare and Dayton were making their rounds by the residence halls when their dispatcher sent out a call that someone had reported a broken window at Padelford Hall. They were the closest, just passing by Haggett, and Dayton radioed in that they would go check it out. These minor cases of vandalism were the most common crimes they dealt with on an everyday basis, and Clare appreciated the simplicity of it. Go find the window. Locate the drunk kid standing close to it, ready to throw another rock. Case closed.

They walked the short way to the hall, passing several students as they went. Eleven o'clock wasn't a busy time on campus, but there were usually plenty of people heading back to the dorms from the libraries or going out with friends. The area around Padelford seemed relatively quiet. She went to the entrance and pulled on each of the doors, making sure they were locked. She peered into the darkened foyer, playing her flashlight over the empty space.

"Looks okay from here," she said. "Let's check the rest before we go in."

"Sounds good," Vance said. "See you around back. He headed left, shining the beam of his flashlight on the first set of windows, checking each pane in turn. Clare went in the opposite direction and did the same.

She remembered Libby telling her how much she disliked this building, and she understood why. Clare had seen some redeeming qualities in Gould Hall and had shared them with Libby, but she couldn't come up with a single one for Padelford. She got the impression that the bricklayers had occasionally thrown in a right angle whenever they got bored following a direct route from one corner to the next. The jutting brick sections were broken up further by inset banks of ground-to-roof rectangular windows. The whole building resembled a bunch of pallets made of brick and glass that had been upended and stuck together. The interior was no less confusing, and the two times Clare had needed to go inside, she had gotten lost in dead-end corridors. Asking students for directions while in uniform and when she was actually inside the building was embarrassing, but judging by the way they responded, she wasn't the first to get turned around in there.

For all its weird shapes, it somehow managed to be an example of really boring architecture. Even the walls alongside the steps and some of the walkways were notched in irregular patterns. Following the Northwest's love of greenery—which was even more pronounced on this campus—the building was surrounded by thick trees and shrubs. The landscapers must have hoped they'd eventually grow big enough to conceal the building. From an aesthetic standpoint, Clare loved plant life as much as anyone, but from a safety perspective, it was a risky choice to have made.

If the broken window was close to the ground, she wouldn't be able to see it through the shrubs, so Clare left the paved path and pushed through a thick clump of rhododendrons to get closer to the wall. She hesitated as she passed by the second bank of unbroken windows. She wasn't sure why the other murders were suddenly looming in her mind. Maybe it was because she was thinking about the design of this building, and Gould and Suzzallo were inextricably combined with the previous deaths in her mind. Or maybe she was just on edge because of the investigation, letting the stress of it seep into her regular duty. Whatever the reason, she wasn't going to ignore her intuition but was going to get herself out of this dense landscaping. She and Vance could check out the rest of the building together.

She was reaching for her radio to contact him while pushing past the fronds of some lacy, thick shrub, not paying attention to the ground in front of her, when she tripped over an exposed root. The forward momentum of her stumble meant the blow to her head merely shoved her forward instead of knocking her out, or worse. Unfortunately, the force of the hit was enough to send her headfirst into the wall of the building with a painful crack. She twisted out of her fall, drawing her gun as she turned, but whoever had hit her was no longer in sight.

CHAPTER NINETEEN

She ran out of the bushes, calling for both backup and Dayton on the radio as she did, but the area around Padelford was empty. She returned to the front of the building, and Dayton appeared seconds later, running over to her.

"Sawyer, are you...Hey, you're bleeding."

"Someone hit me from behind, and then I sort of fell into the building. They ran away before I could get a good look." Or any look. Clare reached up to touch her forehead where she had hit the brick wall. Yep. Bleeding. She tried to focus on Dayton and not on the throbbing headache that was threatening to pop her eyeballs out of her head, and she nearly jumped out of her skin when someone called her name.

"Clare? Is that you? Oh my God—you're bleeding."

"That seems to be the general consensus," she said, stupidly trying to laugh at her own sad joke and wincing at the pain. "Ariella? What are you doing here so late? Ow, what the hell are you doing, Dayton?"

"Checking you for concussion," he said, moving his flashlight's beam out of her eyes.

"You're supposed to use one of those little doctor flashlights, not a high-powered spotlight." She accepted the handkerchief he was holding toward her, feeling slightly abashed when she saw the obvious concern on his face. She would have felt the same if she had separated from her partner and they had gotten hurt, even though it had clearly not been his fault. "But thank you. I'm all right."

She turned back to Ariella. "Did you see anyone run out of those bushes before I did? And why are you here again?"

Ariella exchanged a glance with Dayton, and Clare wondered if she sounded more shaken than she felt. "I met Jazz for a drink after I finished work today, and I was heading back to my car when I saw you. I didn't see anyone else."

"Your car..." Clare repeated. She must have hit her head harder than she thought. Nothing seemed to be making sense. Why was Ariella's car in the middle of campus? She looked around her. "Did you park it here?"

Ariella took her arm and led her over to a bench by the steps, pushing her gently until she sat down. Dayton hovered nearby, alternating between looking at her as if waiting for her to keel over and watching for the arrival of other officers.

Ariella sat beside her. "My car is in Padelford's garage, behind the building. This is Padelford. It's my building, Clare. The English department is here."

"Yes, got it. Thank you."

"Here comes our backup," Dayton said as several other campus officers came jogging toward them. "I'll get an officer to walk you to your car," he said to Ariella. "You shouldn't be in the garage alone right now, in case the attacker ran in there for cover."

Ariella nodded, then turned back to Clare. "I can stay with you," she said. "Do you need me to stay?"

Clare shook her head. Huge mistake. "I'll be fine once I've caught my breath." She tried to reassure Ariella by patting her on the arm but sort of missed. She decided to just pretend she had meant to pat the bench instead.

"She needs to get to the emergency room," Ariella told Dayton. "Or at least get checked by a doctor."

"We'll take care of her," Sergeant Kent answered instead, her voice uncharacteristically gentle. Her quiet tone scared Clare more than anything else had this evening. How close to death did she look if Kent was concerned?

Kent called an officer over to take Ariella to her car. She squeezed Clare's shoulder gently, then left.

"Clare, I need to ask you to show us where you were when you were attacked and to tell us what happened. Then we'll let you rest."

"By *rest* do you mean *die*?" Clare asked. "Just how terrible do I look?"

Kent gave a short exhale of laughter. "You're going to be fine. Come on, up you go."

Kent held out her hand and helped Clare to her feet. She took a deep breath and made sure nothing was spinning when it shouldn't be before returning to the side of the building where she had been hit. With five Maglites beaming around, the shadowy area was now as light as day. She pointed out the attacker's escape route, marked by scuffs in the dirt and fir-needle-covered ground but no clear footprints.

"I didn't turn around in time to see anything," Clare said, angry with herself for missing the opportunity. "I lost my balance when I tripped and didn't recover fast enough."

"Well, since that stumble probably saved your life," Kent said, "I'll forgive you this time. What about you, Dayton? Anything unusual on your side of the building?"

"Nothing," he said, his voice tight with emotion. "I should have been here. It was my fault."

"No," Clare insisted. "We followed standard protocol for a vandalism search of a building. We split up the way we always do."

Kent looked as if she wanted to yell at someone but didn't have a clear target. She apparently chose the entire department. "Yes, it was standard protocol. Not anymore. From now on, you search together, no matter how trivial the call seems. Understood?"

A chorus of *Yes, Sergeant* followed her pronouncement. They spread out and searched the area, and Harris soon called them over to where he stood, just across the path and outside Hall Health. He aimed his flashlight under a willow, where a metal pipe was resting against the tree's trunk. "Probably ditched it here, then ran around the building. It'd be easier to blend in with other pedestrians without it."

"Good job. Guard this until Flannery gets here, Harris. The rest of you, keep searching the area. I'll take Sawyer to the ER."

Clare breathed a sigh of relief. She was back to being Sawyer. She had been a lot more worried when Kent was calling her Clare. She climbed into the passenger seat of one of the four-wheelers the officers sometimes used to get around quickly on the campus pathways, and they drove in the direction of Portage Bay, where the university's medical buildings were located on the south side of campus.

Seeing the pipe, recognizing that it was most likely the same type that had been used to attack Turnbow and Laura, and most likely wielded by the same hand, unnerved her. She had come very close to going from being the detective on the case to the next victim. She wanted to credit her good cop instincts for saving her, but instead she could only thank the twist of fate that had made her trip at the correct time. Well, she had stumbled because her attention was on her radio and not on walking, and her instincts had been the reason she was using the radio, so...

No use. It was just damned good luck, which wasn't something she could rely on with any certainty at all.

Kent parked right outside the entrance to the ER and marched her inside, as if she was a flight risk. Clare, her headache settling into a constant dull roar, sat on a plastic chair while she waited for Kent to explain the situation at the intake desk. She barely had time to register how uncomfortable she was before she was whisked off to a private room. One of the benefits of being an officer in uniform with a bloody head—no long waits in the emergency room. Of course, just the bloody head part would probably have gotten her or anyone else the same treatment.

Kent followed her as far as the doorway to the room, then she held out her hand. "Duty belt," she said. Clare fumbled at the buckle and handed the heavy belt to her sergeant, feeling as naked now without her gun as if she had peeled off all her clothes.

Kent seemed to read her reaction. "Keep your back to the wall," she said. "If you see someone coming at you with another pipe, scream for a nurse. You can have this back once the doctor clears you for duty. I'm going back to the scene, but someone will be out there waiting when you get released."

She hesitated with her hand resting on the doorframe, as if deciding what else to say, then she shook her head slightly and walked away.

Clare perched on the edge of the examination table, crumpling the wide swath of paper that covered it. In the silence of the room, the thought she had been keeping at bay by focusing instead on her headache came to mind strongly and clearly. She didn't know why she was being targeted, or what she could possibly have uncovered that was making the killer squirrely enough to want to murder her next, but she did know one small, undeniable truth. She couldn't let Libby anywhere near this unknown source of danger, which meant she couldn't allow Libby to be anywhere near her.

When Clare finally had been scanned and prodded to the doctor's satisfaction, she went back to the waiting room and found Cappy standing in the corner of the room, where she had a view of both the entrance and the door to the exam rooms. She pushed away from the wall and came over to Clare.

"Well? Is anything cracked? Do I need to stay with you tonight and slap you every time you start to fall asleep?"

"Just bruised, and no thanks. I don't have a concussion."

"Okay, then," Cappy said as they walked out the door. "Can I, just for fun, stay with you tonight and slap you every time you start to fall asleep?"

"Still no." Clare followed her to the designated spot for police vehicles, which Kent had completely disregarded when they had arrived. She slid into her seat, fighting to stay awake.

Cappy started the car and let it idle. "Do you know how mad I am at you? What were you doing, wandering alone through the bushes?"

"It was a simple vandalism call. Dayton was right around the corner, so whoever attacked me wouldn't have had time to stage a murder scene."

"Exactly," said Cappy in a tight voice. "They knew where you'd be, and how you'd handle the call. There wasn't going to be any dragging you around or posing your body. This was meant to be a quick kill."

Clare shivered. She had come to the same realization, but she still didn't like hearing it expressed out loud. If Dayton had gotten to the back of the building and she hadn't been there, he'd have come directly around to her side. The attacker had seconds, at most a couple minutes, to take her out and get away. They had come a long way since Turnbow's sloppy murder.

Clare turned her fear into obstinance. "Haven't you done building checks since we started this investigation? Do you make sure you have a chaperone whenever you do?"

"No, but I don't seem to be the target. You are."

Clare shook her head. For God's sake, why did she keep doing that? She exhaled slowly and focused on their argument instead of the pain. "That's probably more a matter of opportunity than intent. We both have the same information on the case. Why should I be seen as the bigger threat?"

"I don't know," Cappy said, each word sharp with frustration. She put the car in gear and pulled out of the parking place. "We're both off patrol until we get this case solved."

"Why? I'm perfectly capable of—"

"Everything. Yes, I know. But Kent's orders. You're our best shot at solving this, and she's not going to put you at risk by sending you out to handle calls."

"You're as likely to solve it as I am, and neither of us seems close. She should turn it over to Seattle and send both of us back to regular duty." Clare leaned back against the headrest. "Please don't slap me. I'm just resting my eyes, not sleeping."

She smiled faintly when she heard Cappy's quiet laugh. They drove the rest of the ride—mere blocks from the ER to police headquarters—in silence until they were parked outside the station.

Cappy poked her in the arm, and Clare lifted her head, opening her eyes. "Look, Clare, you're the one who understands this case, and if anyone is going to solve it, it's you." Clare started to protest, but Cappy shook her head to stop her. "I mean it. You're the one who understood the position of the bodies. Yes, I know you had Libby's input about some of the symbolism, but you recognized the significance enough to ask her about it. You seem to get the way this killer thinks about the crime scenes, and you just need to trust yourself, trust that you'll figure it out."

Clare was silent. She didn't have nearly the same faith in herself that everyone else seemed to have in her. They seemed to believe she was on the cusp of some big breakthrough, when she didn't feel any further along than she was on day one.

They walked into the station, and Clare had barely made it through the door when Libby launched out of one of the waiting room chairs and flung herself into Clare's arms.

"Oh, I forgot to tell you," Cappy said. "Libby's waiting for you at the station. She's worried about you."

Clare ignored Cappy and instead let herself have a few perfect moments with Libby in her arms. She could feel her trembling, and she cupped her hand on the back of Libby's head. Gently, as if she might break if Clare held her too tightly. She steeled herself for the time when she had to let go.

Finally, she pulled back and led Libby over to the chair she had been sitting in before. Clare sat down next to her, holding Libby's hand in both of her own.

"How did you know what…oh, Ariella?"

Libby nodded. "She called me as soon as she got in her car. I was going to come to the emergency room, but your sergeant said I could wait here. She told me what happened. Are you okay?"

Libby touched the bandage on Clare's forehead, tentatively running her fingers along its border. Clare felt a shiver move through her.

"Oh, sorry," Libby said, pulling her hand away. "Did I hurt you?"

"No," Clare said, careful not to shake her head for emphasis. "You feel good. I love it when you touch me, but…"

"But…" Libby repeated when Clare paused. "But I should stay away from you because it's too dangerous. We shouldn't see each other anymore because if I'm around you, I might get hurt."

"Exactly," Clare said.

"I disagree," Libby said.

Shocking. "Look, Libby, you can't deny what's happened to you this week. You've been to two crime scenes, once as the first person to find the victim. How many dead bodies do you usually see in a week? I'm guessing that two is a record for you. And what about texts from lunatic murderers? Do you normally get a few of those on a Friday night?"

"I agree it's been an unusually bloody week, but I don't want to give you up. If I agree to stay away from you until this case is solved, what will happen the next time you're on an investigation? Will I just get pushed away again?"

No, Clare thought. Because tonight's push had to be strong enough to keep Libby away from her for good. She was right—Clare's life was dangerous right now, but it was part of her job. She would always carry the chance of risk with her and could bring it home to anyone who was important to her.

Libby was watching her face closely and seemed to know what she was thinking. "Oh, Clare," she said quietly, barely above a whisper. "Don't. Don't give up on us because you're afraid for me. How many officers do you know who have people in their lives they care about? Most of them? All of them? Are you planning to be alone forever, like some crime-fighting machine?"

Clare closed her eyes. "Do you know what I see when I do this?" she asked. "The bushes where I was standing tonight before I was hit, but instead of me, I see you there. I see you at Gould Hall, and at the entrance to Suzzallo." She opened her eyes again and met Libby's deep blue ones, shining in the bright lights of the station. "It's hard enough when it's only in my imagination. If I ever..."

She stopped, unable to finish the sentence. Libby sighed, a resigned look on her face.

"Laura wasn't dating a cop," she said. "Her fiancé is a history teacher in high school. That didn't keep her out of danger." She shrugged. "I truly believe that you want me to be safe and happy and alive, but that's not why you're doing this. You're trying to protect yourself from being hurt if something were to happen to me. This is about you, not me."

She stood up and turned to Cappy, who had been hovering near the reception desk, out of earshot but close enough in case they needed her. Libby walked over to her.

"I'm assuming Clare will want someone to take me home and check under the bed again. Do you mind?"

"Of course not," she said, glancing at Clare.

Clare stood up, trying not to look wobbly. Her headache was nothing compared to what was happening to her heart. Libby brushed her hand over Clare's cheek, then turned away.

"Thanks for taking care of her," Clare said to Cappy.

Cappy hesitated, looking as if she was gearing up for a lecture, but she mercifully decided not to deliver it. "No problem. I'll be back soon to drive you home."

Clare sat down again, too tired to protest and say she could drive herself. She really doubted that she could. She watched through the front window as they walked away, backlit for a moment by the streetlights in front of Gould Hall, and then swallowed in the darkness again.

Chapter Twenty

L ibby waited in her living room while Cappy checked her apartment. She paced back and forth the length of her couch, edgy after sitting in the station for hours and then talking to Clare for five minutes. She knew which of those had been hardest to bear. Before Clare got back from the emergency room, Libby hadn't known what was going on. How Clare was, or when she'd be back. Once Clare had sat her down for a talk, she had known exactly what Clare was going to say to her—if not the words themselves, then the painful meaning behind them. Then she longed to go back to the ignorance of the hours before.

In other circumstances, she might have argued for a longer time with her, but Clare looked incapable of handling much more of a conversation than what they had. Libby already had a long list of words she would use to describe Clare—granted, tonight's additions weren't the most flattering—and *fragile* was nowhere on the list. But when Clare had walked into the station, with the white bandage on her forehead adding emphasis to her ghostly pale skin and the dark violet circles under her eyes, it was the first word that had come to Libby's mind. She had looked shaken, walking with the unsteady gait of a drunk person, her arms held slightly out to the side for balance. And dazed. She probably thought she looked perfectly in control of her movement, even though it was obvious to anyone looking at her that she was barely keeping herself upright. Libby had wanted to grab hold and never let go.

Then Clare had started to speak, and Libby went from wanting to hold her and take care of her to wanting to smack her on the undamaged side of her head.

The worst part was being so certain that Clare cared about her with the same intensity as Libby felt for her. She saw it every time Clare looked at her, and she saw it reflected in Clare's actions every time she tried to protect her. Libby felt like two people tonight— one living through the conversation with Clare, and the other watching as if from a distance and seeing the pain etched in the lines on Clare's face as she fought to push Libby out of her life. If she had thought Clare really didn't want to be with her, she would have walked away. She might have cried on a friend's shoulder or gone online and bought a bunch of new books, but she wouldn't have bothered to try to change Clare's mind. Knowing how Clare really felt about her made her want to try, but the simple, physical truth was that Clare needed rest more than she needed an emotional battle. Maybe Libby would let her heal for a few days, then launch another attack.

Cappy came out of the bedroom with Boots in her arms. "You have a cool cat," she said, handing her to Libby.

"I know. Is everything clear?"

"Yeah, except for the guy hiding under your bed in a clown suit. I thought he seemed harmless, so I'm letting him stay." She gave a long-suffering sigh. "Yes, of course everything is clear. You would have heard if I'd had to toss a perp out the window."

"Well, you're in a mood," Libby snapped.

"Sorry," Cappy said, in the same snappy tone Libby had used, which implied she really wasn't sorry at all. "My partner could have died tonight. You have no idea what it was like to sit in that hospital waiting room, with no idea how she was, and imagining what could have happened if she hadn't tripped over that damned tree root."

Libby raised her eyebrows, and Cappy waved vaguely at her.

"All right, you have some idea. Being her girlfriend is almost like being her partner. Sort of."

Libby's breath caught at the term. She and Clare hadn't gotten to the point of putting a name to their relationship, aside from

Libby's playful ways of describing her role in Clare's investigation. "I'm not her girlfriend. And if I was before, I'm not after tonight."

"Please. Give her a break. She was clubbed over the head by someone who most likely murdered two people in the past week, and then she whacked her head against the side of a brick building. To say she's not thinking clearly is a major understatement." Cappy sighed. She had gone from sounding pissed at Clare to defending her. "You know how she is. She's set these impossibly high standards for herself, and when she doesn't live up to them and fails to be Supercop, she gets mad at herself."

Libby frowned. "I get the head issues, but what does the Supercop stuff have to do with her breaking up with me?"

"Nothing," Cappy said, not adding a *duh*, but Libby heard it in her voice. "It's why *I'm* frustrated with her. You have your own reasons."

"Thanks. This has been a really helpful talk," Libby said.

"Anytime," Cappy said with a shrug, either not noticing Libby's sarcasm, or pretending she didn't. Libby assumed the latter. "Be sure to lock the door after I go."

"I will, I will." She put her hand on Cappy's arm as she was leaving. "Take care of her," she said.

"Huh. That's pretty much the same thing she said to me tonight, about you."

Libby shut the door and leaned against it, smiling sadly at Cappy's words. Maybe she would give Clare a few days to sleep and heal. To work on her case with all her concentration, instead of having half her attention on keeping Libby safe. Maybe they could talk after, and—

"Did you lock the door?" Cappy called out from the hallway. "I didn't hear you lock it."

"Jeez," Libby said loudly, snapping the bolt closed. "It's locked! Go home."

❖

Libby got through the next couple of days without giving in and going to find Clare. She felt moments of loneliness without having

Clare in her life—how had she gotten so accustomed to her presence in such a short time?—and she had more than a few moments of anger, too. Most of the time, though, she kept herself too busy to feel more than flashes of emotions. She stayed late at work every night, preparing midterms and grading papers, creating packets for upcoming Denny Hall sessions, and brainstorming new ways she might be able to support her students who were on the fringes of campus life.

Cappy's weird pep talk had, if nothing else, given her a renewed sense of patience. Normally not her strong suit, she knew it was necessary right now if she and Clare were going to have a chance. She would wait and give Clare some time. The sliver of hope she felt was enough to keep her from pining, and she went on with her days, only thinking about Clare about four thousand times an hour.

She turned down her hallway and toward her office after her last class of the day and saw her best friends standing outside her office door. All three of them. Great.

Libby waded through them and unlocked her office. "Look," she said, "if you three are here to give me another lecture about how to live my life, can you save it for a week or so? I'm still trying to recover from the last assignment you gave me. I really think I could use a break."

"We just want to talk," said Ariella, which didn't sound like the break she was asking for. It sounded like the start of another intervention.

They followed her into her office. Jazz walked over to stand by her bookshelves—Libby would bet a year's salary that she'd be reorganizing one of the shelves before the conversation was over. Ariella and Tig had a brief tussle, each trying to offer the other the only chair in the room besides Libby's. Tig lost and sat down in a huff, while Ariella perched on the windowsill.

As they settled in, Libby watched with the detached air of someone who was perfectly willing to kick them right out again if the phrase *try something new* came out of any of their mouths. She appreciated their concern, but she was better off sticking with her regular routine, complete with the predictable pastry of the day.

"Well?" she asked when her friends did nothing more than look at one another without speaking. "I don't think the three of you have ever gone this many seconds without saying something. Go ahead and get this over with so I can tell you to get out and mind your own business. I have quizzes to grade this afternoon, so I don't have all day."

Tig raised her hand as if asking permission to speak. "We're kind of divided on this one, so I'll go first. These two seem to like this Clare person you've been seeing, but I've never actually met her, so I'm neutral. My advice is to get back on the horse."

"What horse?" Libby asked. "Is Clare the horse?"

"The dating horse. Forget her and find someone else. You're a catch, and if she can't see it, then throw her back. There are plenty of fish in the sea."

"You're mixing your metaphors," Ariella offered.

"And using far too many clichés," said Jazz. She pulled out two books and moved them to a different shelf. Libby wished she had found someone to take her bet.

Tig ignored their comments. "I just think you need to stop wallowing and go date someone else."

"I'm not wallowing," Libby protested. She was working extra-long hours to distract herself from thoughts of Clare, but that was being industrious, not *wallowing*. "And it's only been two days."

"Exactly." Tig gestured with her hands as if Libby had just proved her point. "That's what, twenty-five percent of your total relationship? Long enough, I say."

"She doesn't need to date someone else right away," Ariella said, nudging Tig's chair with her foot. "She needs to focus on herself. Get back in touch with who she was before all this happened."

"You mean, the person I was two weeks ago? I think I can remember that far back." Libby sighed and turned to Jazz, who was aligning her books' spines with the edge of the shelves. "Go ahead and give me your advice, Jazz. Then I can boot the lot of you out of my office."

Jazz shrugged. "I think you're fine. We asked you to break out of your rut, and you did so. Who else but our Libby would hear advice to get a new hobby and, instead of taking up needlepoint or learning to play the piano, would give finding dead bodies a go? It was exciting, wasn't it?"

Exciting? Yes. And at times terrifying, infuriating, and nausea-inducing. But the Clare parts of her experience had been wonderful. Life-changing. She nodded at Jazz.

"Good. That's all we wanted. For you to recapture your interest in life, because we thought you were retreating somewhat from the real world." She ran her hand along the smooth line of book spines. "As far as Clare goes, I'd say to just relax and give her time. She's an idealist with a rather overbearing superhero complex, and if you're serious about being in a relationship with her, then this is certainly not the last time she'll do something to drive you crazy. You might as well get used to it. She may be a pain in the ass, but she's a worthwhile one, in my humble opinion."

"Humble." Tig repeated with a derisive snort. "Don't you have dictionaries in that library of yours?"

"She wins," Libby said, pointing at Jazz. She knew all of her friends wanted her to be happy, but Jazz was the one she would most trust to opt for harsh honesty over kind and well-meaning platitudes. Buried in her rather acerbic statements was the core truth that Jazz liked Clare. Libby usually relied on her own judgment, but at times like this—when her feelings for Clare were muddled by wanting her and by the overwhelming emotions from the week's events—Libby was relieved to have some validation for her decision to wait Clare out and see if their relationship stood a chance. Not forever, of course. She wasn't going to throw her life away. But longer than two days? Yes. "Thank you for playing, Tig and Ariella. Your consolation prize is a one-way ticket out of my office so I can get some work done."

"What do I get for winning?" Jazz asked.

"I won't move the books you just rearranged back to the way they were," Libby said, mentally adding *for at least one week*.

"Fair enough. Dinner tonight?"

They all agreed and were discussing where to eat when Libby looked up and saw Angela Whitney standing in her doorway, visibly distressed.

"Hi, Angela," she said. "Come on in—everyone else was just leaving."

Her friends took the hint and filed out, saying hello to Angela, who responded in her usual no-eye-contact way, and saying they'd see Libby later. She shut the door behind them and gestured to the seat Tig had just vacated.

Instead of sitting, Angela stood by the window, backed up against the blinds.

"What is it?" Libby asked. "Is something wrong?"

"Miriam said…" she started, speaking almost too quietly for Libby to hear, then cleared her throat and started again. "Miriam said you talked to her about Professor…Professor Turnbow."

Libby kept her face as smooth as she could, trying not to let it show when she instinctively cringed away from the information. Not Angela, too, she thought, even though she understood the futility of her wish even as she formed it in her mind.

"Angela, if he…if you need to talk to someone, I know a campus police officer who will help you. Her name is Raven, and she can get you connected to people who can help you through this. We can go there now, if you want?"

Angela shook her head, looking terrified. "I'm afraid. Please, I don't know if I can do that."

"I can be there with you, if you'd like," Libby said. For a little while at least. Hopefully long enough to help Angela get comfortable with the officer.

"Can I…can I talk to you about it first?" Angela asked, faltering again, but then the rest of her words came out in a rush. "You've always been so kind to me. You understand me."

Oh, I don't want to hear this. Libby pushed the selfish thought away and nodded. She could listen without giving advice, letting Raven or a counselor help Angela deal with how to handle the experience moving forward. For now, she could just be there. "Yes, of course. I'm here for you."

"Thank you." Angela's relief was palpable. "Can we go outside? It's hard to talk in this building, where his office is."

Libby agreed, feeling some relief of her own. If they were outside and walking, she could steer them toward the police station. "Sure. Let's go."

She walked toward the door, and Angela followed. She was stumbling over her thanks to Libby and bumped her backpack into the desk as she passed, knocking over Libby's pen holder and a stack of journals. She put them upright again, apologizing as she awkwardly stuffed pens back into the jar.

"No harm done," Libby said. "You can leave it—I'll take care of it later."

Angela started talking as soon as they were outside Architecture Hall, as if freeing herself from the building also loosened the hold she had been keeping on her secret. Her story mirrored Miriam's in some ways, even though the details were different, and Libby struggled to keep calm while she went through the helpless pain of listening to it again. They walked through Red Square and past Suzzallo, cutting through the center of the Quad. Libby didn't want to interrupt now that Angela was actually speaking in full paragraphs. She'd get them around to the station as soon as she could.

She stopped when they came to McMahon, one of the residence halls. "We should head back toward the U District," she said, remaining on the sidewalk. Angela continued a few yards, toward the trees behind the hall and the steep hill dropping down to the Burke-Gilman Trail.

"She's not good for you," Angela said, her voice sounding surer than it had been, as if the person Libby had just been talking to had magically swapped bodies with someone much more self-assured. "She's not even a professor. You're so passionate about architecture and buildings and history and *everything*. She'll never be able to share that with you."

"Clare?" Libby whispered, her insides turning to ice as she tried to catch up. Shy, clumsy Angela, one of Jimmy's victims, now looking at her with a self-satisfied smile.

"She was lucky last time. I hurt her a little, but this time she didn't sense me coming. She didn't trip, or have a chance to turn around." She looked away from Libby toward a small dirt trail heading through the trees. "She's down there, and she'll stay away this time. She won't bother us anymore."

Libby gasped, her mind filled with an image of Clare on the trail, bloody and unmoving. Maybe still alive, and needing her help? She ran, pushing past Angela, but as the trees closed in around her, some shred of common sense seeped back into her brain. She heard Clare's voice in her head, as if she was standing right next to her. *Get the fuck out of there. Call the station. Call Cappy. Someone, anyone.* She started to turn around but didn't make it all the way before her head seemed to explode with pain and her world went dark.

CHAPTER TWENTY-ONE

Clare sat at the meeting room table with her forehead resting on its surface, pillowed by a stack of typed notes. The worst part of being pulled from patrol duty was having all those extra hours to spend in this room with Cappy, going through the same information over and over, without any change in scenery. The worst part of *everything* was not having Libby in her life.

She had gone two days determined to stick to her plan to never see Libby again, keeping her far from the dangers associated with Clare's career. She had been right about the risks involved for Libby. But Libby had been right, too, about Clare being selfish in her attempt to push Libby away. She had taken away Libby's choice in the matter, and Libby deserved to make the decision herself. Libby had seen firsthand and up-close exactly what Clare would face. Clare had been treating her as if she didn't fully understand what her job entailed, but she had been wrong.

She had tried calling Libby this afternoon, but she hadn't answered her phone. She wasn't in class—Clare knew her schedule by now—but she had probably been talking to a student or one of her friends and had ignored the call. She would see Clare's number on her cell and call her back. She had tried again a few seconds later, after she was struck by the realization that Libby could have seen her number and decided not to answer. She wasn't sure what the second call had been meant to achieve if Libby really was screening her. Added emphasis? Added desperation was more like it. Clare had decided she really didn't care and called a third time.

Still no answer.

She forced her attention back to the case, sitting up and spreading out three crime scene photos in front of her. Turnbow's body, his ankles crossed and arms at his side. Laura, with her hand pressed against the darkened window. The pipe, hiding under the willow tree not far from where it had been used against Clare. The last one still triggered flashbacks to the moment when she had lost her balance, falling forward and feeling the glancing blow to her head. If she hadn't hit the wall, but instead had fallen on the ground...If she hadn't managed to turn, scaring off the attacker... If, if, if. She swiped the photos together and pushed them to one side, digging through the other pictures they had on the table and replacing the close-ups with distance shots that were much easier to look at.

Suzzallo. Gould. Padelford. Libby's favorite building, which she could talk about for hours. One she had never liked but had started to appreciate, adding it to her class lectures. And one she absolutely and vocally hated. Clare could hear her voice now, ranting about its meaningless angles and convoluted design. She laughed quietly. Sad as she was to be in this limbo state with Libby, she still loved to be reminded of the intensity and passion that were such big parts of who she was.

"Something funny?" Cappy asked, stifling a yawn. She was in her usual position, leaning back with her feet propped on the table. "Or are you having some sort of breakdown?"

"It's nothing. I was just looking at these buildings and remembering Libby talking about them. Investigating this case is like taking an architecture tour with her."

Cappy's chair came back to all four legs with a dull thud. Clare thought Kent might have walked in and startled Cappy into a more civilized sitting position, but when she looked over her shoulder, the door to their room was still closed. She glanced at Cappy, whose expression was neutral.

"How so?" Cappy asked, her voice giving the impression of forced nonchalance, and Clare figured she was just getting tired of hearing her blather on about Libby. She was pretending to be interested, though, so Clare was going to take advantage of that and talk about her some more.

"Well, when she took me to Suzzallo, she said she had once given a two-hour lecture on its history and style. She loves that building, and you can hear it in her voice when she talks about it. And while we were retracing Turnbow's daily life, we spent some time in Gould. She didn't like the aesthetics of that hall, but the more we talked about it, the more she was able to see what other people might admire about it, and what its design might mean to others. She even added those ideas to her class lectures the next day, which is cool. She has definite preferences, but at the same time, she's open-minded and respects other people's opinions, too."

"Hmm," Cappy said vaguely. She reached out and put a finger on the picture of Padelford, inching it closer to Clare. "And this one?"

Clare picked up the photo. "She hates this one. Just like Suzzallo, she can't hide how she feels when she talks about it. I think it just seems wrong to her. The design elements aren't useful or beautiful, they're just...wrong."

"Wrong," Cappy repeated quietly. "She must be a good teacher because she's certainly turned you into a building fanatic. Did you even notice this kind of stuff before her?"

Clare smiled. "No. She's been my ins..." She paused, then whispered, "Inspiration."

She stood up and pushed through the photos, messing up their somewhat tidy piles and pulling out the one she needed. Clark's sculpture. "It's her," she said, flipping the picture across to Cappy. "The sacrifice to Inspiration was made to *her*. Oh God. Why didn't we see it before?"

Cappy went to the door and opened it, calling out for someone to get Kent in there. She came back to the table. "Keep talking, Sawyer. You're saying that someone killed these people for her? She's the key?"

"Maybe. I don't know." Please let it not be true, Clare thought. If it was, then Libby was in more danger than she had thought. "I might have been right about the tenure thing, but I was looking at the wrong angle. What if someone knew about what Turnbow had done? What if they were furious because he was advancing, while Libby—the inspirational one—was overlooked?"

"So they kill him and symbolically sacrifice him to her. Laura?"

"An outsider, trying to get in, but not allowed. Mercy denied." Clare tried to recall everything Libby had said about the crime scene. "She had just added that to her lecture, about Gould Hall being clear and sort of boundaryless, inviting people in, sharing wisdom. But Laura was meant to be seen at night, when the windows were opaque—Libby got the text calling her there, because if the body had been found the next morning, or by anyone else, it wouldn't have had the same meaning."

"Jealousy?" Cappy asked.

"A warning," Kent said. Clare looked up. She hadn't even realized her sergeant had come in the room. Kent continued, "If the killer saw them together at the movies that night and misinterpreted their relationship, they might have sent the body as a warning: Laura doesn't belong here, or in your life."

"There's no misinterpreting what you were starting to mean to Libby," Cappy said, staring at Clare. "The words you used for the building where you were attacked are what the killer would use for you. You're wrong for Libby. They hate you for being with her. Padelford symbolized all that, and the attempt to murder you did, too. It was meant to be violent and fast, without any of the elegance or meaning of the other crime scenes."

Clare took out her phone and called Libby again. "No answer, still. I have to go find her."

"Hold on," said Kent as she left the room.

Clare went back over her reasoning, hoping to find a flaw that would mean Libby really wasn't at the heart of these crimes. "You knew what I was going to say," she said to Cappy. "When I said the photos were like taking a tour with her."

Cappy shrugged, still pushing pictures around on the table. "I didn't know *what* you were going to say, but there was something about your voice, like you were really seeing these photos for the first time. Don't ask me how, but I just had a feeling you were on to something we hadn't seen before."

Kent came back in the room. "I've sent people to her office and apartment. Who are we looking at as the killer, then? One of her students?"

"Maybe," Clare said, thinking back to the night she was assaulted. "Ariella is about five five, wouldn't you say?"

"She was right near Padelford when you were attacked. She was the first person you saw when you came out of those bushes," Kent said.

Clare shook her head. "She teaches in the building—that's why she was there."

"She got to the station soon after we got Libby inside the night Laura was killed," Cappy reminded them. "She would have had time to text Libby, then dump the evidence before coming back to watch the rest of the night unfold. She might have been wearing different clothes, and Libby wouldn't have noticed after what she'd been through."

Clare rubbed her temple. Her headaches had eased but still lingered on the edges. "It doesn't seem right, but maybe. I got the sense she would kill to defend Libby if she had to, but not murder people as offerings to her. I'm going to go talk to her," she said. "We need to send officers to Jazz and Tig, as well. At Suzzallo and Denny Hall."

Cappy and Kent exchanged a look. "She's your partner. You deal with her," Kent said. "I'll cover the other two."

"What does she mean, deal with me?" Clare asked, pulling on her jacket and itching to get out of the room and find Libby.

Cappy sighed. "Listen, Sawyer. *We* are going to talk to Ariella. You've got to stop trying to do everything yourself."

"I'm scared," Clare admitted. "I'm not trying to hog the spotlight or prove I'm the best detective ever. I just need to see Libby, to know she's okay. I'm afraid it took me too long to figure this out."

"That's why you need me with you," Cappy said, pushing Clare toward the door. "You're not alone here."

❖

Ariella's office door was ajar when Clare pushed it all the way open, slamming it into the wall more loudly than she had intended. Ariella was at her desk, reading a book, and she jumped at the noise.

"What's going—"

"Where is Libby?" Clare demanded. She was torn because her instincts told her Ariella wasn't a murderer and was just a good friend of Libby's. But the terrified part of her that needed to find Libby *now* only knew that Ariella had always been there—at Gould, at Padelford, outside the station. Everywhere Libby and Clare were. She fit the physical description, and as a literature professor, symbolism would be her native tongue.

Ariella looked from Clare to Cappy with a confused-looking frown. "What are you—"

"What my partner is trying to ask, in her not-so-subtle way, is where the hell is Libby?" Cappy took an intimidating step forward, and Ariella stood up, not looking intimidated in the least.

"Last I saw, she was in her office, doing some grading. We're meeting later for dinner. Is something wrong? Is she hurt?"

Clare watched her shift from confusion to irritation to concern during their brief confrontation. The changes were subtle, and her expressions seemed genuine. Cappy looked at her with a slight shake of her head.

Clare sighed, feeling the rush of anger ease because Ariella wasn't the one who deserved its full force. "We need to find her. She may be all right and just not answering my calls, but we think she might be in danger."

"What can I do?"

"We have officers going to her office and apartment, and we're contacting Tig and Jazz, too. If you can think of anywhere she might be—a bookstore or coffee shop, maybe—where she might not answer her phone, you could look for her." Clare paused, then clarified her request. "Anywhere public. If you know of any isolated or private spots on campus where she might go for some peace and quiet, then contact the station and we'll have an officer check it out.

Don't go anyplace where you might be putting yourself in danger, too."

Ariella nodded. "I'll get Tig and Jazz and we'll look for her. We know her favorite places."

She and Cappy started out the door, but Clare turned back. "I'm sorry I accused you of...I'm worried about her."

Ariella waved her off. "Save your apologies for Libby. She was weirdly proud that you thought she was capable of murder. She won't be happy to hear that you accused me, too." She picked up her keys and bag, and then looked up again. "I forgot. When we left her office, one of her students was coming in to talk to her. Angela, I think."

Clare barely managed a nod before she was out the door, jogging back through Padelford's halls and hoping she didn't get lost on her way out of the building. Cappy hurried to catch up to her.

"What is it? Who's Angela?" Cappy asked as they pushed through the doors and started a sprint toward Architecture Hall.

"I met her," Clare said, images of the young woman's downcast eyes and hunched shoulders coming back to her. "The day I told Libby she could help me with the investigation, Angela was leaving her office when I came in. I doubt she missed the way we looked at each other." It wasn't easy for Clare to admit the last part, but the time for embarrassment was long past. On that day, she still hadn't known Libby well at all, but she could recall how she felt when she saw her—and she knew it must have been reflected in her expression, just as Libby's pleasure to see Clare was obvious in hers.

"She's one of Libby's special students. They're kids who feel out of place here. Awkward and shy, not able to fit in. She kind of gathers them together and connects them with other students. She does this informal chat session outside Denny Hall, and when I met her after one of them, Angela was there, too. On the outside of the group."

"Someone who would hate Laura for being accepted into Libby's world, while she wasn't, since she was still a student," Cappy added.

Cappy followed Clare up the stairs and down the hall to Libby's office. Harris was standing outside.

"Sergeant Kent told me to wait here, in case she comes back, or someone calls," he said. "Someone from the office downstairs unlocked the door for me." He hesitated, then continued, "I don't think she was planning to go home when she left. Her bag is in there, and it looks like she was in the middle of doing some work."

Clare stepped over the threshold and looked around the office. Harris was right—Libby's satchel was hanging over the arm of her chair. She wouldn't leave for the night without it—otherwise, how would she carry all those extra books back to campus in the morning? Clare smiled faintly, running her hand over the leather shoulder strap. She knew how heavy this thing was. Too bad Libby hadn't taken it with her. It could serve as a defensive weapon.

She put a hand on her stomach, suddenly queasy, and made herself slow down and look around, allowing random impressions to come to her without forcing them. One of the bookshelves was impossibly tidy, standing out among the other haphazardly stuffed shelves. Jazz, maybe? Clare didn't remember Libby's desk being particularly neat the last time she'd been in here, and she couldn't recall where everything had been placed before, but the pen holder seemed wrong somehow. She walked over to the far corner of the desk where half the pens and pencils were in the cup, and the rest were scattered next to it. She nudged them aside and picked up a folded piece of paper.

"You're really creepy sometimes," Cappy said in an awed-sounding voice.

Clare ignored her and opened the note, handing it to Cappy after she read it.

"*The trail to Burke-Gilman behind McMahon. Officer Sawyer come alone.*" Cappy looked up at her. "Okay, we just found someone creepier."

Clare felt paralyzed. Oh, how easy it would have been for Angela to get Libby to go for a walk with her. She needed to talk, she was sad and hurting, and could Libby help. Angela was small, and Libby wasn't the type to give in on anything without a fight. Libby could take her, could defend herself, but not if she wasn't expecting Angela to harm her. Why would she? She'd naturally feel protective of Angela and wouldn't readily believe she was anything more than a shy student who needed support. By the time she realized what Angela might be capable of, it could be too late. It could already be too late.

"Don't look at me like that, Clare. You are not traipsing down that trail by yourself, no matter what this note says."

"She's more dangerous now," Clare said, not really addressing Cappy's comment. "The first two murders were planned. The attack on me was emotional, angry. Now she's delusional if she really thinks she can get away with possibly kidnapping Libby and luring a police officer into the woods, where she probably wants to finish the job from the other night. But delusional people can do as much harm as anyone else, even if they end up getting caught. Maybe more so, especially if she feels cornered, since now her actions are impulsive and erratic."

Cappy looked concerned at her words, as if thinking Clare wanted to rush in alone, which she did, in a way. Angela was likely to be hyperfocused right now, and if she saw Clare coming by herself, she wouldn't look far beyond her.

"I'll go down the trail alone and meet her there. But that sure as hell doesn't mean I don't want you in the woods as backup."

Cappy sighed, relief apparent in her grin. "Don't worry, partner. I've got your back."

CHAPTER TWENTY-TWO

Libby groaned as sensations slowly filtered into her awareness. Pain came first, her head throbbing, pressure behind her eyes. Her hip, bruised and aching, protesting as it supported her weight.

She opened her eyes a little, blinking as the light added to her headache. The world seemed to be nothing more than an impressionistic swirl of russet and green. As she began to focus more clearly, she saw fir trees with reddish sunlight filtering through them. Closer to her, the dirt was covered with needles and cones. Woods. She was in the woods, lying on the hard, cold ground.

Cold. Nighttime? Evening, near sunset. Someone caressed her hair and she recoiled instinctively, bile rising in her throat. Panic, because her mouth was covered.

The piecemeal return of her senses gave way to a sudden shock of awareness as a single name slammed to the forefront of her mind. Clare. Clare was hurt, maybe dead, and Libby was supposed to find her. She thrashed on the ground, not knowing why she couldn't move, until she felt the sharp bite of plastic at her wrists and ankles.

"Shh, calm down Professor Hart. You'll be okay, I didn't hit you too hard."

I think we're at a point in our relationship where you call me Libby, you fucking lunatic. Well, all right, then. Her brain seemed to be back in the game. She shifted—more gently this time, to avoid the cutting feeling of her restraints—and tried to ease the pressure on her hip. Tried to get away from Angela's touch. Each stroke of her hand on Libby's hair shrieked through her mind like grating metal.

She lifted her head as much as she could manage, and realized it was lying on Angela's lap. One of Angela's hands was on Libby, while the other rested on her thigh, holding a gun. She must have turned in her pipe for an upgrade. Libby slithered backward, no longer caring as much about the pain from the plastic ties as she did about getting away from Angela. She'd cut off her hands and feet if she had to.

Angela just watched her as she pushed herself inch by inch along the ground, until she was able to scoot into a sitting position, using a tree trunk for support. She hadn't gotten far and had no real hope of escaping, but she was no longer being touched. She'd count that as a victory at the moment.

"I'll take off the tape if you promise not to scream," Angela said. "We can talk while we wait. I like talking to you."

She reached toward Libby's face, and Libby couldn't keep herself from flinching away. Angela hesitated. "If you scream or make any loud noise, I'll have to hit you again. I don't want to, so don't make me."

Libby whimpered as the tape was ripped off her face, feeling as if it was taking half her skin with it. She bent her head toward her shoulder and wiped her mouth on her shirt.

"Clare," she said, clearing her throat and putting more force into her voice. "You said you hurt her. Where is she?"

"Oh, she'll be along. I was lying when I said I'd already hurt her. They'll check your office when they realize you're gone, and I left her a note. I had to rip up your jacket to mark the trail for her. I'm sorry about that."

Really? She was sorry about the blazer? And apparently not sorry for knocking Libby in the head, or for threatening to kill Clare.

"You killed them," she said, piecing the story together. Angela had admitted to attacking Clare at Padelford before Libby had run foolishly down the trail, but now Libby realized the full extent of Angela's deeds. "Jimmy, Laura. You killed them."

Angela sneered. "That disgusting man. He shouldn't have been allowed to teach after what he'd done, but instead of being punished, he gets rewarded. You deserved his job—the way you teach, how kind you are. You made me feel good about myself, and he only made me feel dirty. I killed him for you."

"As a sacrifice," Libby said, wanting to cry. She choked back her fear and disgust and focused on keeping Angela talking. She didn't know how she could escape, but she might be able to distract Angela enough to let Clare overpower her when she got here. Because of course Clare would come, no matter how dangerous it would be for her.

"Yes, and it wasn't easy." Angela's face crumpled for a moment, as if she, too, was about to cry, but then she smiled again, her mood shifting rapidly. "It was easy enough to get him to meet me in the dark, though. He said he only wanted a hug, but he was more than willing to accept when I offered more." She frowned. "There was a lot of blood."

"And Laura? Why Laura?" Libby asked the question, although she was sure she already knew the answer. Angela had been in her class when Laura had arrived, and she had been at the movies— probably following her, Libby now realized.

"That was supposed to be *me*," Angela said, with barely controlled rage in her voice. "I'd be your favorite student, and after I graduated, I'd stay here to teach. Then we could be together. She tried to steal that from us."

Once Libby figured out that she was part of that *we*, she wanted to gag. "There was nothing between me and Laura. I'd never date a student, even one who had graduated."

"You wouldn't be able to deny what we have. You're not like him. You would have waited for me." Angela smiled at her in a tender way. Libby squeezed her eyes shut and concentrated on not screaming.

"We have something special," Angela continued. "We both love architecture and history. I learned so much from you, and I showed you with their bodies. You understood what I was trying to say with them, didn't you?"

Libby had. She had understood the symbolism because it was patched together from her own lectures. How had she not made that connection before?

"Do you really expect me to be proud of this? You didn't honor me or those buildings. You desecrated them."

"You're wrong. You have to understand what…"

Libby heard the rustle of brush, and both she and Angela looked up. Clare. Damn it. Standing at the edge of the small clearing, her gaze merely flicking in Libby's direction before returning to Angela. Her expression was blank, but Libby could read the subtle signs. Her relief at seeing Libby alive, her determination to get them out of this mess. Her fear. She wondered about that last one until she noticed that Angela had her gun pointed at Libby. Her hand seemed to be trembling slightly, and Libby didn't know if it was a good sign or a bad one. Would she be too nervous to aim well? Or would she be likely to shake so hard she'd pull the trigger without meaning to?

"Throw your gun over there," Angela said, her eyes not leaving Clare, but her weapon still aimed at Libby. Libby carefully bent her knees, curling into a ball. She looked around, desperately hoping to see the rest of the campus police sneaking toward them, ready to stop Angela, but she didn't see any movement. The trees were too sparsely placed to hide them, anyway.

"I'm not wearing one," Clare said, raising her arms. Libby realized she wasn't wearing her duty belt. "I'm still not cleared by the doctors after your attack, so I can't carry a weapon."

"I hit you harder than I thought," Angela said, a note of pride in her voice.

Clare touched her hand to the bruise on her forehead. "Well, I think Padelford should get most of the credit."

Angela grimaced. "We hate that building. You deserved to die there."

Again with the *we*. Libby was getting sick of this. She knew Clare hadn't had a concussion, so she didn't have any reason not to be armed. She wouldn't come out here with nothing, would she? Libby wanted to yell for her to run, to save herself, but Clare never would.

❖

Clare watched the scene unfold before her, fighting to keep her gaze as unfocused as possible. If she let herself look at Libby, her concentration would narrow until she was all Clare would be able to see. Same with the gun, trembling a little but not wavering from pointing at Libby. Angela and Libby were only inches apart, and at that distance, even if Angela was shaking when she pulled the trigger, she'd still be likely to hit some part of her. Her head, her heart. Clare exhaled slowly, willing herself to remain calm. If she panicked now, she'd never get them out of this alive.

She had stood just out of sight for several moments, listening to them talk, before she stepped into the clearing. Her relief at hearing Libby's voice had made her nearly sink to her knees in the dirt. It had taken her some time before she had been able to pay attention to the words they were saying. Angela's voice had chilled her, slipping too quickly from that of a hardened criminal bragging about her kills, to the dreamy tone of a child talking about her fantasy crush on a teacher.

Clare's only goal right now was to get Angela to point the gun at her, not Libby. Wasn't that why she was here? To be another sacrifice to Libby? She had to encourage Angela to get on with the job of killing her, because as long as Libby was in immediate danger, Clare couldn't act. Neither would Cappy.

She took a step forward, but Angela didn't take the bait and swing the weapon toward her. "You can stop this anytime, Angela. Just put down the gun, and it'll end. You'll be safe, okay?"

Angela shook her head. "You tried to steal her from me. You need to pay for that."

Here we go. Clare tried not to look too eager for that to happen. "You're right. I fell in love with her, and I won't stop fighting for her." *So try to shoot me. Come on, turn the gun in my direction.* "As long as I'm alive, I won't give her up."

"Clare, no!" Libby shouted at her. "What are you saying? Run! Get out of here, please!"

Now Clare's world condensed until she only saw one thing—the look on Angela's face as she stared at Libby. As both she and Clare heard the anguish in Libby's voice, her tear-choked plea for Clare to save herself, Angela's expression shifted in a heartbeat from shocked awareness to fury, because the love in Libby's voice was undeniable. And in that moment, Clare was forgotten and Libby—the betrayer, the one who had rejected Angela's sacrifices and had fallen in love with someone else—became the new target.

Clare drew her gun from the waistband of her pants and yelled Cappy's name. Even with the screaming and Clare's weapon, Angela's focus on Libby didn't waver, until Libby's legs swung up, kicking her arm and the gun she was holding to one side. Cappy's shot followed almost immediately, coming from behind Clare and slamming into Angela's shoulder, but not before Angela pulled the trigger.

Clare felt the bullet like a punch in the stomach, but with no pain, just pressure. Well shit, she thought as she dropped to her knees. *The little bitch actually shot me.* She heard voices yelling, but she couldn't be bothered to pay attention to what they were saying because she seemed to have a lot of blood pouring over her hand where it was pressed to her stomach. She saw Cappy's face hovering over her and heard Libby scream her name, and then a white-hot fire seemed to bloom from somewhere inside her, and everything but the pain faded away.

CHAPTER TWENTY-THREE

Clare looked up when she heard the tap on her door and saw Cappy hovering there, half in and half out of the room. "Hey," she said. "You can come in."

She tried to lift herself into more of a sitting position, but the muscles in her core seemed to have disappeared. She flopped back onto the bed with a sigh. Fine. She didn't want to sit up anyway.

Cappy pulled a chair closer to Clare's hospital bed and sat in it, her posture uncharacteristically stiff.

"Are you all right?" Clare asked with concern. Cappy looked nervous, with her hands clenched together in her lap and frown lines between her brows.

"Am *I* all right? I'm not the one who had a bullet pulled out of my gut yesterday. I'm not the one lying there with tubes and wires sticking out of me, like some sort of alien experiment. Yes, I'm fine, thanks. Really great."

Okay, now she looked more like her usual annoyed, sarcastic self. Clare smiled. "Aw, you've been worried about me. It's nice to know you care."

Cappy snorted. "Worried. Yeah, right. What I am is shocked by the lengths you'll go to get attention in this department." She changed to a shrill falsetto. "Look at me, I'm the smartest detective ever. Look at me, I can solve crimes just by looking at the buildings where the bodies were found. Look at me, I'm bleeding all over the fucking ground."

Clare laughed, which hurt despite the pain medication she had dripping into her veins. "The last one was sort of improvised. I have a flair for the dramatic."

"No kidding. I swooped in to save the day and shoot the perp, but you couldn't let me have my moment, could you? You had to steal my thunder and get yourself shot in the fucking stomach."

Cappy's tirade ended with a sort of stifled sob. She rubbed her hands over her face, then through her hair, not seeming to care that she left most of it standing on end. "God, Clare, you scared the crap out of me."

"I can tell. You seem to be swearing a lot more than usual. I'm taking it as a sign of love for your partner."

"Please. I'd ask Kent to reassign me, but I couldn't do that to whichever officer would have to work with you instead. I'm taking one for the team here." Cappy stood up. "I have to go now. Your girlfriend told me I only have five minutes before she was going to come in here and kick me out. She seems to want some alone time with you. God knows why."

She rested her hand on the bump under the covers that was Clare's calf, holding her for a moment, before letting go and walking to the door. She turned back to face Clare.

"You'd better hurry up and get back to work, Sawyer. The rest of us are getting sick of pulling your weight while you lounge around in bed all day."

"Love you, too," Clare called after her.

The word love took on a whole new meaning when Libby appeared in the doorway.

She walked slowly over to the bed, coming to the side where Clare didn't have a bullet hole and IVs in her. She stared at Clare as if needing to reassure herself that she was alive and reasonably well. Clare held her arm out and Libby crawled onto the narrow bed with her, curling against Clare's side.

"Am I hurting you?" she asked as Clare wrapped her arm around her and held her close.

"You're helping. More than all the drugs they're giving me."

She moved her hand, careful not to jostle the IVs sticking in it, and rubbed her finger along the red welt on Libby's wrist.

"I'm sorry," she said, "for what you went through out there. And for pushing you away like I did."

"Funny, isn't it? You were trying to protect me by keeping me out of your life, when I was the one behind the murders."

"You weren't behind anything. Angela was. She's not well, Libby. If it hadn't been you, it probably would have been another professor who was nice to her, or maybe another student who brought out the same obsessive qualities in her."

"I know, but it's not easy to get rid of the guilt I feel about Laura, and even Jimmy. And you. If I hadn't kicked her hand,...I practically aimed the gun at you when I did that."

Clare pulled Libby tighter against her side. "If you hadn't done that, she could have killed you. If you hadn't, then Cappy wouldn't have had an opening to take a shot."

Libby fidgeted with the front of Clare's hospital gown, pleating the fabric between her fingers. If Clare hadn't been full of medication and if she didn't have a gaping hole in her side, she would have been more turned-on by the play of Libby's fingers against her chest. As it was, the feel of her gave Clare a deep sense of well-being, something she couldn't ever remember experiencing to this extent.

"I've been thinking," Libby said. "I suppose I'm the one who should be breaking up with you now. Dating an architectural historian is just too risky. We live very dangerous lives."

Clare laughed and turned to kiss Libby's forehead. "How about no more breaking up, on either side? Life on campus seems to be more dangerous than I expected. We'll be better off if we stick together."

"I like the sound of that," Libby said, lifting her head and kissing Clare on the mouth. "We make a great team. I'm looking forward to the next investigation we get to work on together."

Clare was about to protest that Libby was never, ever going to take part in an investigation again, but before she could start, Libby raised herself on her elbow and kissed Clare again, sliding her tongue into Clare's mouth until she could barely remember what she had been about to say.

Later, she thought as Libby's thigh slid between hers. She would try to remember it later. Right now, nothing mattered beyond this kiss.

EPILOGUE

Clare parked in one of the university's on-campus parking lots, nearly empty at eight o'clock in the evening, and walked down the now-familiar path around Denny Hall and past the libraries. She was wearing civilian clothes, jeans and a heavy black wool sweater to combat the chilly night, since she was still being forced to take time off while her wound healed. She felt perfectly fine, except for the minor inconvenience of abs that refused to function the way they should. She couldn't even get out of bed without first rolling onto the floor and then bracing against her bedside table and hauling herself upright. Not the most dignified of actions, but the university doctors assured her that her core muscles would eventually return to normal.

Aside from the awkward transitions between sitting and standing, she felt well enough to get back to work and had tried showing up at the station a few days after she was released from the hospital. One of Kent's spies had ratted her out, though—most likely Cappy, damn her—and the sergeant had marched into the morning meeting and announced that the other officers had permission to either arrest or shoot Clare if they saw her again on campus in uniform before she was cleared to return by Kent herself. Clare had been getting closer to the other officers in the department and would have hoped they would ignore the directive, but Kent offered an extra week's vacation to whichever officer caught her sneaking back to work. Clare knew she was fair game, then—her growing rapport with her colleagues was no match for the incentive of more time off. So her uniform was hanging in her closet, neatly pressed and waiting for her to heal, and she was stuck in jeans that chafed against her bandages and made her long for the soft sweatpants she wore at home.

She headed from Red Square toward Drumheller Fountain and its surrounding science and technical buildings, surprised at how the structures she passed had taken on individual identities in her mind. When she had first started at the university, they had all looked the same to her and had all been lumped into the single category of brick, academic buildings. The *academic* aspect of them had been more than enough reason for her to want to stay as far from them as she could. Now, partly due to Libby's influence on the way she noticed structural details she never would have cared about before and partly because of the familiarity she was developing as she worked with the people inside those buildings, she felt as comfortable with the physical layout of campus as she did with the rooms in her own apartment.

Clare walked past the Johnson and Bagley Halls, homes of the biology and chemistry departments, and came to the huge, circular Drumheller Fountain. During the day, its jetting water served as an active foreground for a magnificent view of Mount Rainier, but tonight the fountain had been shut off, the water dark and still. A few people walked the paths around her, in singles and groups, but for Clare, at this moment, only one other person mattered.

"Hey," she said quietly, coming up behind Libby where she was standing near the fountain's edge and gazing at the water. Libby turned to face her, and Clare watched an expression of relief spread across her face, smoothing signs of tension around her eyes and mouth. Clare was getting accustomed to having her friends look at her in a similar way every time she encountered them these days. Libby. Cappy. Erin and Zeke. It was as if the image of her lying in a hospital bed was still fresh in their minds, and they always seemed a bit surprised and happy to see her upright, unencumbered by IVs and heavy bandages.

Libby moved forward and wrapped her arms around Clare, her embrace high enough on Clare's waist to keep from jostling her wound. Clare held her close, sliding her fingers into Libby's hair and dropping a sigh of a kiss on Libby's neck. Her friends might still be taken aback when they saw her, but *this* was what filled Clare with a sense of surprised wonder—the easy way she and Libby had developed of falling into each other's touch whenever they met. Clare had been attracted to Libby from the start, and her feelings had grown during their time together while investigating the case, but since Libby had come to see her in the hospital after her surgery, there was a newfound sense of naturalness in their closeness. She supposed near-death experiences tended to break down those last barriers between people. Okay, her bullet wound hadn't been bad enough to be considered extremely *near* death. More like death-adjacent. But Clare would go through it all again, and more, since it had brought her closer to Libby.

Libby leaned back slightly and tugged on the neck of Clare's sweater with one finger. "You always wear black on campus these days," she said, trailing her fingertip along Clare's skin, just under her collar. "Are you planning to dive into the shadows and hide if you see another campus police officer?"

Clare laughed, a breathless sound because of what Libby was doing to her neck. "Possibly. You should have seen the way they were looking at me when Kent offered them a week off. I felt like an innocent little bunny that had hopped too close to a kennel full of bloodhounds."

Libby took the finger that had just been making Clare's skin tingle and poked her in the chest with it. "Innocent, my ass." She shook her head in disbelief. "Back at work even though the doctor hadn't cleared you yet. I'll turn you in to Kent myself if I catch you doing anything even remotely patrol-like while we're out here."

Clare held up her hands in mock surrender. "No police work tonight, I promise. I'm just here to learn, Professor."

Libby grinned and took Clare's hand, interlacing their fingers. "That's the attitude. Come on, then. I usually start my tours over here."

Clare had still been in the hospital when Libby's most recent architectural tour of the campus had been scheduled. She had tried to get released early to join the group—she could imagine how much Libby would light up while sharing her passion with the students and community members—but her doctors had refused. Totally unfair. Of course, at the time she had been barely able to make the short walk to the nurses' station and back during her daily exercise sessions, so managing a two-hour long cross-campus excursion might have proved a bit challenging, but still…Unfair.

Although she was finding it hard to complain about missing the public tour when she was now being treated to a private one. Libby's hand was warm in hers, and the occasional brush of their shoulders and thighs as they walked close together was arousing.

Clare leaned over and kissed Libby's temple. "Maybe after this I can repay the favor by giving you a tour of my bedroom. It's full of design elements you'd probably find fascinating. Walls, a ceiling, a door. A bed."

"Do you need a quick dip in the fountain to cool off?" Libby asked, shaking her head in response to Clare's proposition. Or maybe in exasperation at her persistence. "You know the rules. No bedrooms until you're fully healed and aren't going to start gushing blood again if I touch you."

Clare felt Libby's shudder through their joined hands. After Libby had driven Clare home from the hospital, an innocent kissing session had gotten a little out of hand, opening Clare's wound again. She thought that the joy of having Libby in her arms was worth the slight pain, but Libby felt otherwise. Since neither of them seemed brimming with self-control where the other was concerned, Libby had been very careful to limit their alone time unless they were on campus, like tonight. Apparently, Libby believed they were safe as long as she was within shouting distance of patrolling campus police officers who would probably be only too willing to haul Clare to a detaining cell no matter the reason.

"It's a ridiculous rule," Clare said. "Besides, there was no *gushing*. Just a slight oozing."

Libby just rolled her eyes before pulling Clare off the main path. "Welcome to Sylvan Grove," she said.

A shallow set of paved stairs led them into an open grassy space with four large columns standing on one side. The entire area was bordered by thick trees, with a slender crescent moon peeking through evergreen branches, giving it a sense of separation from the rest of campus. Clare hadn't been here yet while on duty, but she had experienced other nooks and crannies on university property, where people could find an oasis of peace and isolation on an otherwise crowded big-city campus. The romantic possibilities of being in this beautiful and secluded space with her girlfriend warred with her safety-conscious police officer side. Cop won.

"Please tell me you don't come traipsing through here alone at night," she said.

"Alone? Please, I'm usually surrounded by acolytes of my secret murder society when I'm here. So, the university opened in 1861, as Washington Territorial University, since we didn't become a state until 1889. The original school building was in downtown Seattle, and these Ionic columns supported the entrance portico."

In just a few sentences, Libby's voice changed in timbre from playful scoffing to the warm tones Clare always heard when she was talking about some beloved building. Clare listened as Libby spoke about the early days of the university, partially absorbing the details of what she shared, but mostly feeling a deep sense of contentment being in this place with the woman she loved, hearing her speak about architecture and symbolism without it being connected in any way to a murder investigation.

"The downtown building was demolished in 1908, and these columns were the only parts of it that survived," Libby continued. "They were brought to this campus and lived where the Quad is now until it was decided that they didn't fit with the collegiate Gothic architecture of the new Quad halls. They've been here ever since."

"You don't agree," Clare said, smiling. She would like to believe that she was correctly interpreting Libby's opinion on moving the columns because she was getting to know her better every day, but Libby was never shy or hesitant about expressing her thoughts on architecture—anyone listening to her right now could figure out exactly how she felt about this matter. Clare loved that about her, especially since Libby's transparent and genuine nature extended into every part of her life.

Libby grinned at her. "I don't, really. Collegiate Gothic architecture is meant to connect us to the past, and to imbue a campus with a kind of solemn sense of the importance of learning and inspiration. Columns that not only invoke Ancient Greece, but also the specific history of this school seem to fit perfectly well with that aesthetic. I'm not a purist when it comes to architecture. I want tone and intention to blend well, but not necessarily every structural detail." She tilted her head back and looked toward the top of the nearest column. "Still, they're beautiful in this setting, so I'm not annoyed enough to start a petition to get them moved back to the Quad."

"Petition. Right," Clare said with a snort of laughter. "If you thought they belonged there, you'd have already tried to drag them back in the middle of the night, bureaucratic channels be damned."

"You're probably right. If I paid them enough, the people who moved Pierre for me might have agreed to help." Libby's laughter faded into a sigh. "Thank you for this, Clare."

Clare reached over and brushed her fingers across Libby's cheek and into her hair. "For what? I'm the one getting the private tour."

Libby shook her head with a rueful smile. "My last public tour wasn't great. I kept thinking about Angela, and I guess I was censoring myself, trying not to sound too excited about what I was saying. It's nice to be able to just share this with you without feeling so stiff and careful."

Clare gently cupped Libby's chin and made sure Libby was watching her as she spoke. "I love that you feel like you can be yourself with me, Libby. You always can, without any hesitation. But don't change who you are as a teacher and mentor for others because of Angela. She was a troubled young woman, and her decisions and her reaction to you were not your fault. Don't hide your enthusiasm and spirit from other people because you're going to inspire the vast majority of them to be better, to think more and dream bigger and look at the world in new ways."

Libby blinked, her eyes bright with tears, and she leaned forward and kissed Clare. "I love you," she said as she pulled back again.

"I love you, too," Clare said, relieved to see Libby's expression had lost some of its tension. "Now, let's go on with the tour. I don't think I've learned nearly enough about these columns yet."

"Oh, I'm only getting started," Libby assured her. She gestured at the grassy slopes around them. "Several school traditions and ceremonies take place here, usually associated with transition times, such as convocations and graduations, that sort of thing. Beginnings and endings. In one of them, first-year students are brought here and given the same history of the columns that I just told you. They come through one by one and touch each column, and then they come back when they're about to graduate and touch them again. It's meant to encourage a connection to this place, and to get students to reflect on the hopes and plans they have when they start here, and then on everything they've accomplished when they're about to leave."

Clare nodded vaguely, feeling her usual sense of distance from this kind of ritual. She didn't remember much about traditions and ceremonies from her own college—she had likely either daydreamed her way through them or found ways to avoid going in the first place. School had been hard enough without adding emotional connections to any part of campus. She hadn't needed to set aside special times to reflect on how much of a challenge it was just to get through each day, each assignment. Still, hearing Libby talk about this sacred-feeling space made her think she might have missed out on finding meaning where there had only been stress.

"Well, go on, then," Libby said after a pause. "Touch the first column."

Clare startled out of her memories. "What are you talking about?"

"Touch the column," Libby said, pointing at the one closest to them. "It's your first year here. When you're ready to retire or change departments, you'll come back here and touch them again. It's tradition."

Clare put her hands behind her back in a reflexive, protective response. "I'm not a student. It's not my tradition."

"It's a tradition that belongs to everyone who's part of this campus. Now put your hand on the column."

Libby's professor side had suddenly replaced her dreamy, architecture-loving side, and her voice told Clare this was an order, not a suggestion. Clare reached out and put a fingertip on the column.

Libby rolled her eyes—apparently Clare's sulkiness was all too readable on her face. "These columns have names, or qualities, like the statues at Suzzallo. This one is Loyalty. You've more than proved yourself in this way already, with your loyalty to me and everyone else here at the university. You might say you're just marking time here, or trying to advance your career, but if you were really only here for yourself, you wouldn't have risked your life to save me and to stop a murderer. Next one."

Libby pointed at the next column, not giving Clare the chance to argue with her first statements, and to say that she really *had* tried to solve the case because she wanted to prove herself to Kent and the rest of the department. Yes, she cared about Libby, but that was as far as her loyalty went on this campus. Well, she'd grudgingly include Cappy, as well, because she'd had Clare's back when she needed her most. And she was growing to like Libby's friends and would hate to have had anything happen to them if the murderer hadn't been caught. And, well, any of the other people in this community. But only because she was being paid to do a job.

Clare reluctantly put her hand on the second column, glad she hadn't voiced any of her protests about the first out loud since she hadn't even been able to convince herself that Libby was wrong about her growing sense of loyalty to the university.

"I feel like an idiot," she muttered.

Libby ignored her comment and continued with her way-too-personal tour. "This column is Industry. You put everything you had into solving these murders. Although I think you could loosen up a bit on this one, since you try to take hard work to an extreme and are too stubborn to give yourself time to heal. Next."

"Hey, I haven't been back in uniform since Kent kicked me out of the morning meeting. I've just been lazing around doing nothing for *days*." Well, only a handful of them so far, but it felt like ages. She remained silent about the online tutorials she had been taking during her downtime, brushing up on campus policies and city-versus-campus jurisdictions. She had completed them already when she was first hired, but she hadn't paid as much attention as she should have back then, when she had been too filled with regret and worry to let herself focus on her new job. She moved to the next column.

Libby took her through Faithfulness—which bothered her because she had been so adamant about working on her own at first and not being a true partner to Cappy—and Efficiency. She wasn't fond of the last column, either. If she had been more efficient and a better detective, she might have been able to save Laura and to protect Libby from her brief but disturbing kidnapping. She silently vowed that she would improve these two qualities, so she wouldn't be filled with so many regrets when she came back to these columns when she retired from the department. She had already formed that intention before she realized what she was doing. Damn it. Much as she had fought to not find meaning in this weird rite of passage Libby had concocted, she was getting awfully invested in it.

"Powerful stuff, isn't it?" Libby asked, giving Clare a knowing smile as she stepped away from the last column. Clare tried to feign indifference with a shrug, but Libby just laughed. She seemed to have the ability to not just read Clare better than other people could, but also to reach her on levels no one else had ever been allowed to access.

"Please tell me we don't have to end this ritual with a sacrifice or secret handshake or anything equally ridiculous," she said.

Libby stepped closer. "Just a kiss will do," she said. "To mark *our* beginning."

Clare smiled. She might be feeling more connected to this campus and her job here after tonight, but her growing bond with Libby was the one that truly mattered to her. The one she would spend the rest of her life fighting to protect and strengthen. "Now that's a tradition I can wholeheartedly support," she said, pulling Libby into her arms and kissing her.

About the Author

Karis Walsh is a horseback riding instructor who lives in the Pacific Northwest. When she isn't teaching or writing, she enjoys spending time outside with her animals, reading, playing the viola, and riding with friends.

Books Available from Bold Strokes Books

A Long Way to Fall by Elle Spencer. A ski lodge, two strong-willed women, and a family feud that brings them together, but will it also tear them apart? (978-1-63679-005-3)

Barnabas Bopwright Saves the City by J. Marshall Freeman. When he uncovers a terror plot to destroy the city he loves, 15-year-old Barnabas Bopwright realizes it's up to him to save his home and bring deadly secrets into the light before it's too late. (978-1-63679-152-4)

Forever by Kris Bryant. When Savannah Edwards is invited to be the next bachelorette on the dating show When Sparks Fly, she'll show the world that finding true love on television can happen. (978-1-63679-029-9)

Ice on Wheels by Aurora Rey. All's fair in love and roller derby. That's Riley Fauchet's motto, until a new job lands her at the same company—and on the same team—as her rival Brooke Landry, the frosty jammer for the Big Easy Bruisers. (978-1-63679-179-1)

Inherit the Lightning by Bud Gundy. Darcy O'Brien and his sisters learn they are about to inherit an immense fortune, but a family mystery about to unravel after seventy years threatens to destroy everything. (978-1-63679-199-9)

Perfect Rivalry by Radclyffe. Two women set out to win the same career-making goal, but it's love that may turn out to be the final prize. (978-1-63679-216-3)

Something to Talk About by Ronica Black. Can quiet ranch owner Corey Durand give up her peaceful life and allow her feisty new neighbor into her heart? Or will past loss, present suitors, and town gossip ruin a long-awaited chance at love? (978-1-63679-114-2)

With a Minor in Murder by Karis Walsh. In the world of academia, police officer Clare Sawyer and professor Libby Hart team up to solve a murder. (978-1-63679-186-9)

Writer's Block by Ali Vali. Wyatt and Hayley might be made for each other if only they can get through noisy neighbors, the historic society, at-odds future plans, and all the secrets hidden in Wyatt's walls. (978-1-63679-021-3)

Cold Blood by Genevieve McCluer. Maybe together, Kalila and Dorenia have a chance of taking down the vampires who have eluded them all these years. And maybe, in each other, they can find a love worth living for. (978-1-63679-195-1)

Greener Pastures by Aurora Rey. When city girl and CPA Audrey Adams finds herself tending her aunt's farm, will Rowan Marshall—the charming cider maker next door—turn out to be her saving grace or the bane of her existence? (978-1-63679-116-6)

Grounded by Amanda Radley. For a second chance, Olivia and Emily will need to accept their mistakes, learn to communicate properly, and with a little help from five-year-old Henry, fall madly in love all over again. Sequel to Flight SQA016. (978-1-63679-241-5)

Journey's End by Amanda Radley. In this heartwarming conclusion to the Flight series, Olivia and Emily must finally decide what they want, what they need, and how to follow the dreams of their hearts. (978-1-63679-233-0)

Pursued: Lillian's Story by Felice Picano. Fleeing a disastrous marriage to the Lord Exchequer of England, Lillian of Ravenglass reveals an incident-filled, often bizarre, tale of great wealth and power, perfidy, and betrayal. (978-1-63679-197-5)

Secret Agent by Michelle Larkin. CIA agent Peyton North embarks on a global chase to apprehend rogue agent Zoey Blackwood, but her commitment to the mission is tested as the sparks between them ignite and their sizzling attraction approaches a point of no return. (978-1-63555-753-4)

Something Between Us by Krystina Rivers. A decade after her heart was broken under Don't Ask, Don't Tell, Kirby runs into her first love and has to decide if what's still between them is enough to heal her broken heart. (978-1-63679-135-7)

Sugar Girl by Emma L McGeown. Having traded in traditional romance for the perks of Sugar Dating, Ciara Reilly not only enjoys the no-strings-attached arrangement, she's also a hit with her clients. That is until she meets the beautiful entrepreneur Charlie Keller who makes her want to go sugar-free. (978-1-63679-156-2)

The Business of Pleasure by Ronica Black. Editor in chief Valerie Raffield is quickly becoming smitten by Lennox, the graphic artist she's hired to work remotely. But when Lennox doesn't show for their first face-to-face meeting, Valerie's heart and her business may be in jeopardy. (978-1-63679-134-0)

The Hummingbird Sanctuary by Erin Zak. The Hummingbird Sanctuary, Colorado's hottest resort destination: Come for the mountains, stay for the charm, and enjoy the drama as Olive, Eleanor, and Harriet figure out the meaning of true friendship. (978-1-63679-163-0)

The Witch Queen's Mate by Jennifer Karter. Barra and Silvi must overcome their ingrained hatred and prejudice to use Barra's magic and save both their peoples, not just from slavery, but destruction. (978-1-63679-202-6)

With a Twist by Georgia Beers. Starting over isn't easy for Amelia Martini. When the irritatingly cheerful Kirby Dupress comes into her life will Amelia be brave enough to go after the love she really wants? (978-1-63555-987-3)

Business of the Heart by Claire Forsythe. When a hopeless romantic meets a tough-as-nails cynic, they'll need to overcome the wounds of the past to discover that their hearts are the most important business of all. (978-1-63679-167-8)

Dying for You by Jenny Frame. Can Victorija Dred keep an age-old vow and fight the need to take blood from Daisy Macdougall? (978-1-63679-073-2)

Exclusive by Melissa Brayden. Skylar Ruiz lands the TV reporting job of a lifetime, but is she willing to sacrifice it all for the love of her longtime crush, anchorwoman Carolyn McNamara? (978-1-63679-112-8)

Her Duchess to Desire by Jane Walsh. An up-and-coming interior designer seeks to create a happily ever after with an intriguing duchess, proving that love never goes out of fashion. (978-1-63679-065-7)

Murder on Monte Vista by David S. Pederson. Private Detective Mason Adler's angst at turning fifty is forgotten when his "birthday present," the handsome, young Henry Bowtrickle, turns up dead, and it's up to Mason to figure out who did it, and why. (978-1-63679-124-1)

Take Her Down by Lauren Emily Whalen. Stakes are cutthroat, scheming is creative, and loyalty is ever-changing in this queer, female-driven YA retelling of Shakespeare's Julius Caesar. (978-1-63679-089-3)

The Game by Jan Gayle. Ryan Gibbs is a talented golfer, but her guilt means she may never leave her small town, even if Katherine Reese tempts her with competition and passion. (978-1-63679-126-5)

Whereabouts Unknown by Meredith Doench. While homicide detective Theodora Madsen recovers from a potentially career-ending injury, she scrambles to solve the cases of two missing sixteen-year-old girls from Ohio. (978-1-63555-647-6)

Boy at the Window by Lauren Melissa Ellzey. Daniel Kim struggles to hold onto reality while haunted by both his very-present past and his never-present parents. Jiwon Yoon may be the only one who can break Daniel free. (978-1-63679-092-3)

Deadly Secrets by VK Powell. Corporate criminals want whistleblower Jana Elliott permanently silenced, but Rafe Silva will risk everything to keep the woman she loves safe. (978-1-63679-087-9)

Enchanted Autumn by Ursula Klein. When Elizabeth comes to Salem, Massachusetts, to study the witch trials, she never expects to find love—or an actual witch...and Hazel might just turn out to be both. (978-1-63679-104-3)

Escorted by Renee Roman. When fantasy meets reality, will escort Ryan Lewis be able to walk away from a chance at forever with her new client Dani? (978-1-63679-039-8)

Her Heart's Desire by Anne Shade. Two women. One choice. Will Eve and Lynette be able to overcome their doubts and fears to embrace their deepest desire? (978-1-63679-102-9)

My Secret Valentine by Julie Cannon, Erin Dutton, & Anne Shade. Winning the heart of your secret Valentine? These award-winning authors agree, there is no better way to fall in love. (978-1-63679-071-8)

Perilous Obsession by Carsen Taite. When reporter Macy Moran becomes consumed with solving a cold case, will her quest for the truth bring her closer to Detective Beck Ramsey or will her obsession with finding a murderer rob her of a chance at true love? (978-1-63679-009-1)

Reading Her by Amanda Radley. Lauren and Allegra learn love and happiness are right where they least expect it. There's just one problem: Lauren has a secret she cannot tell anyone, and Allegra knows she's hiding something. (978-1-63679-075-6)

The Willing by Lyn Hemphill. Kitty Wilson doesn't know how, but she can bring people back from the dead as long as someone is willing to take their place and keep the universe in balance. (978-1-63679-083-1)

Three Left Turns to Nowhere by Nathan Burgoine, J. Marshall Freeman, & Jeffrey Ricker. Three strangers heading to a convention in Toronto are stranded in rural Ontario, where a small town with a subtle kind of magic leads each to discover what he's been searching for. (978-1-63679-050-3)

Watching Over Her by Ronica Black. As they face the snowstorm of the century, and the looming threat of a stalker, Riley and Zoey just might find love in the most unexpected of places. (978-1-63679-100-5)

#shedeservedit by Greg Herren. When his gay best friend, and high school football star, is murdered, Alex Wheeler is a suspect and must find the truth to clear himself. (978-1-63555-996-5)

Always by Kris Bryant. When a pushy American private investigator shows up demanding to meet the woman in Camila's artwork, instead of introducing her to her great-grandmother, Camila decides to lead her on a wild goose chase all over Italy. (978-1-63679-027-5)

Exes and O's by Joy Argento. Ali and Madison really only have one thing in common. The girl who broke their heart may be the only one who can put it back together. (978-1-63679-017-6)

One Verse Multi by Sander Santiago. Life was good: promotion, friends, falling in love, discovering that the multi-verse is on a fast track to collision—wait, what? Good thing Martin King works for a company that can fix the problem, right…um…right? (978-1-63679-069-5)

Paris Rules by Jaime Maddox. Carly Becker has been searching for the perfect woman all her life, but no one ever seems to be just right until Paige Waterford checks all her boxes, except the most important one—she's married. (978-1-63679-077-0)

Shadow Dancers by Suzie Clarke. In this third and final book in the Moon Shadow series, Rachel must find a way to become the hunter and not the hunted, and this time she will meet Ehsee Yumiko head-on. (978-1-63555-829-6)

The Kiss by C.A. Popovich. When her wife refuses their divorce and begins to stalk her, threatening her life, Kate realizes to protect her new love, Leslie, she has to let her go, even if it breaks her heart. (978-1-63679-079-4)

The Wedding Setup by Charlotte Greene. When Ryann, a big-time New York executive, goes to Colorado to help out with her best friend's wedding, she never expects to fall for the maid of honor. (978-1-63679-033-6)

Velocity by Gun Brooke. Holly and Claire work toward an uncertain future preparing for an alien space mission, and only one thing is for certain, they will have to risk their lives, and their hearts, to discover the truth. (978-1-63555-983-5)

Wildflower Words by Sam Ledel. Lida Jones treks West with her father in search of a better life on the rapidly developing American frontier, but finds home when she meets Hazel Thompson. (978-1-63679-055-8)